Beneath the
Verdant Veil

This book is a work of fiction. Any resemblance to real people, events, or deadly plants is purely coincidental.

Beneath the Verdant Veil
By Veronica Thorne
Liminal Loves #1

© 2025
Mythglow Books

Beneath The Verdant Veil

By

Veronica Thorne

Liminal Loves: Book #1

MYTHGLOW BOOKS

PROLOGUE

1883

The forest had been whispering to him for days.

Not in any way he could properly record in his journal. No rustling of leaves, no shuddering boughs, no animal cries mistaken for words. Its voice was not sound. It tremored through his chest, through the soft place behind his eyes, through the marrow of his teeth.

Come to me.

Horace Pembroke had been a rational man when he entered the Escondido Basin five months earlier. A surveyor by trade, an amateur naturalist by reputation, a skeptic by declaration. Now he was a man who followed whispers without knowing why.

Tonight they led him to a place where the vegetation changed. The air shifted. Even the silence behaved strangely.

His porter, Mateo, walked behind him, muttering prayers. "Señor Pembroke… the villagers do not speak of this place. They bury the name."

Pembroke ignored him. Or tried to. His pulse seemed tethered to something ahead, something that pulled with the gravity of a moon.

The path narrowed into a lattice of arching vines, as though the jungle had woven its own corridor. The light from Pembroke's lamp thinned into pale strands, swallowed by the green gloom.

He pushed forward.

Beneath the Verdant Veil

The trail stretched downward into a root-lined cavern, its yawning passageways dripping with golden sap. Something brushed his wrist as he pressed onward into the cavern: a thin, living tendril supporting a small stone pendant, vine-shaped and faintly warm. He snatched it without thinking, closing his fist around its soft green glow. He never understood why he took it... only that it felt *given*.

The ground before him curved and bulged, forming a smooth rise like the back of some enormous, buried creature.

And at its center, the earth glowed.

Not bright.

Not even enough for shadows.

Just a soft, living luminescence, as though the soil itself inhaled light and exhaled faint color.

Pembroke's breath hitched. "This... this place was not here yesterday."

Mateo backed away. "Señor. No more. Please."

Pembroke stepped toward the mound, lamp trembling. The jade light wavered over the curved surface. It was pulsing. Slowly. Rhythmically.

He pressed a hand to it.

Warm.

Not the warmth of sunlight trapped in stone.

Warm like living flesh.

He jerked his hand back, nearly dropping the lamp. "Good God..."

A tremor passed through the mound.

Or perhaps through the entire cavern.

Pembroke stumbled backward, the breath caught in his throat. Mateo whirled and bolted toward the mouth of the corridor, crashing through the undergrowth and shouting prayers into the night.

"Mateo!" Pembroke called. "Wait!"

But he did not wait.

And Pembroke was suddenly, impossibly, entirely alone.

The mound moved again.

Cracked.

Opened.

Not in a violent way, but like a seed pod splitting when ripe. Earth and root folded aside, releasing a humid exhalation that smelled faintly of orchids and decay.

Pembroke's lamp flickered.

Shapes glimmered inside the opening… not clear, not whole, but suggestions:

curves etched with light;

veins glowing like rivers under translucent skin;

a silhouette suspended in a cradle of luminous roots.

His mind recoiled even as his eyes strained to see more.

He shouldn't be here.

He should run.

Every instinct screamed it.

Yet he couldn't move.

The pulse intensified.

Once.

Twice.

Then a third time, perfectly synchronized with the beating of his own heart.

His knees buckled. He fell forward, one hand sinking into the soft, warm earth.

Something whispered.

Not a voice.

A thought.

A pressure.

Echo-bearer.

He clutched his head, nails digging into his scalp.

"Stop. Stop… please…"

The shapes inside the pod shifted, brightened, flickered. Not limbs, not exactly. Something more abstract: lines of energy, kaleidoscopic patterns blooming like flowers behind his eyes. A thousand green filaments spiraled outward.

He saw:

cities swallowed by vines;

stars through a canopy of leaves;

humans kneeling at the base of an ancient root, hands touching a glowing surface, merging, dissolving;

someone else standing where he stood, long ago, reaching forward before recoiling in terror.

Pembroke's mind tore.

He gasped, tasting metal and sawdust.

The lamp fell from his hand and extinguished.

Darkness swallowed the cavern save for the faint, organic glow radiating from the open mound.

A shape moved inside. Tall, graceful, almost human. But the edges wavered as though made of mist and memory rather than flesh.

Two points of light — eyes, or something that resembled them — opened and fixed on him.

Pembroke froze.

Terror rose in his throat like bile. His body wanted to run, but his limbs felt weighted with organic chains.

The shape leaned forward.

The pulse in his chest synced with the elevating pulse inside the mound, locking him into a rhythm not his own.

Another whisper, sharper this time:

Remember...

And then:

Become.

"No," he croaked. "I can't... I won't..."

He scrambled backward, palms sliding across warm earth. A tangle of vines curled upward, brushing his wrist like a curious animal, leaving streaks of luminescent slime on his skin.

He screamed.

His voice cracked the clearing like thunder.

And suddenly...

the vines withdrew.

Not violently.

Not angrily.

Almost... sadly.

The pathway widened behind him. The walls of vegetation parted just enough to release him.

As if the forest had decided:

Not this one.

Pembroke ran.

Branches slapped him. Roots snagged his boots. He tripped, rose, ran again. His breath tore through his throat in ragged sobs. He did not look back, not once, though he felt invisible eyes on him, watching until the jungle spat him out.

He stumbled into camp just before dawn, wild-eyed, drenched in sap that glowed faintly in the torchlight. His remaining porters recoiled as though he were diseased.

He raved, incoherent, trembling…
of lights in the earth,
of voices that were not voices,
of a Queen beneath the roots,
of being chosen,
of running too soon.
Then he collapsed.

Two days passed and Pembroke remained half-delirious, hands trembling uncontrollably. They assumed fever. Carried him to the nearest settlement. He awoke screaming in the night, clawing at his journal pages, begging to return.

He tried to flee the hospital twice.

The second time he nearly succeeded.

By the time his wife arrived from London, he no longer spoke in coherent sentences. He kept repeating:

"She waited. She opened. I should have… I should have stayed…"

They secured him on a ship bound for home, placed him in an asylum near Bristol. Diagnosed exhaustion, nervous prostration, possible tropical delirium. The doctors wrote long, uncomfortable notes about "visual delusions of a botanical character," "morbid fixation upon a feminine sylvan figure," and "incipient monomania associated with environmental overstimulation."

His journal — erratic, water-damaged, and stained with faint green residue — was boxed and forgotten.

Years later, when he died, his final words were the same whispered phrase:

"The Queen awaits."

CHAPTER 1

The Presentation

The lecture hall at Lakeview University was one of those modern amphitheaters that tried to disguise itself as timeless: honeyed wood panels, brushed-steel railings, recessed lights that warmed the room to a burnished amber. Students filled the lower rows with open laptops; faculty clung to the aisle seats like lifeboats. Above them, the screen was a green sea: an overhead lidar map of the Escondido Basin, its canopy rendered as an undulating surface pricked by ghostly gridlines.

Dr. Mara Ellison stood at the lectern with one hand resting on the remote. The other traced an absentminded circle over the edge of her notes. She wore a charcoal blazer rolled at the sleeves, black trousers, boots scuffed by fieldwork; the kind of practical elegance that made her look more like an off-duty pilot than a professor. Her hair, stark raven black, was pulled back in a loose knot that revealed the cut of her cheekbones and the blunt certainty of her eyes. There was a coolness to her that had nothing to do with temperature, like the feeling that precedes lightning.

She clicked.

The image shifted to a false-color elevation model, the canopy peeled away to reveal something beneath: a set of subdued ridges radiating in rings from a shaded center. Ripples in earth. Or ribs.

"Sector Nine," Mara said. Her voice was lower than the room expected. Measured, intimate, unafraid of silence. "Central Escondido Basin. Each contour you see represents a height differential of two centimeters or less. If it were purely geological, we would expect chaotic variance. Instead, the spacing is rhythmic."

She zoomed in until pixelated lines grew crisp. "The ratios here and here match simple harmonic intervals. Repeated across the surface. A pattern that resists erosion, that maintains structural coherence over time. In other words, a system that behaves as if it selects for stability."

A hand shot up in the second row. Freshman confidence. "Are you saying somebody built... concentric levees? Like, ancient landscaping?"

"If 'somebody' includes a forest acting on itself through growth selection," Mara said. "Not levees. Accretions. Think of it as the jungle playing a note and continuing to tune the instrument until the sound sustains."

A few students brightened; a few faculty exchanged looks.

She advanced to a composite overlay: subcanopy infrared revealing a spiderweb of root-light veining through darker loam. "Infrared picks up what lidar cannot: thermal patterns that hint at what's below. Notice how vascular pathways correspond to mineral seams. There's integration. Not random."

A dry cough from the aisle. "Dr. Ellison, forgive the interruption." Professor Hartwell — silver hair, tenure lacquered onto him like shellac — rose half an inch from his seat. "Every decade we rediscover that nature is efficient. It is not a mind. Your language… *behavior, selection, coherence…* implies intention. We have been down this road. We found crop circles."

Muted laughter. A few phones tilted, recording.

Mara let the room breathe its little exhale and then nodded. "And every decade we move the goalposts. We used to say ants couldn't compute. Then we modeled their foraging. We used to say mycelium couldn't transmit information. Then we measured it. I'm using intention as an archaeological term. Not to anthropomorphize. To listen for design without assuming a designer."

Hartwell's mouth made a shape between a smile and a lemon-soaked pucker. "Trees drafting blueprints. The grants will love it."

"If I wanted to flatter a grant committee," Mara said, "I'd put a drone in a coyote costume and call it Bigfoot."

The students laughed for real this time. The faculty stilled.

She clicked again. On the screen, a small rectangle appeared along the ringed formation: a hollow, perhaps, or a negative space that refused to fill. "Here's what pushed me to present before I was comfortable. This void. Stable by all measures across three wet seasons. Its periphery isn't jagged; it's filigreed. That implies consistent repair or reinforcement."

"By whom?" Hartwell said.

"By what," Mara corrected softly. "We don't have that answer yet. But we do have enough evidence to ask a different set of questions."

She moved through the last slides with the unshowy fluency of someone who knew her material at the cellular level. Cross-correlations. Error bars that refused to budge. Acknowledgments. When she reached her final image, the rings fading to black, she said, "If I'm right, we'll learn something not just about the Escondido. We'll learn how complexity persists. We're archaeologists; our job isn't to worship ruins. It's to hear intention where it has no mouth."

She let the silence settle. Then: "Thank you."

The applause was polite in the way of departmental colloquia: enough to absolve those who didn't like what they'd heard. As the moderator muttered something about Q&A, the first hand belonged to a visiting botanist who asked for a better definition of "information-bearing structure." The second belonged to a graduate student who wanted to know if she had controlled for slumping loess. The third, inevitably, was Hartwell again.

"Last year you argued that anomalous geoglyphs in Peru reflected emergent patterning," he said. "Three months later, a mudslide killed one of your students." He waited just long enough for the room to stiffen. "You must appreciate the optics of returning to the jungle with unorthodox claims."

A heat rose at the base of her skull, but Mara kept her voice steady. "The accident was not related to my methodology."

"I didn't say it was," Hartwell said, gentle as a hammer. "But you might consider whether your language courts belief rather than evidence."

"Evidence is why we go," she said. "Belief is why we don't stop when it's hard."

The moderator called time with obvious relief. Projectors hummed down; the screen went blank.

The Presentation

Around Mara, the air turned to a slurry of murmurs, the little collisions of courtesy that follow an academic knife fight. She stacked her notes, slid them into the crook of her arm, and left by the side door before anyone could corner her for a collegial autopsy.

The atrium outside was all glass and height, a winter garden stripping the city's cold light into planes. Snow flurried across the skylights, then melted into rivulets. She stood beneath a ficus taller than a street lamp and breathed through her nose until her pulse slowed. Her reflection in the glass ceiling was pale and composed. She tilted her head, loosened the knot of her hair, and retied it. There. Control felt like an object she could put back on.

"Dr. Ellison."

The voice was pleasant in the way of hotel lobbies and expense accounts. When she turned, the man approaching was already smiling with the exact wattage required to suggest interest without warmth.

He wore a navy pinstripe suit that suggested tailoring done by someone who cared. Close-cropped dark hair just beginning to gray at the temples. Hands that had never known fieldwork, though the tan line at his wrist marked time in sunnier places.

"Adrian Lorne," he said, offering his hand and then a card. The cardstock was heavy, the logo embossed: a stylized helix from which a pair of leaves unfurled. *Auralis Biotechnologies* in silver.

"I know the company name," Mara said. "It tends to appear near patents."

"Patents are where ideas go when they grow up," Lorne said, genial. "I enjoyed your talk."

She looked at the card, then at him. "Flattery won't get you tenure."

"Tenure bores me," he said, as if she had given him a line he'd been waiting to use. "Discovery doesn't."

That earned the smallest edge of a smile from her. "Then you must be dreadful at academic dinner parties."

"Infamous," he said. "May I steal ten minutes? Not here. The atrium echoes. There's an empty classroom down the hall."

She considered refusing on principle; the principle retreated when curiosity stepped forward. "Ten," she said.

They found a seminar room with a long table and a single window framing the white blur of the quad. Lorne placed a tablet between them and angled it so she could see. The first image that bloomed was a satellite composite of the Escondido Basin: the same region she'd presented, rendered in a richer palette, as if the jungle had been coaxed to speak in full sentences.

"Our platform runs multispectral inference over long time spans," he said, tapping to reveal a time-lapse of faint bands tightening and loosening through rainy seasons. "We've been capturing this for six months. Initially it looked like ordinary hydrology. Then the recursion appeared."

"Recursion," Mara repeated. "I say harmony and you say recursion."

"Different instruments, same chord," Lorne said. He zoomed into a central depression. The void she knew appeared, more definite. Around it, the ringlike ridges rose in delicate steps. "We're seeing rectilinear symptoms underground as well. Not walls; don't look at me like that. Pathways. Think of them as… conduction tracks. Mineral-dense seams."

"And you think the biological system is using them," she said.

"I think there's a conversation," he explained. "Mineral to root to water to air. I don't leap to mystical. I leap to opportunity."

"And what would you like from me?" She tried not to lean closer and failed.

"A field lead," Lorne said simply. "You're the rare archaeologist who can talk to a botanist without either of you filing for divorce. You also aren't afraid to say 'intention' when it's the correct word."

"You've met my department," Mara said.

"I've met every department," Lorne said. "I prefer labs where the work happens."

He swiped again. A short dossier appeared: *Expedition 1749 - Escondido Initiative*. Vessel: Peregrine. She recognized half the equipment list from grants she'd been denied.

He paused to let the equipment gleam in her peripheral vision, then flicked to a personnel manifest. The names were spare and carefully chosen:

- Project Director - Adrian Lorne
- Field Lead (Archaeology) - Mara Ellison
- Field Operations - Elias Grant
- Systems - Kenji Tanaka
- Environmental Data - Amaya Nguyen
- Cultural Liaison - Diego Morales

Elias Grant.

The name tugged at her memory.

Then it clicked. A few years ago, headlines blaring across a dozen gossip sites. All some variation of "TV Archaeologist Exposed in Dig Hoax." The same PR photo of a young man in a field vest, smiling too bright for sincerity. A very public pox on a serious profession.

"Perfect," she muttered. "You're sending a showman."

Lorne coughed. "Tentative," he explained. "We reached out. He hasn't answered emails. He has a habit of not answering emails."

She kept her face still. "I remember the scandal."

"Most do," Lorne said, pleasantness cooling by a degree. "But Mr. Grant's past indiscretion aside, he is good on the ground. And offers essential, perhaps life-saving, expertise on the Escondido."

Mara stiffened, arms crossed. "Safety is key, of course," she stated. "And how do you envision my role on this mission?"

"The scientific spine," Lorne said. "And the hypotheses. Auralis will fund the expedition fully. You'll have autonomy in the field. Publish first, license second. You lead the questions; we'll worry about how to ask them afterwards without being sued."

She exhaled. "You're making a promise your lawyers wouldn't."

"My lawyers work for me," Lorne said, and smiled with just enough teeth to remind her that sometimes money wasn't merely the villain of a story. Sometimes it was the current that carried a thing where it needed to go.

Mara leaned back in the chair and watched the snow try to make up its mind about being rain. The last time she had said yes to a jungle she had come back with a notebook full of erosion models and a name she could no longer bring herself to say. To go again felt like teasing scar tissue. It also felt like waking up.

"What are you really looking for?" she asked.

"Understanding," Lorne said. "Then leverage." He shrugged, unembarrassed. "That's the sequence. But the first is not a lie."

"How does Auralis see 'understanding' translating into 'patentable'?" Mara inquired.

For the first time, Lorne seemed to glow. "Imagine crops that can reconfigure themselves to survive drought. Materials that heal structural damage on their own. Bio-signal networks that replace silicon for certain types of computation. If there's an organism out there capable of that kind of dynamic coordination…"

His smile sharpened.

"Auralis wants to be the first to sequence it."

Mara felt herself almost swept away in the possibilities. "And if what we find looks like sentience?"

Lorne spread his hands. "Then we learn its rules before someone else does."

The lights in the room timed out, leaving just dim strips along the floor. The window brightened by contrast, as though the world wanted in on the conversation. Mara looked down at the tablet again and at the void at the basin's heart. In the margins of the screen, someone, Lorne or one of his people, had left a note: *correlate ring spacing to seasonal river levels*. Another note circled the central depression and wrote simply: *why repaired?*

She glanced at the door. "Half my department will call this a boondoggle."

"The other half will ask if they can come," Lorne said.

"What about the parts you didn't tell me?" she asked.

"I didn't tell you because I prefer not to lead my scientists," he said. "I hire them because they lead me."

She was quiet for a long moment. Then, because there was a thing she had to say to herself before she committed it to the world: "I'm not claiming sentience. I'm claiming order that behaves as if aware of itself."

"Say that to a camera," Lorne said, "and I'll get you a second expedition."

"God forbid," she muttered, and he laughed as if she'd made a joke just for him.

He tapped the tablet and it pinged. Her phone vibrated. An email appeared with the subject line *AURALIS Logistics Packet - Expedition 1749*. Beneath it, a calendar invite. Beneath that, a simple line: Autonomy guaranteed in field decisions - M.E. to set research priorities.

"Is that actually binding?" she asked.

"It is when I send it," Lorne said.

Mara stood, the chair legs making a polite sound on the floor. "I haven't said yes."

"You will," Lorne said, not unkindly. "Because you can't leave that pattern alone. Because you went to sleep last night thinking about it and woke up doing the same. Because if you don't go, Hartwell will, and he'll call it a floodplain."

The Presentation

She looked down at the Auralis card, at the neat helix with its two small leaves, at the way the designer had tucked potential into a logo. Something in her chest that had been clamped for months loosened by a notch.

"What's the ship?" she asked. "You said Peregrine."

"A self-navigating river vessel with a human override for when software remembers it isn't a person," Lorne said. "Quiet engines. Good sensors. Ugly coffee."

"Departure?"

"Five days. San Isidro, Berth Seven."

She nodded. "I have classes."

"You have adjuncts," he said, and when she lifted a brow, he added, "And a dean who will forgive you when the press release lands."

She hated that he might be right. She loved that he might be right.

"Send me the full data set," she said.

"It's already waiting in your inbox. With a secure link. And a nondisclosure that won't insult you."

She picked up the card and slid it into the pocket of her blazer. "I'll let you know tomorrow."

"You'll let me know in an hour," he said, still smiling. "Go walk in the snow first. It helps."

Mara bid Lorne a polite goodbye and left him there in the shadows of the seminar room, helix-leaf emblem still aglow on the tablet. Outside, the atrium had emptied to a few stragglers and a custodian pushing a cart. Snow, having decided against rain, fell with a steadiness that promised to make the city new by morning. She checked her phone, saw the logistics packet waiting like a secret, and did not open it yet.

Instead, she crossed the quad without her hat, letting the flakes find her lashes and the line of her jaw. She thought of Peru… a slope that had looked stable until it wasn't, the sound of a hillside deciding to move, the torn edge of a name that would not leave her throat. She had promised herself she would not be the kind of scientist who sought absolution in new risks. She had also promised herself she would not let fear wear the mask of rigor.

By the time she reached her office, the radiators had come on and Hartwell had sent an email with the subject line "Re: Today's Colloquium" and the first sentence, "I worry that your rhetoric undermines the department's credibility." She didn't open it.

Instead, she clicked on the message from Auralis.

It was all there. Equipment lists that would take a normal grant cycle two years to assemble. A vessel schematic for the Peregrine: a narrow, cat-eyed hull with shallow draft and a squat tower for sensors. A manifest distilled to essentials.

Her hand hovered over her mouse. She heard her own voice from an hour ago, bright and sure in a room that wanted to dim it: *"If we can model it, we could learn how living systems manage complexity far beyond human computation."*

She clicked Reply and kept it to one line, because sometimes one line was the only way forward.

Confirmed. - M. Ellison

She let herself breathe. Then she scrolled back through the packet until the Auralis logo was the only thing on her screen. The helix curled upward; the leaves were not dainty but vigorous, pushing into their form

The Presentation

with the kind of confidence chlorophyll has when it meets light.

It should have looked corporate. It looked like an omen.

CHAPTER 2

The Fallen Explorer

San Isidro was a town that had once believed in its own importance. The dock cranes were rusting statues; the torpid air stung of diesel and fruit rot. Painted letters flaked from corrugated rooftops. Even the gulls seemed to circle slower now, as if time itself had grown humid and heavy.

Elias Grant rented a single room above a boatyard that smelled of oil, mangrove, and regret. The fan in the ceiling wobbled with every rotation, scraping rhythmically against the metal housing. He'd learned to sleep through it. Nights, he sat at his small desk beneath a half-dead bulb, paging through his battered notebooks and a folder of old photographs. Fragments of a previous life and puzzle pieces in a never-ending quest.

By day, he patched hulls, took survey jobs for the harbor office, and carried crates for the fishermen. He was leaner now, the scruff on his jaw too deliberate to be laziness. Sweat left salt maps on his shirts; his hands were cracked, strong, and always faintly stained with grease. Most evenings he ended up at the Cantina Sol, drinking lime-cut rum and listening to the waves slap against the pilings while the locals argued about soccer and ghosts.

But every night ended the same, with the sound of pages turning.

On the desk lay a tattered journal wrapped in oilcloth: "*The Escondido Papers of Horace Pembroke, 1883.*"

The Fallen Explorer

The ink had faded, but Pembroke's hand was precise and strangely modern.

"The jungle speaks, not with words but with order. It arranges itself as though remembering."

Elias traced the line with his thumb, his lips moving silently. He knew the passage by heart. The more he read, the more it felt less like history and more like contagion.

Pembroke had returned from the jungle broken and incoherent, his once-celebrated intellect reduced to scribbled ramblings and muttered references to a "Green Queen" who whispered beneath the soil. He was quietly committed to an asylum overlooking the Bristol Channel, where he died years later.

His belongings were auctioned off in pieces. Elias had tracked down a battered trunk sold in London, dropping half a year's pay in one frenzied bid. Inside, he found Pembroke's field journals, stained and brimming with bound urgency. But the necklace described in those entries, a vine-shaped pendant of pale green stone, went to a separate bidder who hadn't already nuked their bank account. Elias later traced the necklace to a private collection in Madrid. He'd made it as far as the glass display case before security escorted him out.

He hadn't even touched it. And yet he could feel something... waiting.

Elias leaned back now, fingers resting on the glass neck of a soda bottle, and stared through the slatted window. The jungle began where the town ended. He could almost hear its pulse beyond the river, steady, patient, like something breathing.

He told himself he stayed here because rent was cheap, work steady, air honest. The truth was more complicated: It was the closest he could get to Pembroke's phantom within the law or without bankrupting himself. Elias had worked along the *edges* of the Escondido Basin in years past, mapping colonial trade routes and abandoned mission sites — but the interior was sealed off under federal conservation law. Only government or corporate expeditions were granted access.

Every lead, every scrap of rumor about Pembroke's doomed adventure pointed to these jungles. But even if Elias could obtain permission to mount his own expedition, it would cost more than he could beg or borrow. So he worked from the margins, interviewing river pilots, poring over militia reports, listening to the stories that drifted down from the interior; piecing together what he could while the true heart of the jungle remained, for now, out of reach. And, truth be told, he had nowhere else to go.

Three years earlier, Elias had been famous enough to begin hating it.

The network special was supposed to revive public interest in archaeology. *"Worlds Before Memory,"* produced with the slick precision of a travelogue and the moral clarity of a sermon. He had stood before cameras on the Yucatán ridge, wind in his hair, voice-over softening his drawl to something global. "Evidence," he'd said, "of a pre-Columbian seafaring culture that reached these shores long before recorded trade."

They had filmed the artifacts under stage light — bronze clasps, fragments of porcelain — proof of an impossible connection. The internet called it a revelation. For three days. Then the experts arrived.

The Fallen Explorer

The porcelains were modern. The bronze had machining marks. Someone had salted the dig. His local fixer, paid under the table, vanished with the bribe money. The network apologized to the viewing public. The university distanced itself. His co-host stopped returning calls.

Diego Morales, then a rising anthropologist, had been among the loudest critics. His op-ed in *El Mundo* called it "an insult to the discipline and to every culture exploited by academic tourism." Elias still remembered the line that stung most: "*Grant's tragedy is that he believed the myth he was selling.*"

Within a month, the contracts dissolved. Funding dried up. Friends offered sympathy like alms. He sold his cameras, paid his debts, and disappeared south.

Now, when he thought of it, it was less rage than fatigue. He had been wrong, yes, but not in the way they thought. The fakes were fake. But the feeling of discovery was real. There had been something else, too... something permeating the earth, something *watching*. He could still feel it like pressure behind his eyes.

Elias was halfway through the last of the rum and Coke when the knock came.

Three quick raps... knuckles that expected to be answered. He closed his notebook, swept tortilla chip crumbs into a chipped saucer, and opened the door.

Adrian Lorne filled the hallway like he owned the building. Light linen suit, no tie, unbothered by the heat. His expression was one of practiced curiosity, an executive pretending to discover humility.

"Mr. Grant," he said. "Or do you prefer 'Doctor' still?"

Elias blinked once. "Depends who's asking."

Lorne extended a hand. "Adrian Lorne. Auralis Biotechnologies. We tried reaching you."

"People try a lot of things."

"True," Lorne said easily. "Mind if I come in? The hallway feels conspiratorial."

Elias hesitated, then stepped aside. The man didn't wait for permission to sit, choosing the least battered chair. His eyes swept the small room — maps pinned to the wall, compass, the Pembroke journal open on the desk. "You're still chasing ghosts."

"Some pay better than others," Elias said, sitting across from Lorne. "What does Auralis want with me?"

"Straight to it," Lorne said, as if impressed. "We're mounting a survey of the Escondido Basin. Environmental, archaeological, biological… you name it. We need someone who can keep a team alive in a place that doesn't want them there."

Elias' intrigue was tempered by skepticism. "Hire a mercenary," he suggested.

"I prefer explorers who know when not to shoot," Lorne said. "You've been there before."

"Officially. Maybe unofficially," Elias acknowledged. "But you have no reason to trust me."

"Actually, I do. The people who hate you most still cite your data. You see connections where others see noise."

Elias laughed, sharp and brief. "You want me to be your interpreter?"

The Fallen Explorer

"I think you're among the few professionals who won't dismiss unorthodox possibility by default," Lorne said. "On top of that, you've walked the Basin's perimeter. You know its moods, its history, its dangers. That puts you ahead of every specialist with a perfect résumé but no dirt under their nails."

Elias leaned back, chair creaking. "The Escondido doesn't want tourists. Last time anyone went deep into the basin was the late eighties, and the forest swallowed the camp overnight. No signals, no remains."

" I don't want to be on that list," Lorne said. "That's why I'm in your living room."

"Why go at all?"

"I can't not go," Lorne said quietly. "And you can't stay here forever pretending you're finished being an explorer."

Lorne set a small tablet on the rickety table, swiping to bring up satellite maps. Elias leaned closer to the tablet, politely curious, but the image that appeared froze him mid-breath: concentric rings radiating through the green. The same ridges Pembroke had described.

That ridge line.

That bend in the river.

That impossible little clearing Pembroke had drawn as a shaky rectangle in the margin of his journal, labeled with a single word: "Listening."

Lorne kept talking, some clipped explanation about anomalous returns and vegetative overgrowth, but Elias barely heard him. Every fragment of Pembroke's route, long dismissed as fevered Victorian fantasy, was aligning on the screen with uncanny precision.

He forced his voice steady. "Where did you say this was taken?"

"Interior Basin," Lorne said, tapping the center cluster. "Roughly twelve kilometers into the exclusion zone."

Twelve kilometers.

Exactly where Pembroke claimed the ground itself began to hum.

Elias swallowed, nodding as if this were merely interesting academic overlap. But inside he felt something blooming — hope, sharp as a blade.

Lorne narrowed his eyes, noticing the shift. "You've seen something like this before."

"Not like this," Elias said carefully. "But I've... followed the paper trail for a long time."

He didn't elaborate.

"What's the endgame?" Elias asked, shifting.

"The kind of opportunities that rewrite industries," Lorne said with a satisfied smile. He had no compunction about revealing further details because he knew one thing for certain: *Elias Grant was already on the hook.*

"Auralis sees pathways to groundbreaking innovations," Lorne explained, full sales mode. "Adaptive resins. Bio-lattices that reorganize under stress. Tissue that communicates chemically over long distances. If the rumors about this region are even half true, we could be looking at a living architecture. Something closer to a nervous system than a forest. We intend to file intellectual property on any unique compounds or structural behaviors we document."

Elias kept his expression steady, though excitement thrummed through his whole being. If this data lined up with Pembroke's route, if the anomaly he'd dreamed of for years actually existed…

"You'll be compensated handsomely," Lorne added. "Field operations lead, safety oversight, logistical authority."

Elias raised an eyebrow. "Who am I babysitting?"

"Six-person crew. Our lead scientist is Dr. Mara Ellison. Brilliant, if a little idealistic. You handle the route, equipment, and people. Let her chase *her* ghosts; you keep her alive."

Lorne watched the recognition flicker. "You've met?"

Elias shook his head slowly. "I've read her work. Fractals in biological patterning. She's serious."

"Absolutely," Lorne said. "And she'll need someone serious watching her back."

The fan above them ticked its tired circle. Outside, thunder rolled over the bay, slow and theatrical.

Elias looked again at the satellite image. The rings were faint but there… deliberate.

He spoke without meaning to. "Pembroke… the naturalist… wrote that it called to him. That it wanted witnesses."

Lorne's tone was light, but his eyes sharpened. "Then let's go bear witness. Help us get there safely. And leave the chase to her."

For a long time neither man spoke. The rain began, tapping against the shutters like someone asking for entry.

Finally Elias said, "I don't do interviews."

"You won't have to," Lorne said. "This isn't television. It's logistics."

Elias' gaze drifted to the journal. The last line he had read still glimmered in the lamplight: *She remembers all who listen long enough.*

"How long?" he asked.

"Departure in three days," Lorne said. "San Isidro port, Berth Seven. You know where it is."

"I know where everything is," Elias murmured.

Lorne stood, smoothing his jacket. "That's why I'm here. I'll send the formal contract to the harbor office... and your email, if you care to check it. Try not to vanish before then."

He left without waiting for goodbye, footsteps echoing down the narrow stairs.

Elias remained where he was until the rain softened. He reached absently for the drink, decided against it, and instead opened Pembroke's journal to a random page.

"At dusk the forest spoke as one breath. I dared not answer."

He read the line twice, then shut the book. Through the cracked window, the jungle beyond the town shimmered with lightning. The pulse beneath it was slower, older. He imagined the basin waiting, patient as ever.

He exhaled, picked up the phone he hadn't charged in a week, and scrolled through missed messages. The most recent unread: *Auralis Logistics Packet – Expedition 1749.*

"Dammit." He smiled without humor, knowing the devil over his shoulder had already won. "Guess I'm officially on the manifest."

Then, as the fan scraped its next rotation, he began to pack. Elias knew that the door Auralis had creaked open might lead straight to hell. But he had stepped halfway over that threshold long ago…

CHAPTER 3

The Crossing

The Peregrine didn't look like it belonged in San Isidro any more than a scalpel belongs in a junk drawer. Her hull was white and severe, her bow lines impeccably clean, her twin turbines still with the promise of whispering power. She gleamed like a visiting starship; the rusting barges and patched fishing boats around her looked like plastic toys in comparison. Rain pinned the harbor to a pewter sky. Ropes groaned and settled along the dock pilings.

Mara paused at the base of the gangway, fingers tightening on her suitcase handle. She'd expected something older, maybe even charming: diesel stink, rust, tar. Instead the ship glowed with a laboratory's self-confidence, quiet lights banded along the rail as if to discourage sentiment.

"Quite a sight, isn't she?" said a voice from the deck above. Mara gazed upward.

The man leaning on the starboard rail had taut, sun-browned arms and a field vest zipped halfway up an old T-shirt. Stubble roughened his jaw; his hair was sun-bleached at the tips in a way that might have been accidental. He watched her with a sentry's stillness and a boyish grin held carefully in reserve.

"Elias Grant," she presumed.

He nodded, blue eyes wary and amused at once. "Guilty."

The Crossing

Elias glanced at the sprawling Escondido. "They don't usually send boats like this upriver."

"They don't usually send archaeologists," she replied, adjusting her grip on the suitcase.

He grinned. "Then we're both here under unusual circumstances."

She ascended the gangplank and extended her hand. "Dr. Mara Ellison."

"A pleasure, Dr. Ellison." Up close he smelled faintly of oil and rain. He offered a hand; she took it, surprised by the unshowy strength. His fingers were nicked, nails clean, knuckles scarred in small, honest ways. "I'm field ops and navigation on this trip," Elias offered. "Or, as Lorne puts it, the one who keeps people from dying of their own enthusiasm."

"That sounds reassuring."

"I do my best. Results may vary."

Their eyes met for a moment longer than politeness required—hers sharp, assessing; his wry but weary, the look of someone who'd been forgiven fewer times than he'd earned. He was handsome in a way that came from surviving rather than posing; she was composed in a way that came from choosing to be. A gust licked rain across the deck.

Mara released his hand. "To be perfectly honest, I'm surprised Auralis recruited you."

"Surprised they recruited anyone with a sense of adventure?" he asked lightly.

When she didn't answer, his grin softened. "Don't worry, Doctor. I only falsify relics on Thursdays."

She almost smiled. "Good. I'm allergic to scandal."

He stepped aside, motioning her aboard. "Then we'll get along fine."

Inside, cool air washed over them, filtered and dry. The corridor hummed softly underfoot. She caught her reflection in a pane of glass: dark hair pinned back from her face, rain glossing the stray wisps at her temples. The exhaustion left over from a sleepless flight had cast a finer grain to her features, the kind of look critics mistake for brittleness. She straightened.

"Conference room's forward," Elias said. "Or, if you'd rather meet the coffee first, galley's on the port side."

"Briefing," she said. "Then coffee."

"Ambitious," he said. "I like it when the scientist goes first."

"Get used to it."

The corners of his eyes creased. "Working on it."

They turned a corner and nearly walked into a young woman with a tablet pressed to her chest. She wore her hair in a mid-length bob that curled whenever the air dared it; her shirt had a tiny embroidered fern near the collar. When she saw Mara she froze, eyes wide.

"Oh. Wow. You're—hi. Sorry. I'm Amaya. Amaya Nguyen. Environmental systems. I, um, made your paper on coral basin fractals required reading last spring. I should have asked permission, but… it was on the syllabus and nobody reads the footnotes, right?"

Mara felt a small, unexpected warmth unlock. "I'll allow it," she said. "Only because I like your taste."

Amaya exhaled as if she'd been holding her breath since childhood. "I can show you the sensor array after the briefing. We modded a standard rig to ride the humidity flux and — sorry. You're on your way somewhere. I'll just — okay."

"She normalizes after the second coffee," Elias murmured.

"I heard that," Amaya replied, not offended, and peeled off toward the conference room.

"Diego and Kenji are through here," Elias said, pushing the conference room door.

The room was glass-walled, the table a long ribbon of matte black. A topographic projection hovered above it: green dunes shifting over ghosted lines. Two men stood at opposite ends. The first — mid-twenties, lean, longish black hair perpetually falling in his eyes — flicked through menus on a console, as absorbed as a pianist with a new score. The second — early thirties, field shirt faded by sun and detergent, boots quietly expensive — turned toward Mara with an expression that read equal parts welcome and assessment.

"Dr. Ellison," he said, extending a hand. "Diego Morales."

"Cultural liaison," she said. "Anthropologist."

"Among other sins," he said. "My department insisted I come. The Basin has stories. People tend to cut before they listen."

"We cut less when we can model the reasons not to," she answered.

His mouth twitched. "Good. It's been a while since I worked with someone who thinks intention is a measurable phenomenon."

"It is," she said, and held his gaze until he glanced away.

The young man at the console lifted a hand without looking up. "Kenji Tanaka," he said. "Systems and robotics. If it blinks, whirs, pings, or crashes, I'm responsible. Unless it's good news; then it was a team effort."

A door hissed and Adrian Lorne stepped in, the air seeming to adjust itself to his presence. Linen shirt open at the throat, no tie, watch that belonged on a very careful wrist. He smiled with the precision of a metronome.

"Excellent," he said. "Everyone's here."

"Everyone," Diego repeated, and his eyes slipped to Elias before returning to Lorne. On Diego, polite became cool very easily.

Lorne ignored the temperature change. "Let's begin."

He closed the blinds with a fingertip brush; the projection brightened, the green resolving into heights and depressions. Rain ticked faintly on the tempered glass.

"Satellite lidar returned this six months running," Lorne said. "At first glance, geological. Look closer."

Kenji zoomed; the ridgelines multiplied into nested curves. Underneath the green: faint rectilinear hollows, like hallways erased by time and replaced by root.

"Is that…" Amaya began.

"Suggestive of intentional architecture," Mara said. "Or at least a blueprint for such."

Lorne dipped his head toward her. "We think so. The pattern fidelity is… troubling."

"Troubling how?" Elias asked.

"Too precise," Lorne said. "Too persistent across weather events, growth cycles, and seismic nudge. Our modeling shows something is maintaining these ratios. We don't know what or why. Dr. Ellison's paper on biological pattern selection suggests a framework for asking better questions."

He glanced at Mara. "You'll lead the exploratory mapping and interpretative work. Decide what we sample, where we look, how deep we cut, when we cut at all. You'll have *autonomy*." He let the word sit between them a moment longer than casual.

Mara kept her face unreadable, though the word landed like a hand on her shoulder. "We'll need staged protocols," she said. "If there's an active biological system overlaying the stone, we risk collapsing both by guessing."

"Agreed," Lorne said. He cleared his throat and tapped the manifest on the wall screen. "And before we move on, there's one logistical point the Ministry insisted on." He nodded toward Diego. "Dr. Morales isn't just here as a courtesy. The regional government requires an accredited cultural liaison on any deep-basin expedition."

Diego sat straighter, folding his arms. "Any finds of anthropological or archaeological value must be catalogued immediately. That is the law. Especially in a region where unrecorded sites may exist."

Mara raised an eyebrow. "You think we'll find ruins out here?"

"Not *think*," Diego corrected, tone clipped. "Hope, perhaps. Or fear. The Basin has never been fully surveyed. Local traditions speak of settlements swallowed by the Green Heart." He shot a pointed look at Lorne. "And those traditions aren't yours to bulldoze through."

Lorne gave a thin smile. "Hence why you're here to keep us honest."

"Or to stop you from stealing anything that isn't nailed down," Diego muttered.

Lorne pretended not to hear. "Bottom line: should we encounter any structures, artifacts, or sacred sites, Dr. Morales files the first report. He has full authority to halt the mission if he believes cultural integrity is at risk."

Kenji blinked. "Full authority?"

"Yes," Diego said, with no small satisfaction. "Even Auralis must obey federal regulations."

Mara glanced between them, understanding dawning. *So that's why Lorne tolerated Diego on the team.*

Elias leaned back in his chair, smirking faintly. "And here I thought I was the only one brought aboard for my charming personality."

Diego shot him a glare sharp enough to slice marble, but the tension in the room had already shifted — Diego's presence wasn't an inconvenience.

It was a mandate.

Diego pointed a finger at the heart of the projected map. "There's something I don't get. The Escondido Interior's been sealed off longer than I've been alive. How did *you* get in?"

Lorne didn't look up from his tablet. "Auralis negotiated access."

"Negotiated," Diego repeated, flat. "That a polite word for *paid handsomely*?"

Mara shot him a warning glance, but Lorne finally met Diego's eyes. The executive was cool, patient, unbothered.

The Crossing

"Auralis is funding rural clinics, renewing research agreements, and sharing select data with the Ministry. Everyone benefits."

"Except the people whose land has been off-limits for decades," Diego said. "Funny how it opens the moment a corporation wants samples."

Lorne's smile thinned. "If you have objections to government policy, take it up with the government. Our mission is scientific."

Diego leaned back, unimpressed. "Sure. Scientific."

"Auralis has been completely transparent with authorities," Lorne argued. "We're here to establish precedence and proprietary claims. If this ecosystem houses an organism with novel biochemical logic, we identify it, characterize it, and, if feasible, recover a sample for controlled study."

The room held its breath a moment longer before Lorne turned to change the slide, but the unease stayed behind like humidity — quiet, heavy, and impossible to ignore.

Diego cleared his throat. "One more question."

Lorne turned back and gestured with pained magnanimity.

"Why him?" Diego asked, nodding toward Elias. "There are others who can keep us alive without bringing scandal to shore. Mr. Grant's last expedition embarrassed three universities and half my friends."

Kenji looked up, startled. Amaya went very still.

Elias didn't change expression. He watched the projection as if the answer might be embedded there.

Lorne folded his arms. "Because he is the best at what we need most — reading a landscape beyond its labels. He can smell a bad path without a sensor telling him. And because reputations are cheap when weighed against competence."

Diego didn't blink. "Or you like the story his presence tells."

"I like results," Lorne said. "You can quote me on the ship's manifest."

Diego's mouth crooked downward, but he let it go. He turned to Mara instead. "Dr. Ellison, I'm glad you're here. It's easier to respect myth when science shows it where to stand."

"Respect goes both ways," Mara said. "I won't pretend to know your people's stories better than you do. But I'll know when the rocks have a memory they shouldn't."

Amaya made a small, involuntary sound of approval and then blushed when all eyes cut her way. "What?" she said. "That's a good line."

Lorne swept onward. "Kenji, walk us through the toys."

Kenji spun the projection to a schematic of the Peregrine. "Primary sensor mast with multimode lidar and passive bioelectric listeners. Subsurface ground-penetrating radar we can ferry to shore with the skiff. Speaking of which, the skiff, Minnow, is fully powered, shallow draft, aluminum hull, seats six with gear. And drones: two lightweight recon birds with thermal and spectral cameras, plus a heavier survey unit for hovering over canopy gaps. Try not to lose them."

"Try not to give me reasons to," Amaya said.

"And safety?" Mara asked.

The Crossing

"Redundant comms between Peregrine and Minnow, personal transceivers for shore team, sat beacon. First-aid and trauma kits in triplicate," Kenji said. "And Elias." He tipped a thumb toward the Field Ops lead.

Lorne's smile tightened. "Right. Survival and route decisions run through Mr. Grant. He picks the path and the pace, and we trust him to keep us safe. No heroics. Just competence."

Elias gave a crisp, mock salute. "No promises."

The room laughed, some easing of a knot none of them wanted to admit was there.

"Departure in one hour," Lorne said. "We clear the river mouth by nightfall. Any questions?"

Diego raised a hand without putting it up. "Just one," he said. "Have you told your bosses what to do when the jungle doesn't send our bodies back?"

Lorne's smile didn't move at all. "I don't plan for that eventuality," he said. "I plan for you to wax poetic to me about the coffee while we count our samples."

"Then you haven't met our coffee," Kenji said, and the room finally exhaled.

By the time they slipped their moorings, day had rolled itself up. The harbor narrowed to a brown ribbon threading past stilt houses and mangrove roots. Children ran along a rickety dock to pace the ship, shrieking laughter; a dog barked as if the sound were its job. Smoke lifted from cook fires in long, thin columns. A few figures on the shore paused to watch the white vessel slide by. Mara stood at the rail with Amaya and Diego. The air tasted like wet copper.

"Do they know who we are?" Mara asked quietly.

"Maybe," Diego said. "Maybe they just know the pattern. Outsiders come, the forest changes. Some believe it keeps count."

She frowned. "Keeps count of what?"

"Of how many don't come back," he said.

Mara's fingers tightened on the railing despite herself. "I don't intend to add to its tally."

"No one does," Diego said, not unkindly.

For a moment, only the hiss of rain filled the silence.

Behind them, Kenji's silhouette floated from screen to screen on the bridge. Lorne had retreated to his glass office to draft emails that would sound like plans and feel like wishes. Elias moved the deck with the small economy of someone born to it, quietly securing lines that didn't need securing, checking lashings that would probably hold.

The river widened, then narrowed, then wrinkled itself into an S-curve that made the Peregrine shift her shoulders. Ruts carved into the brown banks grew taller, their sides studded with roots like exposed ribs. Egrets lifted off the shoals as the wake slid under their feet. A caiman sank without drama.

"Tell me a story," Amaya said to Diego as the pair carefully strolled the deck, watching the last houses fall away.

"About what?"

"About the Green Heart."

He made a sound in his throat, almost a chuckle. "You don't start with the heart. You start with the lungs. The older people say the basin breathes. That it fell asleep

44

when the miners came, and will wake when the time is right for renewal."

"That's not very scientific," Amaya said, but there was no scorn in it.

"It's precise," Diego explained. "It says what matters."

Mara stared ahead, where the canopy stitched itself into a roof. The first rank of giant trees loomed suddenly, as if the shore had stepped nearer. Branches arched. The light changed — green now, thinner. The air grew cooler while the humidity climbed.

Elias appeared at her elbow, trouser pockets damp with river spray. "You should see the Minnow," he said. "She'll make your scanners blush. Kenji's proud in a way that's almost dangerous."

"We're scrubbing 'almost' from our vocabulary on this trip," she said, eyes still locked on the green border. "Do you hear that?"

"I hear a ship taking itself too seriously," he said.

"No," she said. "Under it."

He fell quiet. At first it was nothing, only the layered noise of water and insects and motors. Then a texture revealed itself, like finding the grain under painted wood. A low tremor. Not quite sound. Not quite feel.

"Could be generators bouncing off the banks," he said.

"Could be," she said.

Neither of them moved for a while. A moth the size of her hand landed on the rail and opened itself like a book. Its wings were patterned with two perfect false eyes.

"Is there anything I should know before we disembark?" Mara asked, watching the moth flutter away.

Elias considered. "Don't step where you can't see ten centimeters into the ground. Watch for trees with roots that look like they're holding hands. Your brain will try to find faces in the lianas; half the time it's right. And if the forest goes quiet, don't fill the silence with your voice."

That last one felt heavier than advice. She tucked it away. "Understood."

"Good," he said, softer. "It will like you more if you pretend you don't care whether it likes you."

"Does that work on people, too?" She cracked a grin.

"Sometimes," he said, and for once the smile reached his eyes.

The Peregrine shouldered into the river proper, and civilization fell away as if it had never been.

CHAPTER 4

The First Steps

By the time dawn broke over the Escondido Basin, the air was already thick enough to drink. The horizon bled from rose to pale gold, and for the first time since leaving San Isidro, the forest ahead didn't look like a simple tree line but a wall — living, vast, and indifferent.

Elias stood at the bow of the Peregrine, scanning the shifting water. "We anchor here," he said, his voice steady over the soft churn of the engines. "Any farther, and we'll be hitching roots instead of river stones."

Kenji frowned at the sonar screen. "Depth's shallow, but it's stable. I'll drop anchor."

Lorne joined them, coffee in hand, white shirt already damp from the humidity. "Stable enough for the Minnow to make landfall?"

"Stable enough for a priest's sermon," Elias said.

Lorne smirked, choosing not to ask whether that was a compliment. He turned to Mara, who stood near the rail, notebook open to a clean page. "Welcome to the edge of discovery, Doctor Ellison."

She gave him a look over the rim of her sunglasses. "Discovery tends to look like mud from this distance."

Elias grinned. "You'll get used to it. Or the mud will get used to you."

The chain clanked through the pulley, and the Peregrine lurched slightly as the anchor bit into the riverbed. Around them, the forest stretched upward in

47

columns of green. Foliage dripped with condensation, vines braided from limb to limb. Somewhere out there, unseen creatures traded calls that didn't sound quite animal.

The Minnow slid down from its rigging with a low splash. The aluminum skiff gleamed under the morning light, its Auralis logo catching the shimmer like a metallic tattoo. Elias and Kenji loaded crates of equipment: mapping tools, sample containers, battery cells, a tent frame strapped in sections along the gunwale.

Mara stepped aboard last, checking the clasps of her waterproof satchel. Amaya clambered in behind her, face flushed with excitement, camera bouncing from her neck.

"You okay?" Mara asked.

Amaya nodded vigorously. "I've never been this close to an untouched system. It feels like being on another planet."

"Planets are easier," Elias said. "At least their gravity doesn't talk back."

She blinked. "Is that a joke?"

"Half of one."

They pushed off. The current caught, and the Minnow coasted the last fifty meters to shore. The prow nosed into soft mud with a sigh. Elias jumped first, boots sinking to the ankles, and secured the rope around a gnarled root thicker than his leg.

The air on land was another element entirely. Dense, vegetal, alive. The scent was a hundred shades of green: wet bark, sap, decay, something floral hiding under it all.

The First Steps

Mara knelt to scoop a handful of soil. "Loam depth's extraordinary," she observed. "You could bury a city in this."

"Some say it already did," Diego said, stepping from the skiff last. His tone was neutral, but his gaze lingered on the trees, reverent. He drew a necklace from under his shirt and touched the charm—a carved wooden heart—briefly to his forehead.

Elias began offloading the gear while Kenji set up a portable drone mast and unpacked sensor poles. "If we're staying here," Kenji said, "I want eyes before dark."

"Then let's start earning the daylight," Mara said.

By midmorning, the clearing pulsed with quiet industry.

Amaya and Diego strung tarps between the sprawling roots of a kapok tree, forming a canopy of faded orange that bled color onto the wet soil. Kenji assembled the sensor poles—thin silver rods with small blinking diodes—around the perimeter. Elias hauled crate after crate up from the Minnow, moving like a man who'd long ago made peace with sweat.

Lorne paced the edge of the camp, tablet in hand, glancing every few minutes toward the deeper green. "We'll need a wide-band scan of this quadrant," he said, motioning vaguely. "Topography, soil conductivity, whatever your instruments can spit out. We're not just here to pitch tents."

Mara looked up from her map. "We have to establish baseline readings first. If we scan before we calibrate—"

Beneath the Verdant Veil

"If we delay, we risk missing something," Lorne interrupted. "We're here to prove something new."

"New doesn't mean reckless," she said, sharper now. "No use analyzing faulty data."

The air thickened a degree. Diego straightened from where he was pegging a tent line. "The forest doesn't like to be measured," he warned quietly.

Lorne laughed under his breath. "Good thing it doesn't get a vote."

Diego's eyes narrowed, but Mara cut in, redirecting. "Kenji, run a limited sweep. Five meters around the base, low power. Amaya, log sample coordinates. We'll expand once we verify there's no interference."

"Yes, ma'am," Amaya said quickly, grateful for the structure.

Elias, half-listening, paused near the tree line where twin vines had grown in a spiral, twisting around a central branch like a double helix. He frowned. The formation was too consistent. Nature loved symmetry, but never this precisely.

He drew a small sensor from his pocket and placed it ten meters away, along the marked perimeter. It blinked amber. Without comment, Elias walked the sensor back to the base of the spiraled vines and saw it turn green. He buried the device there under a layer of leaves.

Mara caught the movement out of the corner of her eye. "Adjusting the grid?" she asked.

"Trusting my gut," he said.

"That's not scientific."

"It's predictive," he said with a half-smile. "You'll thank me if something crawls out of that geometry."

The First Steps

She let it go. For now.

By early afternoon, the buzz of equipment joined the insect chorus. Amaya crouched by the northern array, labeling glass tubes of soil while Kenji checked readouts from his tablet.

"This place breaks every rule of growth mapping," Amaya said. "The mycorrhizal lines form near-perfect radial networks. It's like —"

" —a designed system," Kenji finished, nodding. "Something's organizing the substrate."

"Biological or mechanical?"

"Could be both," Kenji said, scanning the feed. "The conductivity curves are spiking off-scale. It's like the soil itself is listening."

Diego glanced up from his notes. "Maybe it is."

Mara joined them, brushing stray hair from her face. "Let's stay with observation, not interpretation, please."

Diego gave her a dry smile. "Observation is just slower belief."

"Then believe carefully," she said, kneeling to adjust a sensor.

Elias appeared with two canteens and passed one to her. "You're running on fumes."

"I'm running on professionalism."

"Same thing, most days."

"You worked with Auralis before?" she asked.

"Once," Elias said. "They'd found a microbial bloom near the Maracura cliffs, something they thought might have pharmaceutical potential. My job was to certify that the sampling zone wasn't sitting on top of cultural remains."

Mara raised an eyebrow. "And?"

"It was."

"And they didn't care."

"They cared," he said. "Just not enough to slow down their timeline."

"Marketable over responsible," she said.

"Something like that."

They shared a brief smile before he glanced toward the dense wilderness ahead. "You feel that?"

She listened. The air held a low vibration, not quite sound. "Maybe an approaching storm."

"Or the forest thinking," he said.

"Don't get poetic on me."

"I wouldn't dare," he said. "You'd require I cite sources."

By late day, tempers thinned along with the light. The heat, the insects, the damp had a way of abrading patience.

Lorne wanted progress reports. "We've been here eight hours and I don't have a single headline-worthy anomaly," he said. "You're telling me the jungle's symmetrical and damp. I could've told you that from my office."

"Science isn't performance," Mara said evenly. "It's patience."

"It's also funding," he countered. "Auralis didn't send us for pretty patterns."

Elias, nearby, said without turning, "Then maybe they sent the wrong people."

Lorne ignored him. "Kenji, boost your scanner range. Let's see beneath the root line."

The First Steps

Kenji hesitated. "That might overload the signal. The forest floor's wet enough to ground the entire circuit."

"Do it anyway."

Diego stepped in. "The last people who ignored warnings here are bones the roots haven't finished yet."

Lorne turned, irritation sharp. "I didn't invite superstition."

"And I didn't invite arrogance," Diego shot back. "But here we are."

The silence after that carried the weight of thunder.

Mara broke it. "Enough. Kenji, continue baseline mode. No full sweep until I say so."

Kenji nodded gratefully.

Lorne stalked off toward his tent, muttering. "Fine. But I'll expect something tangible by morning."

Elias watched him go, expression unreadable. "That man's going to dig a hole until something climbs out to eat him."

Diego snorted. "The forest might find him indigestible."

For the first time, Mara laughed, not loud, but real. "I'd like to keep everyone intact at least until day three, please."

The forest began to change as the light bled out. The greens deepened to blue-black; mist crawled along the ground in sheets. Amaya hung small LED lanterns along the ropes between tents, their light tinted soft amber to avoid attracting too many insects.

Kenji logged the last of the day's data. "Soil activity fluctuated around midday, then stabilized. Energy readings show faint rhythmic pulses about two hertz."

"Mechanical?" Mara asked.

He shook his head. "No metal. It's like the dirt's breathing."

"Everything breathes," Diego said from his hammock.

"Not like this."

Mara leaned back against a crate, her hair damp and curling against her neck. The jungle beyond the circle of light seemed impossibly still. No wind. No rustle. Even the insects had gone quiet.

"Too quiet," Elias said softly, as if he had read her mind.

Then the ground shivered.

It wasn't violent, just a deep, slow undulation that rolled through the camp like the exhale of something buried far below. Cups rattled. Instruments flickered. The LED lanterns swung once, twice, before stilling.

Kenji checked the readings. "No seismic activity."

Lorne emerged from his tent, hair mussed. "What now?"

Amaya whispered, "It felt like… a heartbeat."

Another pulse came, slower this time but stronger. The air vibrated.

Elias crouched, pressing his palm flat to the soil. "It's definitely not mechanical."

Mara knelt beside him. The sensation climbed up through her bones, a rhythm too deliberate to be random, too vast to be human.

"Could be groundwater shift," Lorne said, voice brittle with forced logic.

"Or something moving under it," Elias said.

The First Steps

Diego just stared into the darkening trees. "It knows we're here."

Lorne scoffed, but the sound died quickly. No one moved for a long minute, listening. The pulse faded, leaving the night impossibly empty.

Finally Mara exhaled. "Log it," she said quietly. "Tomorrow we find where it came from."

Elias looked toward the murky tree line, where glimmers of their firelight painted faint highlights on the impenetrable darkness. "And what happens," he said softly, "when it finds us first?"

CHAPTER 5

Echoes of the Past

Night made a second jungle on the riverbank, one woven of lamplight and shadow, of steam drifting like breath and moths haloing the tarps. The camp settled into its small routines: Amaya cataloging samples by headlamp, Kenji coaxing a reluctant data burst from his tablet, Diego sharpening a stick to a pointed tip because hands needed work when minds wouldn't rest. The Peregrine glowed faint in the distance, a low constellation on the water. Closer, the Minnow clicked as it cooled in the shallows.

Elias fed slivers of dry heartwood into the stove's little mouth until the small flame steadied. He didn't look at Mara, though he felt her attention as surely as the heat on his shins. The day's pulse still lived in the soles of their feet. It had been brief, two breaths rolling through the ground, but every conversation since had bent around it like reeds around a stone.

"Story time?" Amaya said, trying for lightness. Her voice carried the thin brightness of a person insisting on normal.

Diego's mouth tugged. "Careful what you wish for in this place."

"Careful is why we brought you," Kenji said, smiling without quite lifting his eyes from his screen.

Lorne emerged from his tent with a mug and an impatience that reeked like cologne. "Not too careful.

56

We're not writing field poems." He took the empty camp chair, crossed one leg over the other, and studied the four of them as if they were instruments he might yet play in harmony. "Dr. Ellison, what did you make of this evening's event?"

Mara closed her notebook. "The pulse wasn't seismic. The sensors picked up synchronized voltage changes in the soil lattice. Very low, very broad. It felt... organized."

"That word again," Lorne said, half-amused. "Organized."

"I'm not calling it sentient," she said. "I'm calling it non-random."

Diego looked toward the dark, where the trees leaned over one another in postures that could have been sleep or listening. "On this river," he said, "random is just a word we use when we don't like the intention."

Lorne sipped, unconvinced. "And what intention did you hear, Mr. Morales?"

Diego didn't answer him. His gaze had shifted to Elias, who had set his hands palm-down on his knees as though steadying himself against a swell no one else could feel. "Tell it," Diego said quietly. "The story you've been asking every librarian and historian in Central America about. The old one."

Mara's attention sharpened. "What old one?"

Elias watched the stove's flame-lit plume rise in a straight line before the damp air caught it. He slid a folded paper from the inner pocket of his vest — edges feathered soft from years of being handled — then hesitated. The hesitation was the first unguarded thing he had offered them all day, and it softened the set of Diego's jaw a fraction.

"It's a clipping," Elias said. "From 1883. London paper. The headline is grand, the way headlines always are when the writer can't believe his luck. *The Madness of Explorer P — .*" He smoothed the fold. "The article is a summary of a longer account by the man himself. Pembroke. First initial H. It never gives the full name here, which is both coy and very 19th century."

Mara leaned in, elbows on knees despite herself. "And he was where we are?"

"Further inland. He'd followed a map hand-drawn by a hired boatman who refused to go beyond the second bend. Said the river forgot you there." Elias glanced up, as if expecting someone to laugh. No one did. "Pembroke describes being drawn off the water by music that wasn't music. That was his phrase: 'a music without tone.' He claims it came up through his feet when he stood still, and through the handles of his instruments when he set them on the ground."

Amaya rested her chin on her fist. "Like our pulses."

"He camped three nights," Elias went on. "On the fourth day, he says the forest 'presented him with a corridor' — his words again — roots and vines parting just long enough for him to walk twenty paces into a cavern that had not been there before. There he found what he calls a 'fibrous temple,' though he admits there was no stone. Only columns of living filaments, threaded like embroidery, and within a shape he could not see without remembering other objects, places — and people — he had loved."

"Poet," Diego said softly, not insincerely.

"A scholar in poetic panic," Elias said. "He writes that something spoke to him. Not a voice in the air, a thought that arrived already in the shape of words. He tried to answer aloud. He asked what it was, and it answered only with a sensation that he struggled to name. He wrote the word 'queen,' and then scratched it out, then wrote it again."

"'Queen Beneath the Roots,'" Diego said, the phrase a familiar bead on his tongue.

Elias nodded. "He tried to step closer. When he did, he felt a physical pull in his chest, as if a hand had reached inside him and found a rope. He believed he was being asked to choose. He also believed he might never return if he chose the thing that was asking. He ran."

Kenji exhaled. "He took off."

"He ran," Elias repeated. "Back to the river, barely made it to the nearest settlement. Pembroke was fevered and swore the trees were calling him by name. He refused to leave at first and then refused to stay. They dragged him out. Within a year he was confined to a private asylum in England. The last line of his account reads, 'There is speech in the roots. They braid their memories through the bones of the earth, and if you listen long enough, they will tell you what the soil dreams.'"

Silence lay down with them for a long minute. A moth skimmed the edge of the campfire light and vanished again, unscorched.

Mara's body did the thing it had trained itself to do in the presence of a seductive story: it wanted to lean forward while her mind planted both feet. "Nineteenth-century travel writing wasn't journalism," she said. "It was a parlor trick. Sea serpents and wild men and mermaids in bathtubs. If Pembroke didn't make it up, an editor did."

Elias didn't flinch. "He could be a liar and still be right."

"He could be a liar and be dangerous," she said. "Believing people like him is how we end up with sunk costs and dead students."

The stove ticked once as a rivet cooled. Amaya stared at the forest floor.

Diego's voice came cold, cutting the damp. "You would know, *señora doctora*, about dead students."

Mara met his gaze. "That was unkind."

"It was," he said. He didn't look away. "So was the joke about bathtubs."

She felt heat rise under her collar. "The joke was not at your people's expense."

"You don't have to name my people for it to land on us," Diego said. "We had plenty of Pembrokes. They sat on our fire circles and listened until we trusted them. Then they left with our words and came back with maps we weren't on."

Mara noticed Diego's gaze lingering on Elias with a tension that wasn't just academic disagreement. "You tell the stories well," he said, tone flat. "Almost like they were yours to tell."

Elias blinked. "I'm just repeating what Pembroke wrote."

"Mm," Diego murmured. "Funny how some people get praised for repeating what others were scolded for preserving."

Before Mara could intervene, Amaya nudged Diego lightly. "Hey. Maybe the forest just likes a good storyteller."

Diego didn't smile, but the edge softened.

Lorne cleared his throat, plucking at the thread as if he could unwind the scene. "We're not here for folklore rivalries. We're scientists. We let data correct us. Right now we have a nineteenth-century melodrama and a low-frequency anomaly. We don't have a queen."

Diego's mouth bent. "You have already met her borders."

Mara kept her tone level. "We're not dismissing anything. We're assigning it a shelf, that's all."

Amaya finally spoke, small but steady. "I also assigned your paper on canopy collaboration," she said to Mara. "I argued you were right when you said systems have intention. Not minds, intention. Doesn't this… feel like that?"

Mara looked at the girl's face. Amaya was trying to be careful and brave at the same time. "Intention is not the same as person," Mara said, gentler now. "We can name what we felt today without building it a throne."

"Someone already did," Diego murmured. "Long before us."

Lorne stood, mug empty. "Enough for tonight. Tomorrow, Kenji, I want a more ambitious sweep. Dr. Ellison, prioritize anything that looks engineered, whether by fungus or men. Mr. Grant, you keep us out of the quicksand and the more literal kinds of trouble. Mr. Morales, collect your… narratives. They make good sidebars when we publish."

Diego's jaw tightened, but he didn't answer. Lorne went to his tent.

The smaller conversations drifted apart. Kenji muttered a goodnight and slouched into his hammock with the tablet on his chest, the screen dimming to ambient light. Amaya stayed by the stove, poking the embers into careful symmetry.

Elias started to rise. Diego's voice stopped him. "You carry that clipping like a totem," he said, not unpleasant now.

Elias folded the clipping along its crease. The newsprint had softened to cloth in places. "It was a map I wasn't steadfast enough to follow."

"You followed another map, once," Diego said. The words were soft and very sharp. "You humiliated our people. You brought cameras into our saints' houses and asked them to pretend."

Elias didn't reach for defense. "I let a man I worked for plant what he wanted to find," he said. "I suspected. I didn't stop him. That's my sin, not his. If it helps, and I know it doesn't, I didn't get rich. I got emptied out."

Diego considered him through the blanket of darkness. "Why are you here, then? To refill?"

Elias looked into the stove, where the last blue flames licked at a dry twig. "This time," he said, "I'd rather find something that can't be filmed."

The answer surprised them both in its simplicity. Diego's face changed, very slightly. Some knot loosened, not forgiveness, but the space that precedes it.

"You hear her," Diego said, as if confirming something he'd been avoiding. "Even if you don't say it."

"I feel something," Elias said. "I first felt it in the Yucatán and now I feel it here, more distinctly. It could be the story I fed for too long. It could be the jungle. I'm willing to be wrong in the right direction."

Mara, who had paused five paces away, pretended to study the cathedral-like kapok roots that anchored their tarps. She heard every word. She had wanted to dismiss Elias as a good-looking ruin with instincts that would get them all killed. Instead, he kept saying things that bent her towards him against her will, like a compass to a magnet buried under the floor.

"Tomorrow," she said into the air, as if speaking to the sleeping vegetation, "we map the corridor on the north side. If the pulse has a source, my guess is it's along that spine."

Diego and Elias looked over. "Yes, Doctor," they said in unison. The title had no mockery in it.

"Don't make it sound like a promotion," she objected, but her mouth was almost a smile as she said it.

CHAPTER 6

The Lost Drone

By noon the heat had the texture of burlap. Fog lifted off the river in slow sheets, and the trees wore their own weather, a luminous sweat that beaded at leaf-tips and dropped in soft metronomes onto the understory. The camp had come to life like a disciplined anthill. Tarps re-tensioned, lines coiled, the Minnow ferrying another load ashore: dry boxes, a second gravity filter, a bright orange case that Kenji cradled the way a violinist carries his instrument.

He set the case on a folding table he'd hammered level with a rubber mallet and three curses. The lid unfolded to reveal foam cutouts: rotors, gimbal assembly, a camera the size of an apple, two spare batteries gleaming like river stones. The drone itself lay in the center, matte and patient.

"Say hello to Kestrel," Kenji said, palms hovering theatrically over the airframe before he lifted it free. "Lightweight composite body, stabilized 3-axis gimbal, on-board lidar, thermal, hyperspec bands in the near-IR." He paused. "And a personality."

"More than some men," Amaya said, deadpan, and then flushed when she realized she'd said it out loud. "I mean—"

Kenji grinned and spared her. "She flies docile in a breeze and mean in a headwind. Top speed forty knots. If anything can thread the needle in there…" He angled his chin toward the knotted green interior. "It's her."

Lorne stood with his hands behind his back like a captain whose ship was a spreadsheet. He was crisp even in the heat, a small miracle of starch and stubbornness. "We need coverage out to five kilometers," he said. "Grid first, then adaptive sweep if you find anything that looks like a pattern of right angles."

"Right angles are the jungle's favorite joke," Diego mused, watching from the shade of a buttress root. "It lets you see them when it wants."

"We'll ask nicely," Kenji said, and snapped the last rotor in with a satisfying click.

Mara adjusted the brim of her field hat and checked the handheld spectrometer clipped to her vest. "I want to fly a spiral out from the last known pulse maximum," she said. "If the soil voltages are spiking regularly, we may get a harmonic that repeats with distance."

Lorne's mouth did a small thing that might one day become respect. "Spiral, then a lattice overlay," he agreed. "Grant, you're point on the ferry. If Kestrel goes down in recoverable terrain, I want eyes on it."

Elias, crouched at the edge of the clearing, had been tracing the damp loam with a twig, mapping something only he saw. He stood, brushed his hands against his trousers, and shouldered the dry bag he'd prepped an hour ago. "Copy," he said. The word had the clean snap of habit, the frenzied routine of TV production still lying dormant in his bones.

They used the Minnow to get a clean launch lane over the river. Kenji sat amidships with Kestrel balanced on his knees, Elias at the tiller, and Mara on the bow with binoculars, eyes narrowed against the glare. Amaya straddled the orange case, hugging it with her calves; Diego remained on shore, a silhouette under towering river palms.

At mid-channel, Elias eased the throttle until the Minnow drifted in place. The jungle crowded the banks, roots like wrists, branches like grasping fingers. Somewhere deep, a bird made a noise like a sheet of tin being torn. The air smelled of wet stone and things that had never seen direct sun.

Kenji lifted Kestrel one-handed and released her. The rotors hummed into clarity, a precise, insectile voice. She rose, wobbled once while her gyros worked out where the world had put itself today, then steadied, camera checking yaw, pitch, roll like a dancer finding balance.

"Telemetry green, radio green," Kenji said, fingers moving on the controller's sticks with surprising delicacy for a man who wore a ring of tools like a belt. "Begin spiral."

They watched as Kestrel took her first long arc over the opposite bank, skimming just above the canopy. Data streamed across Kenji's tablet: altitude, heading, real-time imagery. The screen showed a quilt of leaves stitched with shadow. Every now and then, the canopy made a polite attempt at geometry. Then, like a magician revealing the trick, it softly unraveled.

"Nothing too anomalous," Kenji said. "Wait. Hold. Spectral spike in near-IR. Switching bands."

On the screen, green drained to ghost. The canopy became a map of heat and water content; in the false-color palette he'd chosen, stress showed up as smoky lavender. A faint ring bloomed.

"Back twenty meters," Mara said. "There."

Kenji nudged the stick. Kestrel banked, obedient. The ring resolved into a series of concentric ovals, shallow as brush strokes. In the middle lay a depression, the suggestion of a rectangle worn smooth by centuries of something heavier than rain.

Mara exhaled. "It's the same harmonic spacing we detected previously in Sector Nine," she said, and heard the tremor she couldn't entirely keep out of her voice. "Two centimeters average variance, repeating at — Kenji, throw me the ruler."

He passed her his stylus instead. She measured against the scale, did the math. " — repeating at a ratio that matches the lidar's frequency band from the satellite pass." She looked up at Lorne on the bank, far away and impatient. "It's not random."

Kenji changed to lidar. The screen dotted with points and then, slowly, a phantasmal structure: the suggestion of corridors under the leaf skin, not deep, maybe a meter down, each line so faint you could have called it noise if the world was quiet enough.

Lorne's voice crackled over the handheld. "Report."

Mara swallowed dryly. She didn't look at the Minnow's wake, suddenly very narrow and very far from shore. She looked only at the tablet and said the thing she had taught herself to say only when the data left her no room for doubt. "We have rectilinear subsurface features beneath a biologically organized canopy. It's… consistent with intentional arrangement."

"Say it," Lorne said. "Say the word."

Mara met Elias' eyes by accident. He wasn't gloating. He looked — what? — sorry for her, almost, that she would be the one to carry the word and be punished for it. "Architecture," she said softly. "Biological architecture."

"Jesus," Kenji whispered.

Onshore, Lorne's "Yes" carried across the water like the release of a held breath. "That's our proof," he said. "Push to the center. Let's see our temple."

Diego's voice cut in, low enough that the radio barely caught it. "Careful."

Kenji zoomed the camera as Kestrel eased down through a break in the canopy. The image juddered, leaves nudging the lens, then steadied. The clearing was perhaps twenty meters across. No trunks inside it, only a woven floor of roots, tight as a basket. The center held a feature that might have been a hollow, might have been a mouth. Around it, the ovals were narrower, more insistent, as if the earth itself had repeated something it loved until the repetition became memory.

Elias felt his tongue find the back of his teeth and press as if against a word. He did not speak. He did not need to.

Diego was a dark shape on the bank, hand flat to the rough skin of a tree trunk. "El Corazón Verde," he said, and though he used the radio now, the phrase came as if it had been waiting in the air for someone's tongue. "The Green Heart."

The Minnow drifted. A wider, older pulse came up from the floor of water and touched the aluminum hull. It wasn't the same rhythm as the previous night. It wasn't a rhythm at all, more like the notion of one.

The Lost Drone

"Kenji," Mara said, keeping her voice level. "Altitude two meters over the clearing. Let's get a full sweep, then pull back. No contact."

Kenji nodded, focused. Kestrel obeyed. The gimbal tilted. The hollow filled the screen. For half a second, the camera tried to make sense of the contrast, failed, and applied a softening that turned the image into a painter's wash.

Something on the edge of the frame moved. No, not moved, recomposed. A coil of vine lifted as delicately as a cat moves a whisker. It touched the tip of Kestrel's rotor guard like a blind person greeting a hand in the dark.

The feed glitched.

"Back," Mara said.

Kenji eased the stick. The drone rose, clearing the lip of the anomaly. For a moment the screen was full of leaf, leaf, more leaf, as a bough pushed forward like a thought changing course.

"Telemetry?" Elias asked.

"Solid," Kenji said, but his voice was thinner.

"Bring her back for diagnostics," Mara said.

Lorne's voice cut across the radio like a knife. "Negative. If there's a central feature, I want it mapped."

"One pass, then out," Mara said quietly to Kenji. "We don't want to risk crash recovery deep inside."

Kenji swallowed. "Copy." He took Kestrel along the eastern arc. The image cleaned up as the drone climbed a meter and the canopy stopped touching. The ovals revealed smaller ovals nested inside, the geometry of a shell, the language of nature.

"What does your paper say this is?" Amaya asked, unable to keep quiet. "Is there a name for—"

"Pattern selection," Mara said. "Self-reinforcing structures that preserve stability."

"Like coral," Amaya said. "Like —"

"Like temples," Diego said.

Kenji breathed out. "Telemetry spike," he said, almost conversationally, the way a person says *the stove is on fire* in a polite restaurant. "Electromagnetic noise coming up from below."

On the screen, a ripple crossed the clearing. It wasn't wind. The leaves didn't move. The light changed, as if the sun had blinked. A jade whip briefly flashed past the camera.

"*Kestrel*," Kenji said, and for the first time he spoke to the machine as if it was a person who could hear the shape of care.

The feed tore, just a single line across the frame.

Then black.

Kenji froze. His thumbs made small, helpless circles over the dead sticks. He tapped the restart sequence. He checked the radio channel. He flicked the mode toggle out and back like an old superstition. "Signal loss," he said, and though it was an obvious sentence, saying it made it truer than he wanted it to be. "Last coordinate logged. Battery at eighty-one percent." He stared at the tablet as if he could think a picture back onto it. "She's... she's just gone."

Elias felt the bottom drop a degree under the Minnow. Or maybe that was simply his body registering the absence, how every machine makes a sound, and only when it stops do you hear what it kept quiet. "Bring us around," he told himself, as if he were not the one holding the tiller. He eased the nose toward shore. "We'll mark the GPS."

"Recoverable?" Lorne asked, his tone already deflecting blame.

"Maybe," Kenji said, betraying worry that went beyond a budget line. He held still and listened for the faintest cough of a returning signal, the way a person at a deathbed waits for a breath and tells himself he hears it.

Mara put a hand on his forearm. "We've got coordinates and a drone recovery kit. We'll get her back."

"Tomorrow," Lorne said, from the bank, cursing under his breath. "First light of day. With cutters. Proceed with today's scheduled groundwork."

They ferried back. Kenji packed the empty case as if it were a coffin. Amaya inventoried the loss. "Was that… did a vine grab her?" she asked, voice faltering. "Did we see that?"

"Probably a downdraft," Lorne said. "Mechanical artifact."

"Like how the forest sent a pulse through the soil last night that was just 'thermal expansion,'" Kenji murmured, not quite under his breath.

Mara recorded the numbers and tried not to interject her feelings. She wrote, "Oval ratios consistent, and subsurface points suggest organized voids," and not, "*It seems like the jungle is toying with us.*"

They worked until the light went soft. The Minnow rocked in its moorings like a dog asleep in a hammock. The river went from bronze to brushed pewter. Mosquitoes brandished their small swords and found no gaps in the camp's armor.

Dinner was packet stew made edible by Diego's handful of crushed chilies and the good mood of men and women who have solid work to do the next morning. Lorne ate standing, the way men eat when they want the people around them to remember they're supposed to move. When he finally retreated to his tent with a satphone that might as well have been a scepter, the camp exhaled a different air.

Eventually, Diego's gaze became lost in the flickering of the fire.

"You okay?" Amaya asked quietly.

Diego hesitated. "This place... it reminds me of things I tried not to remember."

"Like what?"

He thumbed the carved talisman hanging from his neck. "My wife used to say the world speaks in signs. I thought losing her meant the signs were lies."

Amaya's voice softened. "Or maybe you just stopped listening."

He gave her a surprised look, not offended, but unsettled. And heard.

Mara drifted toward the edge of the clearing, where the ground sloped to a patch of bare soil. The day's footprints had already softened. Elias knelt there, palm spread on the earth the way old sailors touch their ship's hull when no one's watching.

She eased down beside him until their shoulders matched height. The soil was warmer than the air. "What's it saying?" she asked, half-grinning.

"Here," Elias said softly. "Hold your hand like this."

The Lost Drone

He slid his hand two inches under the leaf litter until his fingertips met the cool damp crust where today becomes yesterday. She mirrored him. For a while there was only the little drum of small lives: ants, roots, the machine-song of beetles milling over one another.

"Now," he said. "Stop listening for sound."

"What else is there?" she asked, but she obeyed. She opened a different kind of attention, the kind that catches the feeling of being looked at from across a room before your eyes have found the gaze.

The earth under their fingertips shifted. Not shove, not shock. A shift the way a sleeping child turns their face into the pillow to catch more of a pleasant dream. It wasn't a rhythm yet. It was the hint of one.

"I feel it," she said, and the admission cost her less than she'd imagined. It felt good to be simple.

"It's stronger where the humus is deep," Elias murmured. "Like the... like the voice has more to hold."

"Don't call it a voice," she said, reflex snapping. Then, almost laughing at herself, "Not yet."

"We'll find you a better word," he said. His shoulder brushed hers. The contact was accidental and careful at once, the way people who have been lonely for a very long time learn how to touch. "And I'll stop talking before we ruin the silence."

She turned her head to look at him. In the low light his face had lost the hard angles that made him look like a man who carried around his past like an anvil. He looked younger with the work on him, younger and more himself. The stubble along his jaw shone like gold filings.

Behind them, Amaya laughed at something Kenji said, and the laugh carried a relief that belonged to another life. Diego hummed a tune under his breath, one of those minor-key songs that have no beginning and no end. The river moved the way old men move when they decide to pretend the pain isn't there tonight.

They withdrew their hands at the same moment, as if on cue from a conductor neither could see, and stood. For a beat, neither of them stepped back from the other. The moment had the fragile perfection of a glass bead in a palm; you can't throw it in the air to make it more beautiful without losing it.

"Sleep," he said, low.

"Right," she said. "Sleep."

The night slid over them in careful increments. Camp quieted. The mesh of insect song settled into a far-off roar, the universal static of the tropics. Mara lay in her tent with the flap half-open to the idea of air. The curve of the buttress root along her right side felt like a wall made by a living architect with a beat in its plan. Her body did the inventory it performed after long days in the field: ankles complaining in a minor register, calf throbbing from the fracture she suffered in Peru. The surgical scar was a faint echo of the gaping wound she carried in her mind's eye.

The handheld radio by her head rasped, a whisper of electronics settling. Then it rasped again, longer, oddly toned. Static, she told herself. The jungle's humidity plays havoc.

The static took shape.

" — *closer* — "

Mara sat up fast and knocked her elbow against the tent pole. "Kenji?" she hissed. "You on?"

The Lost Drone

Only a snore from the engineer's tarp. Amaya stirred in the next tent, mumbling a dream-logic list of Latin names.

" – come – closer – "

The voice was human, but wrong. Not Lorne, not Elias, not Diego. The syllables were stretched, as if they had been pulled through a screen and hung to dry and then put back together by a toddler. The aspirated *c* of *come* became a soft sigh. The *s* in *closer* dragged with a hint of leaves.

Mara swallowed. "Who is this?"

Only the river answered, patient as sleep.

She clicked the radio off, then on again. Nothing now but the honest night. She lay back down, heart daring itself to slow. A minute later, she rolled onto her side, closer to the flap, closer to the silent giants who stood like wooden sentinels over their heads.

"If you're learning," she muttered, feeling like a fool breaking her own rule, "learn this: we don't want to hurt you."

No answer came, and that was somehow worse than any whisper could have been.

CHAPTER 7

The Wall

They left just after dawn while the river still wore its night-cool breath. Condensation unspooled from the surface in tattered veils that caught at the Minnow's bow and clung to their boots when they stepped ashore. Elias led, machete low and lazy, more an announcement than a threat. Behind him, Mara picked footholds with a surveyor's thrift. The shadowed half-moons under her eyes betrayed a restless sleep and a strangeness she wasn't ready to admit. Amaya carried a compact logger at her chest like a second heart; Kenji had the recovery kit slung high; Diego brought up the middle, with a battered field camera hanging from his hip and a dislike for everything that gleamed; and Lorne came last, immaculate and impatient, as if he were late to his own ambition.

Elias made a narrow trail, turning his blade sideways to push ferns rather than slice them. It only felt right to give such deference. Whenever he did cut, he did it clean, and muttered a soft apology. If Mara heard it, she didn't say so. The forest opened around them like a crowd that parts when a stretcher passes.

They stopped for a bit to check readings. "Marking," Amaya said, reaching out to pin a reflective tab to a liana. "Every fifty meters."

"Make it thirty," Kenji said. "The path is knitting behind us." He held up a strip of flagging tape he'd tied himself a few minutes earlier; the vine it circled had already begun to grow over the knot.

"It did that to roads my grandfather's crew cut many years ago," Diego said. "They put in culverts; it swallowed the culverts. They bridged a ravine; the ravine expanded. This place refuses to be tamed."

Lorne checked his watch as if time could be shamed. "Kestrel went down at 10° north-northeast from camp," he said. "Another two hundred meters."

They kept marching. Elias, at the forefront, soon came to a crackling halt on the undergrowth and lifted a hand. "Might be a long two hundred meters," he said. One by one, the team joined him in stunned silence.

Before them was a wall, but not in the human sense. It had not been raised. It had grown. Vines as big as thighs braided with buttress roots, mismatched bark fused together, all of it interleaved with layers of fibrous tissue that had the satin sheen of healed bone. The structure curved away left and right, out of sight. Not perfectly circular, more like the turned rim of a colossal bowl. Where it met the ground, the loam pinched together like a welded seam.

Mara stepped forward until the shade of the thing cooled her face. She did not touch it. Her fingers hovered, reading temperature, moisture, the small electric prickle that is the skin's way of admitting it does not know what it knows. Up close, she saw the pattern most clearly: spirals nested in spirals, the growth rings of a tree translated into geometry and then translated back into flesh.

Kenji exhaled a sound that wasn't quite a laugh. "That's not... possible," he said, which was exactly what people say when something is.

Lorne crouched beside the living wall, running one hand along its surface with an almost reverent intensity. "Feel this," he said, knocking lightly. "It isn't just bark. It's a composite, layered like engineered fiberwood. That means there's internal structure. And if there's structure, there's a seam."

Mara folded her arms. "And you think cutting it will somehow tell you where that seam is?"

"Exactly," he said. "A ten-millimeter core will give us the growth orientation of the fibers. Once we know the angling, we can model the whole lattice. Find the weakest vector. That's how we get inside without blasting half the basin open."

Kenji shook his head immediately. "That's not how plants work. That's not how forests work. These growth patterns aren't natural. Look at the alignment. It's too uniform. If it's constructed biology, its reaction to injury could be defensive. Or worse."

Amaya touched the wall very lightly, almost flinching at its faint warmth. "It's... organized," she murmured. "Not like normal cambium layers. More like muscle tissue."

"Which is why we need a sample," Lorne said. "We can't model what we don't understand."

"That's exactly why you *don't* cut into it," Mara fired back. "We don't know how it reacts. And whatever this is? It's an ecosystem. You hurt one part, the whole thing responds."

The Wall

Diego's eyes stayed fixed on the wall, expression dark. "She will feel it."

Lorne scoffed. "Plants don't feel."

Diego didn't move. "This one does."

Elias exchanged a tense glance with Mara. Even he wasn't sure he believed Diego's folklore, but the hair rising on the back of his neck was harder to dismiss.

"It's just wood," Lorne said.

"It's not," Diego returned, the flatness in his voice more effective than heat. He tipped his head, listening. "That's the border of her breath."

"Whose?" Amaya asked, less to argue than to make Diego say it.

Diego's eyes stayed on the braided mass. "The one you forget to fear until you enter her domain."

"Local myth," Lorne said, already bored with someone else's reverence.

Mara stepped sideways along the curve. In some places the vines had grown tight and dense like tendon; in others, sap had welled and dried, a varnished luster. There were scars, places where something had cut once, long ago, and the tissue had mounded up around the wound like a lip. She felt the memory of force in those places. Not just pressure. Conviction.

"We could find another way around," Elias said quietly. "Maybe."

"The day's too early for lost opportunity," said Lorne. He turned to Mara with palms open in a mockery of collegiality. "Doctor Ellison, we are here to prove there's an underlying architecture. We are not going to do that from the riverbank like pilgrims at Lourdes."

"Lorne," Elias tried to reason. "We're here seeking purposeful design. This wall was put here for a reason."

"One shallow core," Mara said at last. "Low-force, minimum heat, minimal tissue disruption. If the sap rises, we stop. No blades. Chuck drill only. And we log three minutes of baseline bioelectric first."

Lorne inclined his head as if she had agreed with him and not given a condition that could turn into a refusal. "Tanaka," he said.

Kenji looked at Elias, not at Lorne. Elias said nothing, and in that nothing Kenji found what he needed. He set down the recovery kit, unlatched his toolkit, and assembled the palm-sized corer with movements that were all apology. The bit was a hollow cylinder with fluted teeth no sharper than a butter knife. He fitted a torque-limiting chuck. "Three seconds on, three off," he said to no one. "If she warms, she'll tell us."

Amaya squatted beside the wall, fingers hovering a centimeter off the surface, logger in her lap. "Baseline," she whispered. The graph traced a slow wave, not steady, not random—like the sea's long breath under a chop.

Diego stood with his hand flat to his chest, thumb on his talisman as if it were a rosary he refused to show anyone. He watched Kenji as he might watch a surgeon operating on a living thing that didn't know it had agreed.

"Okay," Mara said. "Now."

Kenji braced the corer and brought the fluted end to the junction where two vine-bolts had grown into one another. He kept his arms loose, let the tool find center. The motor engaged with a thrumming purr. The wood, if you could call it wood, accepted the first bite. There was almost no resistance. The bit sank three millimeters. Kenji lifted, waited, felt the heat-bloom. Mara eyed the logger. The wave form altered, barely. The second pass took them to five millimeters. Nothing bled.

"Last," Kenji said, and pressed.

At seven millimeters a bead welled around the bit, so small you could have mistaken it for dew. It was red. Not wine-red. Not maple-syrup red. Rust, like weathered iron.

Amaya made a small sound. "Stop."

Kenji lifted. The bead trembled, fattened, and then, without falling, retracted. The hole closed a fraction. Around it the surface knit into a new pattern like an armadillo shell.

"Enough," Mara said. She hadn't realized how loud her own breath was until she heard it stop.

"Sample," Lorne said. "We've already —"

The wall moved.

Not back, not aside. It tightened, the way a muscle does on reflex. The closure wasn't local. The vines above their heads hunched together; the seam at the ground pinched. A smell rose, wet iron and cut stems, and under that the raw sweet of green tissue exposed to air.

"Back," Elias said. He didn't shout. He gave the word the same weight he gave to "*stop*" when a cliff began a meter earlier than the map claimed. He reached without looking and closed a hand on Diego's shoulder. Diego obeyed a stranger's hand as if it were a cousin's warning.

The wall's surface rippled. The ripples rolled outward in concentric rings, and everywhere a ring passed, the vines thickened and the gaps closed. A thin thread dropped from a branch and touched Amaya's wrist like a question. She flinched; Mara batted it away with the logger, and the thread recoiled with such speed that Amaya yelped as if stung.

"Move," Elias said, already moving.

They retreated along their own fresh track and found it narrower. The forest didn't slam doors; it arranged furniture. Ferns leaned. Lianas that had hung like casually tossed laundry now draped like dungeon chains. The sense wasn't of being chased but of being kept from forgetting that they had crossed a line.

"Kenji," Mara said, pointing to the ground. "Markers."

He tried to toss a strip of flagging ahead to a visible branch. The strip hit a curtain of fine tendrils which wrapped around it like tongues. "Nope," he said, too calmly. "Nope, nope."

Amaya stumbled. Vines around her ankles flexed, not snaring, but testing. Elias spun, machete up now, and slashed. He sharply chopped the creepers at her legs but carefully swatted the hangers that were falling like a net, using the flat side of the blade. "Don't hack what's holding its own weight," he said through his teeth. "You don't want a curtain on your head."

A root heaved under Diego's boot like a crossbar. He pitched forward and would have put his hand straight into the sharp spines of a black palm if Elias hadn't hauled him aside bodily by the straps of his pack. Diego's breath left with a *whuff*; a beat later he registered the near-miss and went a little white.

"Gracias," he managed.

"Don't mention it," Elias said absently.

The Wall

A tendril slid over Lorne's sleeve with the moist sound of peeled tape. He slapped it off and swung his machete wildly, jaw set in fury more than fear. "It's a reflex," he said, because the alternative was admitting the world had opinions. "A plant's *thigmonasty*. Stimulus-response."

"Your textbooks can call it whatever they like," Diego said sharply. "But don't pretend you didn't feel it *reach* for you."

They entered the last bend before the river and found their path reduced to the size of a drainage pipe. The jungle had compressed there not into a barrier, but a funnel. Elias didn't think. He surged forward, shoulders sideways, and pushed through the living curtain, blade working like a swimmer's hands in rough water. No big gestures, only the necessary ones. The light beyond blared as if from another country. The river's silver lay ten body-lengths away.

"Come on!" Elias said from the far side, and his voice was a rope for the others.

Mara lightly shoved Amaya ahead. Kenji ducked, hunched around his gear like a running back guarding a football. Diego waited half a beat to force Lorne through before him. The curtain, having learned them, adjusted. It dropped threads for their faces and licked their limbs blindly with rows of moist suckers. It did not hold. It wanted to, Mara thought, and didn't. The intention of the place was not to capture; it was to compress. To teach.

They tumbled into light that felt rude. The river took their noise and spread it thin. The Minnow bobbed, tied short to a root that now looked less like an anchor and more like a clawed hand.

The explorers piled into the skiff without grace. Elias flicked the knots free with the tip of his machete and kicked the motor over. The little engine coughed, then caught. He shoved them into the channel; the current did the rest.

From midstream, the expanded wall, if you could call it a wall, looked less like a human obstruction and more like a giant, green amoeba sealing itself. The curtain they'd come through shrugged, and the gap disappeared as if it had been a mistake the forest had corrected.

Amaya reached for Mara's hand without pretending she wasn't. Mara squeezed back with her left; her right stayed on the gunwale, white-knuckled.

Kenji stared, the engineer in him offended by an elegance that had not been prototyped. "It... closed," he said, as if putting a verb to it might reduce the magic to size.

"It didn't want us," Elias said.

Diego shook his head. "It wanted us to learn the word, '*No.*'"

Lorne stood at the stern and looked at what he'd been denied: the clean geometry of it, the way the curve promised the satisfaction of an answer if only you could get inside the right question. His face smoothed into something that would have looked like composure to a stranger. To the people who knew to read hunger in a blink, it looked like calculation shedding its skin.

Over the mutter of the motor and the river's chatter, the forest made a sound that might have been wind and might have been the memory of wind. The scent of iron thinned, replaced by something sweet and dry that made

Mara's mouth water and her stomach turn at the same time.

By the time they nosed into their little cove below camp, the light had shifted toward afternoon and the heat had gone flat. They stepped out in a sequence that had already become ritual: Elias steadying the bow, Mara hopping onto riverside roots, hands reaching for the cases, Amaya calling inventory, Kenji checking the motor even after it had already proved it wanted to live. Lorne stood with one boot braced on a bench, like Washington crossing the Delaware.

No one spoke for a while. They didn't need to. The story the day told itself was loud enough, and none of them wanted to make the mistake of talking over it.

When Lorne did finally break the silence, his voice carried like a thrown rock. "We saw the barrier," he said. "We know where to apply pressure."

Diego's head came up, dangerous as an old bull's. "You didn't just see a barrier," he said. "You saw defense."

Lorne ignored him. He turned to Kenji. "Since the jungle 'told' us we couldn't take a sample, then let's argue back." He clenched his hand as if grasping inspiration from the heavens. "We'll make a signal that opens it. Since it shuts at touch, we'll try it at a distance. Harmonics tuned to last night's ground pulse, plus two decibels. We learn to speak its own language."

"That worked out so well for Babel," Elias said.

Mara, who could feel the heat where a vine had brushed her hand, couldn't quite get her voice through her throat. When it did emerge, the words were raw as if she'd been through a windstorm. "We wait, Adrian," she said. "We log. We breathe. Then we decide. If we push too hard, we may not get a second push."

Lorne smiled without teeth. "Doctor Ellison," he said softly, "did you come to study a door or to walk through it?"

She looked at the green barricade that now ballooned over where the path had been. It looked back.

"Both," she said. "But in that order."

The river pressed on. Something large turned under the surface a dozen meters away, just a roll, a suggestion. The sound was a punctuation none of them could read.

Lorne lifted his chin to the trees as if he were addressing a boardroom through a two-way mirror. "We'll break through, and soon," he said confidently over the water's hiss and the forest's old whisper, making the promise to his reflection and to the part of the jungle that might enjoy being dared.

The wall, already sealed, said nothing at all.

CHAPTER 8

The Pulse

By the time they broke camp and the Peregrine slid back into midstream, the forest had withdrawn into a silence that felt personal. The living wall loomed behind them as a dark band inside the retreating daylight, its woven surface outlined in the spill of the ship's floodlamps. Where their machetes had absently bitten in the frenzied expulsion from the trees, the bark still gleamed with rust-red sap.

Mara stood at the bow rail, one hand resting on the cold metal, the other clamped around the strap of her field bag as if she expected the river itself to tug it away. Water slapped gently against the hull. It should have been a soothing sound. It wasn't.

"They're not supposed to move like that," Amaya said beside her, watching the jungle edge through the curtain of drizzle. She whispered it as if speaking too loudly might bring the wall surging toward them.

"Trees?" Mara asked.

"Any of it." Amaya's breath smoked in the damp air. "They reacted as a unit. When Kenji cut, the sap pressure spiked across multiple trunks. It was like they shared a vascular system."

Mara remembered the way the barrier had sealed behind them, vines knitting together with terrible speed, turning open air into a clenched fist. "Remember that," she said quietly. "We may not get another chance to see it up close."

Elias stepped out from the cabin, coat thrown over a damp shirt, hair still dark from the rain. "Kenji's firing up the lab equipment," he said. "Lorne's on a tear."

Diego emerged next, rubbing his forearms where the vines had brushed him. Sucker marks had already started to bloom, small bruised constellations beneath his skin. He stared over at the sealed wall of vegetation, shaking his head.

Amaya stepped closer to Diego. "You look pale."

"Not out of fear," he calmly refuted.

"Didn't say it was," she replied. "But… you're shaken."

Diego let out a breath. "I lost faith once. I thought I'd buried it with her." A beat. "And now the jungle is picking at old scars."

Amaya placed a hand on his arm, firm but warm. "Then let it. Doesn't mean it wants to hurt you." She hadn't noticed the sucker marks.

"My grandmother used to talk about places like that," Diego said. "Borders between worlds. You cross them at your peril."

"Your grandmother did not have access to satellite imaging," Lorne's voice cut in.

They turned. He was on the upper deck above them, hands braced on the rail, suit jacket gone, sleeves rolled to his forearms. In the harsh light he looked less like a corporate director and more like a tired predator, too used to getting his way to recognize when something had finally said no. "That wall proves we're close," he announced. "Whatever is inside does not want us there. Which means it is worth the trouble."

Mara's fingers tightened on the rail. "Or it means we've already done enough damage for one day."

Lorne smiled thinly. "If you're worried about ethics, Dr. Ellison, we'll settle that debate once we know what we're dealing with."

He turned away toward the stairs that led to the lab.

Elias watched him go. "That man thinks consent is a problem to be solved," he muttered.

"Most grant committees aren't much better," Mara said. "They just have less expensive toys."

The wind shifted. For a moment, the deep green band of forest seemed to lean slightly toward the ship, as if straining to hear them. Then the movement was gone and only the rain remained.

"Whatever he is planning, he'll start tonight," Elias said softly.

Amaya's eyes were already drawn toward the portholes of the lab. Banks of equipment glowed behind the glass, halos of soft blue light. "If he's about to wake something up," she said, "at least we'll be recording the moment."

Diego snorted. "Doctora, if the forest gave us a warning, we should hear it. Not talk over it with more machines."

Mara met his gaze. "I don't intend to talk over anything. I intend to listen. If Adrian's going to start a conversation, I'd like at least one person in the room who cares about what it says back."

Diego opened his mouth, then closed it with a small sigh. "Then I'll say a prayer."

Elias watched them all peel away toward the companionway. He looked at the living wall one last time. Bleeding sap winked in the floodlight like an open eye.

"We're coming back in, aren't we," he murmured, not quite a question.

The wall shivered. Just once.

He went inside.

The Peregrine's lab smelled of ozone, disinfectant, and river mud that no one had quite managed to keep off the equipment. Racks of instruments lined both walls, all harmonizing in their own minor keys. The long central table was dominated by the transmitter array, a cluster of boxy black modules and polished aluminum plates wired into the ship's power core.

Kenji bent over the main console, fingers moving rapidly across the touch panel as scrolling numbers reflected in his glasses. Lines of code marched upward, each tagged with a time stamp and frequency band.

"Phase-cancellation filters in place?" Lorne asked as he entered.

"Yes," Kenji said. "We can shape the output so it doesn't fry our own systems."

"'Can' being the operative word," Elias said from the doorway.

Lorne ignored him. "And the harmonic sweep?"

"Programmed. We'll start low and step upwards, watch where we get a response."

Mara slid in on the far side of the table, Amaya close behind. Diego took up his post near the bulkhead. He touched the talisman under his shirt with two fingers, unseen by Lorne but not by anyone else.

"What exactly are you attempting?" Mara asked.

Lorne gestured at the array like a magician unveiling his assistant. "A conversation. We send a clean signal, then listen for a reply. That wall responded physically to our cutting. I suspect this will be subtler."

"You're assuming it can interpret electromagnetics as language," she said.

"Everything in that basin is saturated with conductive pathways," he countered. "Roots, mineral veins, groundwater. If there is an organizing intelligence, it will use whatever channels are available. We're just speaking up on one of them."

"And if we're shouting?" Elias asked.

Lorne smiled without humor. "Then something will hear us."

Kenji finished a sequence and tapped his stylus against the console. "Power at standby. Emission bands ready to cycle. We're linked to the hull plating, forward sensor mast, and both dorsal arrays."

"The whole ship," Diego said. "You're turning this boat into a tuning fork."

Lorne tipped his head, conceding the point. "Poetic, Mr. Morales. Yes. A tuning fork in a very large, very belligerent bell."

Mara stepped closer. "If we do this, I want continuous data capture. Bioelectric readings from the surrounding canopy. Thermal imaging. Any shift in the river's conductivity."

Amaya nodded. "Already set. We'll run the sensors in passive mode. Watching, not pushing."

"Good," Mara said. She looked at Lorne. "Then we have no excuse to keep doing it if we see dangerous stress patterns."

Lorne's eyes hardened, but he spread his hands. "If it shows we're harming our subject, I will revisit parameters."

"*Subject*," Diego repeated softly.

Lorne pretended not to hear. "Let's begin," he said.

The transmitter warmed with a soft, rising whine. Kenji's fingers danced across the panel as he initiated the sequence. The overhead lights dimmed by a fraction, compensating for the power draw.

"Baseline at ninety hertz," Kenji reported. "Output at twenty percent. Contact points stable."

Mara watched the graph bloom on her tablet. The emitted wave was smooth, controlled. For now.

Outside, nothing moved. The forest thinned slightly in the wash of the ship's lights, leaves glistening from the rain. The living wall was a darker smear against the sky, its surface unreadable.

"Give it a little time," Lorne said.

They waited. Amaya's eyes flicked between the external cameras. Elias watched the waterline, where the reflection of the hull stroked the slow current. Diego's lips moved in what might have been a prayer or just a list of curses.

After a few seconds, Kenji shook his head. "No measurable deviation in ambient noise. No shift in field readings."

Lorne frowned. "Increase amplitude."

"By how much?"

"Ten percent."

The Pulse

Kenji thumbed the control. The whine deepened. The lab floor vibrated faintly, like the sensation you get standing too close to a heavy speaker.

Mara felt it in her jaw. "Easy," she said. "That's enough to cause structural resonance if it couples with the right frequency."

"We need a stimulus," Lorne said. "We aren't here to whisper and hope."

On the external feed, a few leaves quivered. It could have been the smallest breeze. It could have been nothing at all.

"Do you see that?" Amaya asked. "Camera three."

They all leaned closer.

A tangle of vines that draped from a low bough had begun to sway. Not side to side, but toward the ship, then back, in the same slow period as the pulsing line on the console.

"Synchronization," Mara said under her breath. "It's entraining."

"Probably coincidence," Lorne said, but his pupils had dilated. "Increase another ten."

Kenji hesitated. Elias moved closer, standing at his shoulder. "Push this too hard and you'll cook your own boards," Elias said. "I've seen what faulty resonance can do to older hulls. They tear themselves apart from the inside."

"This hull was built three years ago," Lorne snapped. "It can take it."

Elias did not move. "You're not listening. If you start a rockslide, you don't get to decide where the stones stop."

Beneath the Verdant Veil

Lorne's jaw clenched. "Grant, if you cannot keep your nerves in check, step away."

Kenji looked between them, then at Mara. She held his gaze. "We're observing," she said carefully. "Let's treat this like any other experiment. Gradual increases. Real-time monitoring. No arbitrary jumps."

Lorne exhaled sharply through his nose, anger contained only by the need for results. "Five percent increments, then. But we are going up."

Kenji turned the dial.

The tonal quality of the hum changed. It was no longer just heard; it was felt. The air itself seemed to thicken, molecules crowding closer. Mara's skin prickled. Her hair, damp from the earlier rain, tugged at her scalp as if caught in an invisible breeze.

On screen, more vines began to sway. Tendrils uncoiled from trunks, reaching out with slow, tentative movements, like sleepers stretching in their beds.

Diego's fingers tightened around the edge of the console. "She heard you," he said. "Now you should stop."

"Do you smell that?" Amaya asked.

A faint scent had risen, threading through the filtered air. Not the usual mix of river rot and metal. This was greener, sharper, with a sweetness like torn leaf and warm syrup.

"That scent was in the clearing," Mara said. The memory surfaced with full sensory clarity. The vines closing. The shudder of the earth. "Right before it closed itself."

The Pulse

Lorne looked almost delighted. "We've engaged some part of the system. This is exactly what we wanted."

Mara turned on him. "We wanted to observe, not provoke a systemic response."

"You can't observe without there being something to see," he replied. "Science is not a one-way mirror."

The thrum climbed another notch. A hairline crack raced across one of the overhead light covers with a sound like ice breaking. The bulb inside flickered, then steadied.

"Kenji," Mara said sharply, "check hull vibration."

He skimmed his hand across the data. "Within tolerance. Barely. If we hit a resonant frequency with the superstructure, we'll know. Rapidly."

"Radiation levels?"

"Normal. It's just sound, Dr. Ellison," said Lorne.

"Sound can kill," Diego retorted. "Ask anyone who has seen a bridge fall because someone marched in time."

Another vine dropped from the canopy on the screen, its tip swinging toward the camera. It held there, wavering in place as if tasting the air.

Something tapped, softly, against the hull. The sound came from somewhere below them. A light, almost polite contact.

Everyone froze.

"Probably debris," Lorne said.

The tap came again. Louder.

Elias had already moved to the nearest porthole. He cupped his hand around the glass to block the lab lights and peered down toward the waterline.

At first he saw only warped reflections. Then the reflection shifted. Something pale was pressed against the steel below the surface: a cluster of vines, slick and slender, writhing in a slow knot. They slid along the hull, searching.

"They're touching us," he said.

Amaya joined him. "Oh my God."

On the other side of the glass, tendrils thickened, more of them joining until a rope of plant tissue had formed. It tightened and the ship listed a fraction of a degree toward that side, just enough for everyone to feel it underfoot.

"We need to cut output," Mara said.

Lorne shook his head. "No. We're at the edge of something important. If we stop now, it may withdraw entirely."

"If we keep going, it may crush us," Elias said.

"It hasn't," Lorne said. "We are still very much afloat."

The ship lurched again, harder this time. The lab's hanging cables swung like pendulums. A metal tray slid two inches along the table.

"Kenji!" Mara snapped. "Power down to baseline, now."

Kenji's hand hovered over the controls.

"Tanaka," Lorne said softly. Warning and promise layered together.

Kenji's jaw worked. He swallowed.

Elias stepped in, voice low but carrying. "Kenji," he said. "You know what a feedback loop is. You know what happens when you let it run longer than you can control."

The Pulse

Kenji's fingers tightened on the dial. For a heartbeat, he looked like a man trying to decide which god to anger.

Then he cut power.

The hum died so abruptly that everyone staggered. It left behind a ghost tone in their heads, a phantom ring that made silence feel unreal.

"Tanaka!" Lorne hissed. Kenji avoided his glare.

For a moment nothing happened. The entwined tendrils at the porthole hung there, suspended, drifting gently with the slowing motion of the ship.

Then every vine touching the hull convulsed.

The tap became a thud, the thud became an impact. The ship shuddered as if a giant hand had given it a single, contemptuous shake. Somewhere below, something groaned, a long, low complaint from the ship's metal belly.

Alarms pinged on Kenji's console. "Contacts along port side. Multiple points of pressure."

"Propeller?" Elias demanded.

"Still free, I think. I can feel a slight rotation through the deck."

"Bring auxiliary power online," Lorne ordered. "We may have to move."

"Auxiliary runs off the same grid," Kenji said. "If we spike it again, we'll be blind and dead in the water."

Outside the porthole, the vines began to withdraw, unraveling from around the hull. They did not drift away randomly; they sank back toward the dark in synchronized undulations, like waves retreating into the surf.

The ship rocked once more, then steadied.

Beneath the Verdant Veil

The scent in the air changed. The sharp floral aroma dulled, leaving behind something heavier. It smelled like wet earth tamped over fresh graves.

Diego exhaled shakily. "She answered," he said. "And she decided to let us be. For now."

Lorne released a breath he had not seemed to know he was holding. His hands trembled once before he clasped them behind his back. "Recordings?" he asked, voice hoarse.

Amaya was already scrolling. "We got everything," she said. "Field strength, hull vibration, external movement, atmospheric chemistry. It's... a lot."

Mara rubbed at the bridge of her nose. Her skull felt too tight. "I want copies of all of it," she said. "And we're not doing that again until I've gone over the data."

Lorne straightened slowly, a man rebuilding his composure brick by brick. "We have proof now, Dr. Ellison. Physical interaction, likely directed by some organizing principle. That's worth the risk."

"Worth whose risk?" she asked.

He smiled. It didn't reach his eyes. "Ours, of course."

Elias looked from Lorne to the porthole where the last of the tendrils slipped back into the murk. "You keep telling yourself that," he said quietly. "But the risk isn't yours alone."

"Fine," Lorne acquiesced. "Perform a full ship diagnostic. We'll regroup in the morning."

Kenji began rebooting non-crucial systems. The lab lights dimmed to their nighttime level. The consoles glowed softly, like coals banked in ash.

The Pulse

In the lull that followed, a faint vibration moved through the floor. It was not loud enough to set off any alarms. It did not rattle glass or make loose objects dance.

It just was.

Mara felt it through the soles of her boots, a slow, deep throb that had nothing to do with the ship. She glanced at Diego. He was standing very still, eyes half-closed, fingertips pressed lightly to the wall.

"You feel it too," she murmured.

He nodded once. "It is under us. In us."

Elias laid his palm flat on the metal bulkhead. The warmth there did not feel mechanical. It felt organic, as if something enormous had pressed its body lightly against the hull in some secret, inhuman version of a handshake.

"What is it?" Amaya whispered.

Mara listened. The pulse was slow, measured. After a few beats, she realized why it felt so unnerving.

It was keeping time with her own heart.

"I think," she said, "that we just gave it a piece of our rhythm."

The pulse continued, steady, patient.

Outside, the jungle lay quiet, its silhouettes etched sharp against the starless sky. The wall did not move. The vines did not surge. On the surface, nothing had changed.

Inside the Peregrine, the ship floated in the center of its own small universe of data, sensors humming, consoles quietly recording.

And beneath the floor, in the metal, in the rivets, in the faint film of condensation on the walls, the forest's answering heartbeat kept time with theirs, a shared tempo waiting for the next note.

CHAPTER 9

The Green Tide

The storm broke well before dawn.

Mara woke to the sensation of being watched. For a disoriented second she thought she was still in the forest, cheek against the damp earth, the sky a low ceiling of branches. Then the thin mattress under her shoulder reminded her of the Peregrine, the muted hum of generators a soft presence in the walls.

Her cabin was a narrow rectangle: bunk, locker, a porthole the size of her head. Condensation had filmed the glass during the night. When she wiped it with the heel of her hand, the smear revealed the river, a murky mass under a still darkened sky.

The living wall loomed where the floodlights struck it, a massive and impassive tangle of fused trunks and interwoven vines. The ship lay anchored just off its shadow, a white tooth against a dark gumline.

Beneath the hang of vines, the forest looked perfectly still.

Mara dressed quickly, pulling on damp trousers and her field shirt. The faint taste of yesterday's oscillations still lingered in her mouth, as if the pulse had rewired her taste buds. When she stepped into the corridor, she heard voices from the lab, low, tense. She followed.

Kenji's words met her first. " — saying we're not built for another run like that."

The Green Tide

"You're overly cautious," Lorne replied. "We barely grazed what this system can do."

They were bent over the main console again when she entered, the lab lights dimmed to conserve power. Outside the reinforced windows the river slid past, flecked with bits of floating debris. The forest watched warily from the riverbank.

Elias leaned against the doorframe, arms folded, expression set somewhere between resignation and anger. Diego sat on a stool nearby, eyes blaring and bloodshot. Amaya hovered behind Lorne, afraid to tear her eyes off the sensors for one moment.

"What's happening?" Mara asked. "We were supposed to discuss this in the daylight."

"Mr. Tanaka is attempting to veto scientific progress," Lorne said without looking at her. "We're going to run a controlled follow-up. Lower amplitude, narrower band."

"'Controlled' is doing a lot of work in that sentence," Elias said.

Kenji shot Mara a look of relief, as if she'd arrived with reinforcements. "We still don't know the full structural stress from last night. I've rerun the diagnostic three times and we're fine on paper, but paper doesn't account for… that." He gestured toward the shoreline.

Mara stepped closer. "What's the plan, exactly?"

"Not a broad sweep like before," Lorne said. "We have terabytes of raw response data already. This time we match a few of the frequencies the forest seemed to respond to most clearly and send a brief, discrete pattern. More like a knock than a shout."

"Why?" she asked.

"Because," he said, as if explaining to a stubborn child, "we need repetition. One event is a curiosity. Two is the beginning of a model."

"And Auralis doesn't fund curiosities," Diego murmured.

Lorne's lip twitched. "No. It funds breakthroughs. Which reminds me…"

He keyed in a command. One of the auxiliary monitors shifted from sensor readouts to a simple interface bearing the Auralis logo and a status bar: UPLINK STANDBY.

"Data packet?" Mara asked.

"Last night's preliminary findings," he said. "Condensed field data, hull recordings, the works. Our satellite window is open. We'll send a burst, then begin the second trial while we still have comparable conditions."

"You're calling in the cavalry," Elias said flatly.

"I'm informing our stakeholders," Lorne corrected. "What they choose to do with the information is their concern. Ours is to provide it before someone else does."

Mara stared at him. "You think someone else is pursuing this?"

He smiled without humor. "You don't seriously believe we're the only ones who noticed the anomalies on those scans? Auralis was simply the first to move."

Kenji muttered in Japanese under his breath, something sharp-edged. He caught Mara's eye and translated dryly, "He's worried about losing priority."

"I'm worried about losing the signal," Lorne said. "We've already disturbed the system. It's aware of us. It may choose to change. We need this moment captured and transmitted before it goes away."

Diego lifted his head. "Moments like this don't go away. They go deeper."

Lorne ignored him and focused on Kenji. "Power up the uplink. We'll send the packet and then begin the targeting sequence."

Kenji hesitated, then entered the command. On the auxiliary screen the status bar flicked to UPLINK ACTIVE: 12%... 24%...

A soft vibration moved through the deck as the satellite dish on the mast above them rotated into position, seeking its line of sight.

Mara watched the percentages climb. Somewhere in a climate-controlled building thousands of miles away, someone in a suit would soon have a piece of their nightmare on a screen. Whatever came next would not be just theirs.

At 100%, the bar flashed UPLINK COMPLETE. LOG SENT.

Lorne's shoulders loosened by a hair. "Good. Now we make it worth their while."

He flicked back to the main array controls and dragged a series of sliders up, eyes bright. "Targeted harmonics only this time. No broad-band noise. Think of it as... picking out her name in a crowded room."

"*Her?*" Diego repeated. "You use the word now."

Lorne waved the observation away. "Kenji, lock it to the bands that gave us the strongest return last night. Short pulse train. We'll be under the stress tolerance curve before the system has time to react structurally."

"That's you guessing," Kenji said. "Not calculating."

"Then calculate faster," Lorne snapped. "Ready on your mark."

Kenji's fingers hovered over the keys. The sensor graphs from last night glowed on the adjacent monitor: peaks and troughs, harmonics, interference patterns. Against his better judgment, he locked the transmitter profile to three frequencies spiked by the forest's response.

"Profile set," he said quietly.

Mara put her hand over the console. "Adrian," she said. That was unusual enough that everyone stilled. "If you escalate the interaction again, it won't stay one-sided. Last night, it touched us because we touched it. What happens when you start trying to tell it how to behave?"

"That's the point of an experiment," he said. "Perturbation and observation."

"Not when the system can hit back," Elias said.

Lorne's patience finally snapped. "You wanted field autonomy, Dr. Ellison. You wanted the freedom to test your wild theories about intention in natural systems. That's what I've given you. I'm not going to stand here and let you turn timid because the forest swayed in the breeze."

"It wasn't the breeze," Amaya said softly.

He turned on her. "I expect you to interpret data, Ms. Nguyen, not poetry."

Her cheeks flushed, but she didn't lower her eyes. "The data said it wasn't the breeze," she persisted.

For a heartbeat, Mara thought Lorne might actually explode. Instead, he exhaled, clipped and controlled. "We're done arguing. Tanaka, execute pulse on my mark."

The Green Tide

Kenji looked at Mara, then Elias. Neither spoke. Diego's eyes spoke for him.

Lorne leaned over the console, voice low with something like triumph. "Mark."

Kenji pressed the key.

The transmitter's hum rose from the bowels of the ship, subtle at first, then more insistent. It wasn't sound so much as pressure behind the eardrums, a rearrangement of the air. The lab's equipment rattled in tiny sympathetic quivers.

On the forward monitor, the green wall filled the frame. As the pulse built, the vines along its edge shivered.

"Look at that," he breathed. "She hears us."

The fused trunks along the barrier's seam flexed. Slowly, like a crack spreading in a windshield, a narrow crease opened in the living mass.

"There," Kenji said, horrified despite himself. "We're forcing a deformation—"

"Not forcing," Lorne said. "Inviting. Push the amplitude point-five up."

"That exceeds the predicted—"

"Point-five," Lorne repeated.

Kenji swallowed and nudged the slider.

The hum intensified. It ran through the soles of Mara's boots, up her spine, into her teeth. She felt the fillings in her molars buzz. She imagined roots shivering in the river mud beneath them.

On the screen, the crease in the wall widened. The vines at its edges strained, some snapping, sap spraying in dark arcs. Behind the opening, something glowed faintly, as if a throat lay beyond.

"Adrian, that's enough," Mara said. "We've proved response. Shut it down."

"No," he said softly. "We've proved she can *move*. Now we see how far."

He dragged the amplitude slider again, not waiting for Kenji this time.

The hum spiked from discomfort to pain. Amaya clapped her hands over her ears. Diego flinched, gripping the wall. Elias swore and took a step toward Lorne.

"Cut it," he shouted. "You're going to break something we can't fix—"

The first impact hit like an enormous punch.

The lab lurched. Mara grabbed the table; Amaya staggered into her. An equipment case skidded across the floor and slammed into the bulkhead.

"Contact on the hull," Kenji gasped, eyes jumping to the sensor array. "Multiple points, port side. Pressure spike—"

A second blow. The deck tipped harder, sending a tray of sample vials skittering, glass shattering when it hit the wall.

"That's not just current," Elias said. "She's grabbing us."

On the external camera view, the river erupted. Thick clusters of vines surged up from below the waterline like tentacles, latching onto the Peregrine's flank. Their surfaces glistened with slime; their suckers grabbed and adhered.

"Shut it down!" Mara shouted.

"I'm trying," Kenji said, fingers flying. "The interface is—"

The transmitter controls flickered, then went dark. The hum didn't stop.

"Feedback loop," he said, voice almost a whimper. "She's feeding it back through the hull. It's not just us broadcasting anymore."

Lorne stared, something like awe washing over his face. "Do you see?" he said, almost laughing. "She's completing the circuit. This is… this is beautiful."

"Beautiful is not the word," Diego said through his teeth as the lab floor rolled under them.

The ship groaned under the growing constriction. A deep, rending sound came from somewhere below, metal protesting.

"Enough," Elias said. "We need to get off this thing. Now."

Alarms began to wail, triggered not by human hands but by the sheer number of systems screaming past tolerance. Red lights strobed at the corners of the ceiling.

Kenji stared at a rapidly reddening schematic of the Peregrine. "Port hull breaches in mid compartments. We're taking on water! List at four degrees and climbing."

"Grab gear," Mara snapped, slipping into the cool, ruthless register of triage. "Life vests, med kit, beacon. One bag each. Nothing we can't carry at a run."

Amaya flinched, then moved. She snatched the med pack from its hook and the satellite beacon from the emergency locker, hands shaking. Kenji shoved tools into a canvas bag with frantic, economical motions. Diego shouldered his field pack and slung his machete.

Mara dropped to one knee, snapped the latch on a waterproof case, and stuffed her notebooks and the most crucial samples inside. If the Peregrine went down, she wasn't letting the story sink with it.

She looked up and found Lorne still frozen at the console, his eyes locked on the widening seam in the wall.

"Adrian," she said. "We're leaving."

His jaw flexed. "We are not abandoning this vessel. If I can get us rotated off the bank, we can ride the channel and —"

The deck bucked harder. Somewhere forward, something massive tore free with a scream. The lights cut for a second, plunging them into dim emergency glow.

"You'll ride her straight to the bottom," Elias shouted. "You want to be at the helm when she goes, that's your choice. The rest of us are getting to the Minnow."

Lorne's mouth flattened. He looked, for a heartbeat, almost humanly torn.

Then he grabbed the edge of the console, hauled himself upright, and snarled, "Get to the skiff. I'll try to pull us clear enough that you don't get swallowed."

It wasn't altruism. It was control. He couldn't bear the idea of the jungle deciding how he died.

"No heroics," Mara pleaded.

"Too late," he said, and shoved past them into the tilting corridor, heading for the stairs that led up to the bridge.

Elias caught Mara's arm. "Go," he said. "Now."

The hallway had become a slanted tunnel. They half-climbed, half-scrambled toward the deck, boots slipping on the wet metal as the list increased. Fluorescent tubes swung on their mounts or dangled by wires. Water sloshed along the lower wall, carrying loose papers and a drifting pen.

They burst out onto the deck into chaos.

The Peregrine lay at a sickening angle, port side low, starboard gunwales high above the water. Vines as thick as bridge cables had wrapped around the hull, squeezing, their surfaces rippling with peristaltic motion. Others flung themselves up and over the rails, lashing across the deck, seeking purchase.

Glass from the bridge windows lay scattered in glittering drifts. Through the ragged openings, the pilot's console and wheel stood askew, lights flickering. Lorne was climbing toward the bridge, one hand on the rail, the other braced against the tilting doorway.

"Life vests!" Elias shouted.

They skidded to the emergency locker bolted near the starboard hatch. He yanked it open and shoved bright orange vests at whoever's hands were free. Mara shrugged hers on and buckled it with shaking fingers, then turned to help Amaya with hers.

"Breathe," Mara said, steady despite the chaos. "Look at me. In. Out. We're getting off. Do what I say and you'll be fine."

Amaya's fingers found the clips.

Kenji had one arm through his vest when a vine lashed across the deck and snapped around his ankle. He went down hard.

"Kenji!"

Elias dropped to one knee, knife already in his hand, and hacked at the fleshy coil. The vine tightened, dragging Kenji toward the listing port rail.

The plant's surface was slick, but when the blade bit, sap sprayed — dark, viscous, flecked with something that shimmered faintly. The vine spasmed. Its grip loosened just enough for Elias to get both hands on Kenji's leg and haul.

Diego lunged in, brought his machete down in a clean chop. The vine severed. Its free end thrashed, then recoiled across the deck like a maimed snake before slithering back over the side.

Kenji scrambled to his feet, chest heaving. "I hate this place," he gasped.

"It doesn't like us much, either," Diego said.

Above them, the bridge shuddered. Lorne lurched toward the wheel, grabbing for the controls. Through the fractured windows, they saw him slam a hand down on a manual override, trying to coax the engines to respond.

The hum from the transmitter still vibrated through the hull, but it was ragged now, out of phase, as if the forest were chewing the signal and spitting it back in pieces.

"Cut loose!" Elias yelled, pointing toward the Minnow.

The skiff hung off the high starboard side, metallic hull swinging wildly as the ship rolled. One of the hoist cables groaned under the strain, strands beginning to fray.

"I'll get the stern line," Diego said. "Kenji, the bow."

They slid and clawed their way along the tilting deck toward the davits, using railings and cleats as handholds. Below, the river boiled with movement. Vines writhed just beneath the surface like undersea power lines come to life, tightening around the Peregrine's submerged flank.

Mara kept a death grip on the waterproof case with one hand and Amaya's wrist with the other.

"Do not let go of me," she said.

"I won't," Amaya breathed. Her eyes were wide, but there was steel under the panic.

Diego braced himself against the slant and sawed at the stern cable with his machete. Strands popped one by one. "Now, Kenji!"

Kenji hacked at the bow line. Two wires snapped; the last few held, shrieking.

"Come on, come on —"

From the corner of her eye, Mara saw movement on the bridge roof.

A cluster of vines had found Lorne.

They'd been climbing the superstructure with horrible purpose, moving not in random flails but in deliberate arcs, tracking him as he moved from lab to corridor to helm. Now they converged, pouring over the roof's edge like a slow avalanche.

"Adrian!" she hollered as the vines slithered after him.

Lorne slammed his palm onto the bridge's comm panel at the same time, a loud crackle of static drowning out Mara's warning. "This is Dr. Adrian Lorne of the Auralis expedition team," he shouted, voice trembling not with fear but triumph. "The anomaly is hostile! Repeat, HOSTILE. We are under full biological assault. Immediate armed retrieval recommended. Burn clearance if necessary. Clear a line to the core. That's where the intelligence is."

Mara stared at him, stunned. "Adrian, what are you doing?"

But he wasn't listening. His eyes were bright with the fever of discovery, not survival.

"Auralis, do you copy? The forest is reacting to the pulse. It's… it's waking up! You'll have to cut your way in!"

The vines punched through the bridge roof. Lorne's transmission dissolved into a grinding collapse of metal. He looked up sharply, eyes wild. Through the shattered glass, Mara saw him yank futilely at the wheel as if the ship weren't already in the jungle's hands.

"You're real," he said, not to her, but to whatever he envisioned beyond the wall. Awe and terror mingled in his voice. "My God. You're —"

The vines struck. They hit like netted muscle, wrapping around Lorne's arms and chest, pinning him to the console. He tried to wrench free, but the pressure was absolute. For an instant his face twisted, not in scientific ecstasy, but in pure animal fear.

"Adrian!" Mara yelled again, useless across the maelstrom.

The vines tightened like anacondas. They dragged Lorne outward and down, away from the windows, into the seething mass. His hand clawed once at the broken frame, fingers whitening, then disappeared as the metal warped under the pull. His scream cut off mid-breath as the jungle took him, lost in a writhing throng that dragged him across the listing deck. The tangled mass retreated over the side and back into the river with a sickening slurp. The wheel spun freely for a moment before another tendril wrapped around it, holding it fixed in a grotesque parody of control. Mara's brain recorded but couldn't yet process the horror.

Diego's last stroke severed the stern cable. Kenji's blade parted the bow line. The Minnow dropped in a stomach-lurching plunge, hull slamming into the churning river. One of the paddles snapped free and disappeared in the current.

"Go!" Elias bellowed.

Mara half shoved, half lifted Amaya over the rail and into the skiff, then jumped after her, landing hard on the slick deck. Kenji followed, nearly falling, Diego right behind. Elias vaulted in last, boots skidding as the Minnow bucked under them.

"Push off!" he roared. "Now!"

Diego used the remaining paddle like a lever, shoving the skiff away from the Peregrine's tilting flank. The Minnow scraped along the bigger ship's hull, then slid free into the hungry current.

From their new vantage, the full nightmare was visible.

The Peregrine was cocooned.

Vines wrapped her like a constrictor's coils, bending steel, crushing compartments. Smaller tendrils swarmed over her skin, seeking every seam, every weld, every porthole. Where they found anchorage, they burrowed, splitting metal and glass alike.

In places, the vines glowed from within, a dull, poisonous emerald, pulsing in sync with the deep hum rattling the hull.

The larger ship groaned. The sound was almost articulate: a long, descending wail as the hull's integrity failed.

"Keep her straight!" Elias shouted, grabbing the skiff's gunwale. "Line up with the channel. Don't let the backwash flip us."

Diego dug the paddle into the water, muscles straining. The Minnow's bow swung toward the open river.

Behind them, the Peregrine rolled.

The starboard rail rose, the port side disappeared under foaming water. For a few surreal seconds the ship hung nearly on her side, masts and antennas reaching horizontally. Then the jungle pulled harder.

The vessel tipped past the point of return and went under.

Water boiled as air rushed out, geysers of bubbles erupting where compartments flooded and collapsed. The vines sank with the ship, still wrapped tight, dragging their own mass down into the murk.

The hum reached a screaming pitch. Sparks spat from the Peregrine's superstructure as the transmitter array, crushed and drowned, finally blew itself apart. The sound cut off like a severed wire.

In its wake, the silence roared.

The wave from the sinking ship hit them broadside. The Minnow lurched violently. Frothing water crashed over the sides, knocking Mara to her knees. Amaya screamed as the skiff tilted, one edge dipping perilously close to submerging.

"Shift!" Elias shouted. "Starboard, now!"

Mara threw her weight toward the high side, dragging Amaya with her. Diego jammed the paddle against the opposite gunwale like a brace. Kenji flattened himself along the centerline, grabbing whatever he could reach.

For one sickening heartbeat, the Minnow hovered at the tipping point.

Then it thumped back down, sloshing but upright.

"Bail!" Kenji gasped. "Hands, hats, I don't care, just get water out!"

They scooped and flung with frantic efficiency, using cupped palms and a plastic storage bin. Every bit over the side made the skiff ride higher.

Behind them, the river where the Peregrine had been frothed and fumed. Bubbles rose and burst. A few severed lengths of vine writhed briefly on the surface, then slid under, following their main mass into the depths.

The glow below dimmed, retreating. The hum dwindled to a faint, residual vibration, like the dying ring of a struck bell.

No wreckage floated up. The ship had been claimed cleanly. The only proof she had ever existed was the absence she left behind.

"How far to shore?" Mara asked hoarsely.

Elias scanned the bank. The living wall was no longer uniform.

A gap had opened.

Where there had been an unbroken curtain of fused trunks and twisted vines, there was now a narrow inlet, just wide enough for the Minnow to nose into, if they dared. The vines at its edges arched back, held taut as if by invisible hands. The interior beyond was a void of green shadow.

"That wasn't there before," Amaya whispered.

"No," Diego said. His voice shook. "No, it was not."

"Any other landing?" Mara asked Elias.

He looked upstream, then down. The bank beyond the wall was a tangle of roots and fallen logs, the current too fast and cluttered to attempt a landing.

"Not one we can reach in this," he said. "Not before we're too cold and too tired to swim."

"So our choices are drown out here or saddle up to the vegetation that killed our boat," Kenji said.

"That about sums it up," Elias said. He met Mara's eyes. "You know what this is."

"An invitation," she said.

"A test," Diego added quietly.

"Right now it's also a shore," Elias said. He took the paddle and dug it down over the port side, angling the Minnow toward the gap. "We can argue metaphors after we're not in a bathtub with a monster."

No one stopped him.

As they slipped through the shallows toward the overhang of the wall, the temperature dropped a few degrees. The air thickened with the scent of wet earth and resin. The river seemed to still, its surface smoothing as if the forest pressed down on either side. Vines layered over roots layered over trunks, all knitted together in patterns that echoed the spirals and tessellations Mara had modeled in lecture halls oceans away.

Sound changed, too. The slap of water on aluminum dulled. Their own breaths sounded louder. Over everything, she heard it again, that slow, steady exhale.

The forest's breath.

The Minnow bumped gently against a bank where exposed roots cupped a pocket of mud and discarded leaves. Elias jumped out first, boots sinking, and hauled the skiff closer so the others could disembark without falling in.

Mara clambered up, then reached back to help Amaya. Kenji followed, knees almost buckling when his feet met something that didn't move under him. Diego was last, jumping lightly from hull to bank.

They sprawled on the slick riverbank, coughing up mouthfuls of mud and river water, each of them trembling from the violent escape. For a long moment, none of them spoke. The only sounds were ragged breaths and the distant churn where the Peregrine had vanished beneath the vines.

Then, slowly, impossibly, the living wall ahead of them began to move.

Not violently, as it had when it crushed the ship. Not defensively, as it had when they tried to cut through it the day before.

This time the lianas pulled apart with deliberate grace, like heavy velvet curtains in a theater. Branches bowed away from one another. Thick woven roots relaxed, loosening their grip on the soil. A corridor formed, narrow at first, then widening by degrees, its edges strangely smooth, as if shaped by a phantom architect.

Amaya rubbed her eyes with the back of her fist. "Is… is that really happening?"

"It's opening," Kenji whispered. "Not attacking. Not reacting. Opening."

Diego knelt, touching the moss with his fingertips. The ground beneath was warm, not from the emerging dawn, but from something alive beneath the surface, radiating heat like a breath warming unmittened hands on a winter's day.

"It knows," he murmured. "She knows."

"Knows what?" Mara snapped, her voice still raw from screaming over the wreckage.

"That the threat is gone."

Elias stood last, watching the corridor with a strange mixture of awe and dread. "Lorne," he said quietly. "It shut us out when he was here. Took him when he pushed too hard."

"And now it's... welcoming *us*?" Mara asked, struggling to keep the tremor out of her voice.

"Or allowing us," Elias corrected. "There's a difference."

The paddle-shaped leaves of cigar plants along the corridor's edge swayed gently, not toward them, but *away*, like French doors opening for guests.

The forest was no longer defending itself.

It was choosing.

CHAPTER 10

The Listening Ground

They stood there, five soaked, shaking figures on a threshold, the river at their backs and the gaping green ahead. Neither direction was particularly appealing.

Elias hauled the skiff a little higher onto the riverbank moss. When he pulled, the Minnow tilted, and a thin sheet of water sloshed across her interior, more than had been there when they exited.

"Hold up," he muttered.

He jumped back into the skiff, boots splashing in a film that already covered the deck. He knelt, ran his palm along the inside of the hull, then hissed. "Damn it."

Mara felt her stomach clench. "What now?"

Kenji leaned in beside Elias. On the starboard side, just below the waterline, a jagged puncture was blown through the aluminum where the Minnow had slammed against the Peregrine. Each flex of the hull made it bend a fraction and weep a steady bead of river water.

"Yeah, that's how today is going," Kenji sighed.

"Can you patch it?" Mara asked.

"Not with what we've got," he said. "Maybe if we were in port with sealant and a day in dry dock. Out here?" He shook his head. "Best I can do is slow the leak, not stop it. She might last for short hops along the bank, but not hours. Not against current."

Diego frowned at the crack. "So if we stay on her…"

119

"We sink," Elias finished. "Not immediately. But eventually. And it'll happen when we're tired and far from shore."

Amaya hugged her arms around herself. "So we can't ride her all the way back out of the basin."

"We were never riding out of here on this bathtub," Elias said gently. He patted the gunwale once, almost apologetically. "She got us off the Peregrine. That's the last favor she had in her."

Mara exhaled through her nose, feeling the last illusion of an easy exit drain away. "Strip what we can carry," she said. "Rope, water, the med kit. Nothing we'll curse in an hour."

They moved quickly, hands working by instinct more than thought. In minutes they'd pulled a coil of rope, the compact first-aid kit, two water bladders, the gravity filter, and a multi-tool from the lockers. The Minnow rode lower with every ripple, its cracked hull taking on water in thin, relentless threads.

Kenji shook the satellite beacon once and grimaced; river water dripped from a seam in the housing. "She's waterlogged," he muttered. "I'll dry it out, but don't expect miracles. Half the antenna probably thinks it's a fish now."

Elias straightened, breath hanging in the damp air. "That's it. No boat, no clean way downriver. Whatever path we have now…" He looked into the natural tunnel. "…it's in there."

Mara nodded. The pulse they'd felt through steel and water now thrummed through soil and wood… a low, bass heartbeat under her feet, in her chest, urging them forward. The decision felt less like a choice and more like a verdict finally spoken aloud.

"Then we stop pretending we have another option," she said. "Inland it is."

For the first time since the Peregrine began to die, there was no screaming metal, no rupturing glass, no human voice raised in panic. Only the long, slow inhale of something older than language and their own ragged breathing trying to find a place inside it.

The forest waited.

Finger-like Philodendron leaves draped over the newly opened passage, as if quietly pointing the way. The air beneath the archway carried the faint, electric scent of ozone after lightning.

Mara's voice came out steadier than she felt. "Stay close. No one wanders. Not even a step."

Elias touched her arm. Not reassurance. Agreement.

They shouldered what little they had. Elias slung the med kit and one of the water bladders; Diego took the other water bladder and the rope; Kenji carried the multi-tool and the sat beacon's inert shell, more talisman than equipment now. Amaya slipped the gravity filter and her notebook into her pack, tightening the straps. Mara took the waterproof case. It felt heavier than its contents justified.

They left the riverbank and stepped beneath the jade arch, the damaged Minnow drifting behind them like a fading memory. The forest floor entwined their boots with a soft, deliberate embrace, as though acknowledging that, at last, they had accepted the welcome.

Mara straightened and looked down the corridor. The path ahead was not a trail in any ordinary sense. No boot tracks, no cut branches. But it was a path. The roots and ferns fell away in a subtle trough, as if a redwood trunk had been pressed lengthwise against the forest floor, again and again, until the ground accepted its new shape.

Diego eyed the corridor with a mixture of awe and dread. "Inland is where the stories go thin and the skeletons pile thick," he murmured.

"Diego," Mara said, gentle but firm. "I'm not asking you to like it. I'm asking if you see any other option that doesn't involve drowning or starving on the bank."

He held her gaze for a moment, weighing something that had nothing to do with her and everything to do with the forest. Then he shook his head. "No, doctora," he said. "She's made up her mind about our direction."

"Then we follow. And we keep our eyes open," she said.

Amaya's hands gripped the strap of her bag. "Do you really think... it's making a path?"

Mara took a breath. "I think the arrangement of this corridor is statistically unlikely to be random," she said. "And our odds of survival are better if we assume intention and plan accordingly."

Elias gave her a brief, approving look. "Translation," he said to Amaya. "Yes."

Before they marched out of sight, Mara glanced back toward the river. The Peregrine's absence sat on the surface like a fresh gash. For a second she imagined its white hull rising again, exhaling trapped air, Lorne bursting from the water cackling, telling them it had all been part of the experiment.

The Listening Ground

But the river was just river again, brown and opaque, the only mark the faint swirling scum of sap where the vines had retreated.

She set that picture aside and faced the verdant path.

"All right," she said haltingly. "Let's see what you want to show us."

They stepped into the corridor.

The soundscape shifted with each meter. Near the river, the noise of water still dominated, a constant, sibilant backdrop. As they moved away, the water faded, and other sounds emerged: distant bird calls, the crackle of a branch shifting under its own weight, the tiny scritches of insects moving through dried leaves. Over it all, like a bass line under a song, the low, steady hum.

It wasn't constant, she realized. It rose and fell in gentle waves, a slow modulation. If she stopped and listened with the part of her mind that, back in the lab, had spent hours staring at spectrograms, she could almost hear layers in it, like a chord, not a single tone.

"Hold up," she said.

They paused. She knelt and pressed her palm to the ground. The hum was strongest there, where roots converged under the soil.

Elias crouched beside her, his hand a warm presence near hers, not quite touching. "You feel it, too."

"Yes." She closed her eyes. "Now it's… rising and falling. Like it's listening for something."

"Or like it's talking to itself," Amaya said, voice small.

Kenji shifted his grip on the beacon. "Is it… following us?"

"Hard to say," Mara admitted. She opened her eyes, scanning the undergrowth. Chestnut trees growing along the path did seem angled slightly inward, glossy leaves turned so they "looked" toward the corridor. "But I don't think it wants us to go back."

Diego snorted softly. "Then it agrees with us about the river."

They resumed walking.

The jungle path wound inward in long, lazy curves. Sometimes it narrowed enough that they had to pass single file between buttress roots; sometimes it opened into wider spaces where shafts of milky light speared down from gaps in the canopy. In those pools of illumination, Mara could see that the earth was disturbed not by footprints, but by the slow, incremental push of roots and rhizomes reorganizing themselves.

"Look," Amaya said once, pointing. "These ferns—"

The ferns on the left side of the path were all curled in, their fronds tight coils like sleeping fists. On the right, they were unfurled, broad and open, as if in greeting.

"It's not random," Amaya said, half to herself. "It's... directional. Like an arrowfield."

Mara felt a flush of something like pride, watching the younger woman's mind slot new data into place even as fear tugged at its edges. "You'll map this when we get back," she said. "Turn it into a paper that gives your reviewers headaches."

"If we get back," Kenji said under his breath.

"When," Mara repeated, sharper than she intended.

The hum underfoot seemed to answer, swelling for a few beats, then subsiding.

The Listening Ground

By midday, the air had turned heavy. Sweat slicked the backs of their necks, dampening their collars. Words felt too heavy, swallowed quickly by the forest's vastness. The deeper they walked, the more symmetrical everything seemed. Trees angled toward one another like mirrored pairs. Moss grew in fractal lattices. Even the insects moved in rhythmic clusters, their wings beating in pulses instead of random intervals.

Mara could not stop cataloguing it all.

"This isn't natural," she announced at one point, as if telling the jungle what it didn't know.

Elias stepped closer. "Depends on your definition of natural. The jungle has its own way of organizing things."

She shot him a look. "Order this precise doesn't evolve by accident."

"And who says it's an accident?"

The tone was too calm, and that made her nervous.

They continued.

"Not to complain," Kenji said, batting at a lone insect, "but if the forest is listening, I would like to formally request that it ask the mosquitoes to stop biting us."

Mara scanned the canopy. "Keep an eye out for anything that looks like fruit, but don't pick it. We don't know what's safe."

"Is anything safe?" Amaya asked.

"That depends," Diego said. "On whether she thinks we're guests, pets, or lunch."

The banter kept them moving. So did the fact that there didn't seem to be any viable place to stop until the forest decided there was.

The corridor widened into a space where low stone outcrops pushed through the soil like the knuckles of buried giants. These weren't the towering monuments of ancient civilization. No pyramids, no ornately decorated temples. They were half-swallowed by roots, mottled with lichen, unremarkable except for the fact that they appeared in clusters—and were clearly chiseled and arranged by human hands.

Diego approached first, fingers brushing over the stone. "These should not be here."

"What do you mean?" Mara asked.

"There is no tradition of stonework in this region. Not like this."

"Then who made it?" Elias asked.

Diego's jaw tightened. "That's what I'd like to know. It's just what I hoped to find."

Kenji crouched beside one of the stones. "Look at this." He brushed off wet moss and revealed faint markings carved into the surface, straight lines and spirals that curved inward, intersecting in organized patterns.

"Glyphs?" Amaya whispered.

Mara knelt beside her. "Not just glyphs. Anatomical diagrams."

They stared at her.

She pointed. "Here, these repeating shapes? Neural clusters. And there, vascular patterns. These are organic systems. Someone carved biological schematics onto stone."

Diego admiringly waved a hand above the design. "Why?"

The Listening Ground

Elias leaned in beside Mara. "Maybe they were trying to explain something they saw. Something they didn't understand."

"Or honor something they worshipped," Diego said quietly.

A silence settled over them, thick as syrup.

Mara stood and scanned the surrounding earth. "There's more. Spread out but stay within sight of each other."

They fanned out into the clearing. Amid the stones, Mara found additional clusters, some half-buried, some overtaken by delicate rootlets. None bore writing, but all carried the same unmistakable intention: to make the invisible visible. Nervous systems. Root systems. Fractal mirrors of life.

"Doctor Ellison." Diego's voice was low, reverent.

She hurried to him.

He had brushed away soil from a larger stone, twice as tall as the others. At first glance, it was just another tangle of careless vegetation over rock. But Diego parted the overgrowth, and Mara's breath halted.

Carved into the face of the stone was a depiction of a human torso, open like a dissected diagram. But where organs should have been, there were roots. A heart formed from intertwining vines. A spine made of woven stems. Lungs represented by the unfurling of leaf clusters.

A human becoming plant.

Or plant becoming human.

Elias approached slowly. "Well," he murmured. "That's new."

Amaya's voice trembled. "This… was this what Pembroke wrote about?"

"No," Elias said softly. "Pembroke never mentioned this. He only described hearing a voice. Seeing patterns. Becoming obsessed."

Elias moved… felt pulled… toward another stone, one that lay cracked open, its interior hollow. He reached inside and pulled something out.

A scrap of metal. Old, tarnished, pitted with corrosion.

A transmitter plate — brass, wires trailing — and unmistakably from the 19th century.

Mara froze. "Is that — ?"

"What's left of it," Elias said, turning the device in his hands. "Pembroke's field transmitter. He carried one. It was primitive even for its time, but it was experimental tech, early attempts at long-range communication using atmospheric charge."

"That doesn't make sense," Kenji said. "Even if he had that kind of device, why would it be fused with the vegetation?"

Elias held up the fragment, revealing where a thin vine had grown through its frame as though it had been part of the mechanism.

"He must've dropped it," Elias said. "Or buried it. Or… it was taken."

"Taken?" Diego echoed, a tremor in his tone.

Elias turned to him. "She took it."

The pronoun sat like a stone in the clearing.

Mara swallowed. "Elias, don't start personifying anything. We need clear heads."

The Listening Ground

"I'm not personifying," he said evenly. "I'm interpreting."

Her face hardened. "Same thing."

"Of course, she talks to you first," Diego muttered to Elias.

Amaya raised an eyebrow. "Jealous much?"

He didn't deny it. His jaw flexed. "Some people spend their whole lives studying these stories. Some people stumble into them and get answers."

Elias heard, and didn't know how to respond.

Before their argument could escalate, the ground beneath them pulsed.

Not a vibration. Not a tremor.

A heartbeat once more.

Amaya gasped and pressed a hand to her chest. "It's matching us."

The ground thumped again. This time more forcefully. Mara knelt, palm flat to the soil. The rhythm was unmistakable. Subtle, but insistent, as though the Earth was testing the cadence of their bodies.

Kenji checked his tablet. "No seismic activity detected. No magnetic anomaly. This is biological."

"It's her," Diego whispered.

"Stop that," Mara snapped.

"It is her," he repeated. "The Queen. La Reina Verde. She's listening."

The pulse grew stronger.

Elias stepped back, scanning the perimeter. "Something's happening."

Then, faintly, almost imperceptibly...

A voice.

It came from the trees. From the vines. From the stones.

"…*La Reina Verde*…"

Mara tried to deny it, tried to tell herself it was wind, resonance, anything. But then she heard it clearly:

"…*closer*…"

A whisper repeated from the voice on the ghost transmission. Distorted. Imperfect. But recognizable.

Her pulse hammered.

Amaya clutched Mara's arm. "She's echoing us."

"*echo-ing*…"

"Reflections?" Amaya asked, too quickly, clinging to the word like a rope. "Acoustic… something?"

Mara shook her head slowly. "There's no surface geometry here that would produce that kind of phased repetition," she said. "And echoes don't… adjust. They don't pick up syllables and drop others based on… on what's easier to… replicate."

"Then what is it?" Amaya's voice had gotten small again.

Mara looked at the trees. Leaves shifted in the faint breeze. Vines twitched minutely, as if fighting the urge to move more vigorously.

"It's learning," she said.

It felt like a key turning in a lock she hadn't realized was there. The words themselves were mangled, consonants softened into rustles, vowels stretched thin, but she heard fragments in the susurration of leaves above them.

"…*learning*…"

"It's not the first time," Mara admitted. "The other night, I thought I heard it talking through the radio."

The Listening Ground

Kenji looked over at her palely. His tablet suddenly flickered with green static, and he nearly flung it away into the trees.

The heartbeat intensified.

"...*closer*..."

"...*closer*..."

"...*clo – sshhh – er*..."

The distortion felt wrong now.

Too raw.

Too desperate.

"We need to move," Elias said sharply.

"Agreed," Mara said, but her voice shook.

"Did you get everything?" she asked Amaya, glancing from her recording equipment to the petroglyphs. Amaya breathlessly nodded.

Diego stared at the stones, eyes wide with both terror and awe. "She remembers. The forest remembers."

"I said enough," Mara hissed.

But even she couldn't tear her eyes away from the carving of the human-root figure. The eyes etched into the stone seemed to glow faintly in the filtered light.

"We're leaving now," Elias ordered.

No one argued.

They backed away from the clearing as the whispers tangled with the pulse of the soil. The forest didn't follow, but the sound did, sliding between trunks, tracked by the vines above, as though carried on invisible wires.

After ten minutes of swift movement, the whisper faded.

But the heartbeat continued, softer now, more distant.

Beneath the Verdant Veil

As though the forest was… watching.

They continued down the endless corridor. The air thickened. The path wound through increasingly organized clusters of plant life: spiraled roots, arched branches, repeating motifs too clean for coincidence.

Leaves trembled as they passed, as if cataloguing their presence.

As the sun began to sink, everyone was dragging. Their canteens sloshed half-empty. The humidity pressed in, heavy and wet.

Amaya stumbled once, catching herself on Elias' arm.

"You okay?" he asked.

"Just… dizzy. Like the air's vibrating inside my head."

"It is," Kenji muttered. "Everything is humming."

"Not humming," Elias said. "Talking."

Mara shot him a glare.

He didn't retract the statement.

They marched on, their shadows stretching long and thin. Fireflies emerged, except these weren't ordinary fireflies. Their bodies glowed a soft green-blue, flickering in synchronized pulses like nodes on a circuit.

Kenji stopped walking, breath catching. "Oh. My god."

The fireflies shifted patterns.

Flicker. Pause. Flicker-flicker. Pause.

A repeating beat.

Heartbeat rhythm.

Mara's eyes widened. "It's the same pattern we felt under the ground."

The Listening Ground

Amaya stared upward. "It's everywhere. She's speaking in light."

Diego knelt on the moss. "A language of breath… and root… and spark…"

Mara whispered, "It's communication."

The fireflies brightened.

A soft hum rose.

A wind carried the scent of blooming orchids, though none grew nearby.

Then the fireflies' glow shifted color, green to gold to white, cascading outward in ripples, like a wave moving across the canopy.

The forest answered with bioluminescence as a blanket of indigo evening spread over the jungle.

The moss glowed.

Then the roots.

Then the trunks.

Then the vines overhead.

A wave of light ran through the trees like a neural signal, lighting the world in breathtaking phosphorescence.

Everyone froze.

Even the air paused.

Mara's hand found Elias' without thinking, fingers trembling against his.

He didn't pull away.

The pulse reached a peak…

Then extinguished.

Leaving behind the deepest silence yet.

Elias drew a breath.

"Mara," he said quietly. "That wasn't a warning."

She swallowed. "Then what was it?"

"A greeting."

CHAPTER 11

Dreams Beneath the Canopy

As they wound around a bend in the forest, the trail opened abruptly into a circular clearing about twenty meters across. No undergrowth filled its center, just a smooth, gently sloped depression carpeted in dry leaf litter and fine roots. Around its edges, trees rose like pillars, their buttresses flaring outward to form natural alcoves. The canopy overhead parted, not fully, but enough that a soft, diffuse light trickled in, washing the space in green-gold.

Mara stopped at its edge. Something about the geometry tugged at her brain. The circle was too clean, the arrangement of trees too evenly spaced. It was like standing inside the projection of a lidar scan made real.

"Okay, that's not natural," Kenji said.

Mara's mouth quirked. "Define 'natural' in this context."

He gestured helplessly. "This place looks like someone planned it in CAD."

Diego stepped into the clearing and turned slowly, head tilted back, eyes half-lidded as if listening. "This is a sleeping room," he said softly. "Old stories called them that. Places where the forest rests its thinking."

Mara looked around again. The buttress roots made sheltered hollows for sleeping; the slight bowl of the clearing would divert rain toward the edges; the break in the treetops let in just enough light without exposing them to the full sky. It was, objectively, an ideal campsite.

And everything in her that loved patterns whispered that this was not coincidence.

She lowered her half-empty pack. "We need rest. And we need to keep our strength for whatever comes next. The forest has given us a room. We might as well use it."

Amaya shivered. "We're going to just… set up camp in its brain?"

"Yes," Mara said. "We are."

Elias studied her face. "You sure?"

"No," she said honestly. "But I'm sure we can't keep walking until we drop. And if it wanted us dead, we wouldn't have made it this far."

"That's a comfort," Kenji muttered, but he set down the sat beacon's useless shell like it mattered, anyway, a ritual object from a world that still obeyed physics.

They settled into the bare-bones rhythm of making camp.

Kenji and Amaya tied rope between the stilt roots of two walking palms to create a simple line for hanging their damp clothes. Diego gathered fallen leaves and twigs from the perimeter. Nothing green, nothing that looked remotely alive. Mara spread the med kit, gravity filter, water bladders and provisions along a buttress root, mentally sorting their meager inventory. No tarp. No stove. No spare batteries. No redundancy.

Just the bare minimum to keep five people alive.

Still, the act of arranging what little they had felt grounding, like pressing a small human pattern gently over the larger one they had stepped into. A declaration, however fragile, that they still had a place in this story.

Elias moved around the perimeter, eyes scanning for threats, but his gaze kept snagging on small details: tiny white fungi pulsing faintly where they sprouted from decayed wood, a fern whose fans turned to follow their movements the way a young sunflower follows the arc of the sun.

Diego watched Elias stare into the border of the clearing as if listening to someone invisible.

Amaya noticed his expression. "You're frowning again."

"He hears things I don't," Diego said. "It feels like the forest is choosing him."

"Maybe it's not choosing," she said softly. "Maybe it's calling whoever's willing to listen."

He didn't answer. The hurt in his eyes said enough.

Elias paused beside one of the trees, laying his palm flat against its bark. Mara noticed the way his shoulders eased for a moment, as if some of the tension in him was being drawn off into the trunk.

"You keep doing that," she said, approaching.

He glanced at her, hand still on the tree. "Doing what?"

"Checking in," she said. "Like you're listening to see if it's still on our side."

"I'm listening to see if there's a side at all," he said. "And whether we're on it or… just passing through its mouth."

Amaya, standing nearby tying a knot, winced. "Please stop talking about mouths."

"Seconded," Kenji said.

Elias walked a short distance and placed his hands in his pockets, gazing steadily into the arboreal void.

Mara followed. "You're not surprised," she said quietly.

"I'm a little surprised."

"But not alarmed."

"Oh, I'm alarmed," he said with a humorless smile. "I'm just not shocked."

Mara rubbed her forehead. "You really believe Pembroke heard something alive down here."

"I believe he heard something intelligent."

"Elias…"

"Tell me everything we saw today was random," he said gently. "Look me in the eye and say that."

She opened her mouth.

Closed it.

He nodded. "Yeah. That's what I thought."

"Mara?" Amaya approached, hesitant. "Do you think it's possible… that she's trying to talk to us?"

Mara exhaled slowly. "I think it's possible that something is responding to our presence. But that could be bioelectric mimicry, environmental resonance, chemical—"

Elias interrupted softly. "It wasn't chemical."

Mara glared. "We can't assume intent."

"We can't ignore it either."

The thought made her skin crawl. The anthropologist in her wanted to call it projection. The part of her that had felt the ground pulsing under her boots could no longer be so sure.

They managed a small fire, more for comfort than cooking. Diego insisted on building it in a shallow pit he scraped in the center, away from any exposed roots. "We do not burn her hair," he said. "You don't pull a god's braid unless you want to see her teeth."

Mara didn't correct the theology in that. The warmth and the faint smoke felt human in a way the rest of the clearing didn't.

They ate ration bars softened with a bit of hot water, the flavorless paste improved by Diego producing a small bag of dried guava. The fruit was leathery but sweet, the burst of sugar almost painfully welcome.

Amaya sat close to Mara, knees drawn up, hands clasped around her tin cup. "I keep thinking about the lab," she said. "The way the vines went for the seams first. It was like watching something probe a skull for the easiest way in."

Mara pressed her tongue against the back of her teeth until the image blurred. "Engineers and neurologists are going to have a field day with our notes — if we get those notes out."

"When," Amaya corrected, in a small echo of Mara's earlier insistence.

Mara's chest tightened. She bumped her shoulder lightly against the younger woman's. "Right," she said. "When."

For a while, they sat in companionable almost-silence, listening to the fire snap and the forest breathe.

The heat of the day slowly bled away. One by one they settled in, the fire crackling low. Amaya was the first to doze, head lolling sideways until it found the rolled jacket she was using as a pillow. Kenji soon followed, glasses slipping to the tip of his nose as his chin sank to his chest. Diego chanted under his breath in a language Mara didn't speak but recognized as prayer; eventually, the words blurred, syllables slurring into sleep. Elias, laid with hands crossed behind his head, the swaying of the jungle ceiling having already lulled him into a contented sleep.

Mara opened her field notebook and, by the light of the fire, scrawled line after line. Not coherent analysis — her mind was too scattered for that — but fragments. Corridor geometry. Leaf orientation. The echo game. The way the hum had changed since the river. Lorne's last words.

At the margin of one page, almost without thinking, she wrote: *We are inside a learning system.*

She stared at it until the ink blurred.

Eventually, exhaustion pried the notebook from her fingers. She slid it back into the waterproof case, set the case beside her as if it could serve as a pillow for her thoughts, and curled on her side with her back against a kapok root.

Mara glanced over at Amaya. In sleep, the young woman looked peaceful, the lines of fear smoothed away. Mara felt a familiar tightening in her throat — the same tightening she'd felt watching her grad student the night before the slide, the girl's face dappled with firelight and hope.

"I've got you," she whispered, so quietly she wasn't sure if she'd spoken aloud. "I won't let go this time."

Mara knew she was fighting sleep, but the hum beneath her — soft, steady, like a pulse thrumming through the ground — drew her under despite herself. It felt like lying atop the chest of something vast and sleeping, feeling its respiration through the soil.

Her last waking thought was bitter and strangely calm:

If the forest wants your dreams, it'll take them.

The dream came immediately.

She was back in the Andes. The air thin. The slope steep. The ground trembling just before it gave way.

She could smell it again, that cold, mineral scent that comes just before rock decides it no longer wants to hold itself together.

Her grad student, whose name she couldn't say even in her sleeping mind, slid past her in a blur of red jacket and terror.

Mara lunged, catching the girl's wrist, cold fingers slick with meltwater, slipping through her grasp.

"No—no—no—hold on!"

The mud roared. The slope collapsed. A falling rock slammed painfully into her left leg. The girl screamed her name as she vanished beneath the wave.

"Mara! MARA!"

Sound dropped out. The world narrowed to the desperate strain in her arms, muscles tearing as she clung to a hand that was already gone.

She dug until her hands bled. She screamed for help no one could give. Her nails ripped; dirt packed under what was left. Her leg shot fresh, shocked agony up her spine. Her breath came in sobs that tasted like iron.

She felt again the moment she lost the grip, the subtle give in tendons and bone, the second where the girl's weight changed from something she might haul back up to something the mountain had already claimed.

And then...

Something green pushed through the mud.

A vine, glistening with bioluminescent ooze, coiled around the girl's wrist, lifting her up toward Mara.

But when the face emerged from the soil, it wasn't her student's.

It was a woman with eyes full of chlorophyll light, skin traced with fine leaf-veins, hair like a spill of moss and blossoms. The mud slid off her as though repelled.

She leaned close, and the jungle hissed through her teeth:

You cannot hold the past.

But you can remember.

Mara recoiled...

And woke with a strangled gasp.

Elias was standing at the edge of an impossible canyon made of roots instead of stone, the walls tangled and knotted, pulsing with slow rivers of light. Far below, something vast and green breathed in the dark.

Pembroke stood beside him, or the ghost of him. Victorian beard, hollow eyes, hands ink-stained. He looked smaller than Elias had imagined, his shoulders bowed under a weight that wasn't physical.

"She called me," Pembroke said in a voice like brittle paper. "And I went to her. But when she opened herself, I... we... I ran."

The canyon shifted; roots rolled like the tide.

Dreams Beneath the Canopy

"You came back?" Elias said, his knowledge of the explorer's last days in an asylum clashing with his presence before him.

Pembroke shook his head. "My body never did. But my mind stayed. In pieces. In leaves. In whispers. She remembers me because she cannot forget what she has lost. And I remember her because I cannot forget what I refused."

He turned, and his eyes were green and wet and full of chlorophyll. They shone with the same dim green pulse Elias had seen threading the tree roots. Around the explorer's neck hung a vine-shaped pendant, the same one Elias had traced through auction records. It glowed faintly, as if answering something unseen.

"Don't run," Pembroke said. "Not when she opens to you. It kills something inside you both."

Elias woke with his heart pounding, the taste of loam in his mouth.

For a moment, Mara didn't know where she was.

Her vision blurred, breath ragged. Tears tracked down her temples, cold in the night air. The canopy above her was a dark mesh, not a white sky over unforgiving rock and mud. The vibration beneath her was the life pulse of the Escondido Basin, not tectonic shudder.

In the dying firelight she saw motion beside her. Elias.

He had snapped upright at the exact same time she had.

He was panting, chest rising and falling quickly, eyes wide and glassy, staring at something only he could

143

still see. A faint sheen of sweat glittered along the stubble of his jaw.

"Elias?" she whispered.

He turned toward her sharply, and the haunted expression in his eyes startled her. There was fear there, yes, but also a kind of wonder, raw and unguarded.

"Mara," he said, breathless. "I saw Pembroke."

Mara swallowed hard. "That was a dream."

"No," he whispered. "It wasn't."

She flinched at the certainty in his tone, because it matched something in her she didn't want to acknowledge.

He crawled nearer and reached toward her, hesitated, then rested a trembling hand on her arm. His palm was warm, the calluses familiar.

"You cried out," he muttered. "Was it… was it the Andes?"

She jerked her head toward him, heart hammering. "How did you—"

"You've mentioned it," he said quietly, unsure. "Only in passing. But I know that tone. I know what nightmares born from guilt sound like." He gave a hollow little smile. "I've earned a few of my own."

She opened her mouth to snap at him, to say he didn't know anything about her nightmares, about her student, about the way the word *mentor* had curdled in her mouth after the reports and the inquiries and the condolences.

But something broke inside her instead.

She sagged forward, covering her face. For a moment she didn't care that her breath hitched or that her shoulders shook. The forest had seen her at her most desperate already; what did it matter if a man did?

Elias shifted closer, the moss whispering under his weight. "Mara…"

She didn't lean into him.

But she didn't pull away either.

After a long moment, she lowered her hands. He was still watching her, not pitying, not prying. Just… present. He looked more vulnerable than when she'd first seen him on the Peregrine's deck, the lines at the corners of his eyes carved deeper by stress and chaos.

Their foreheads nearly touched.

She exhaled shakily. "My student. I should have… I should have been able to hold her. I felt her slip. I felt the moment she stopped fighting and—"

Her voice cracked. The rest stayed locked behind her teeth.

Elias reached up, slowly, as if approaching a startled animal, and brushed a tear from her cheek with his thumb. His touch was careful, a question rather than an assumption.

"Mara," he whispered. "You did everything you could. Sometimes the mountain chooses, not us."

She let out a broken laugh. "That's not scientific."

"No," he agreed softly. "It's human."

He hesitated, then added, "And you're still here. That counts for something."

Their eyes met—and held.

Something in the air shifted. The purr beneath them seemed to deepen, as if the forest tilted its attention, curious.

His fingers brushed her jawline, hesitating.

She didn't hesitate.

She leaned in.

Their lips met gently at first, a soft, tentative searching. Then deeper... brief, warm, trembling at the edges. A moment that felt both inevitable and forbidden, a spark striking dry tinder in the middle of a living, watching wilderness.

The kiss tasted of smoke and salt and all the unsaid things between them: apologies, accusations, admissions. For an instant, the jungle and Auralis and old scandals and tragedies dropped away, leaving only two people who had nearly perished that day, clinging to whatever warmth they could find.

When they finally broke apart, both of them were breathless for different reasons.

"I shouldn't have —" she began.

He shook his head. "We're alive. Right now, that's enough reason for anything."

She wanted to argue.

She didn't.

Because she was afraid he was right. And because a small, desperate part of her was relieved to feel something other than fear.

Mara leaned in next to Elias, resting her head on his shoulder. "Why is Pembroke so important to you?" she asked gently.

Elias pulled the yellowed newsprint out of his vest pocket, brushing a thumb across the antiquated text crammed into its columns. "Most people read this article and laugh," he said quietly. "Victorian sensationalism, jungle fever, a man who lost his mind staring at trees. But when I first read it..." He hesitated, then gave a small, crooked smile. "It didn't scare me. It pulled me in."

Mara listened, curious. The warmth between them grew amidst the cool jungle air.

"My dad found the clipping in an old bookstall when I was twelve. I must have read it fifty times that summer. Pembroke wasn't describing a monster." Elias tapped the paragraph detailing the vine-shaped pendant. "He was describing wonder. Terror and wonder at the same time. Like he stood in front of something ancient enough to change him, and he couldn't let it go."

He exhaled softly.

"That was the first moment I knew I wanted to spend my life chasing what everyone else insists can't exist. Not ghosts, not myths, but the truth beneath the myth. Pembroke didn't lose his mind. His own papers make that clear. He found something he couldn't explain."

Elias looked at her, eyes barely visible but somehow more vulnerable.

"And I've spent most of my life wanting... desperately... to understand what he saw."

A rustle broke the moment.

Diego jolted awake with a shout, his hand clutching his talisman. "The spirits! *Madre de Dios.*"

He looked around wildly, eyes wide, chest heaving. For a second he seemed not to recognize where he was; then the present settled over him like a damp cloth. He slumped, rubbing his face.

"No dream is only a dream here," he muttered to no one in particular.

Across the clearing, Amaya wasn't asleep but seemed to be replaying a waking nightmare before her eyes. She sat upright, knees drawn to her chest, eyes fixed on the far side of the camp where a curtain of vines hung from a bowed branch. The vines pulsed slowly, light chasing through their veins in a pattern that almost… almost… resembled a waveform.

"She's… listening," Amaya whispered, voice thin with awe. "She's listening to us."

Mara stiffened.

Elias' hand brushed hers for the briefest second before he pulled away deliberately, settling back on his forest floor bed as if nothing had happened between them. The distance he put between their bodies felt louder than any sound.

Mara didn't know if she was relieved or disappointed.

"Go to sleep, Amaya," she said quietly. "We need clear heads."

Amaya didn't look away from the vines. "What if this is when she understands us best?"

"Then she can wait until morning," Mara replied. "We're not much use to anyone half-conscious."

There was no sharpness in it, only weariness. Amaya finally nodded and curled onto her side, though her gaze lingered on the softly glowing veins until her eyelids drooped.

As he rested beneath the canopy, Elias reached into his pack and pulled out a photocopy from Pembroke's journal, a detailed sketch of the mysterious necklace. He had only seen the real necklace once, briefly, during his ill-fated visit to Madrid. But now, as the jungle pulsed around them, he realized what Pembroke had only guessed.

The pale green stone wasn't just ornament. It was a conduit.

Elias could feel it even now, not in his hands, but in his blood. As though the necklace had recognized him through time. As though it had always belonged to the one who would speak for her.

CHAPTER 12

The Call of the Deep Green

Dawn came reluctantly to the Escondido Basin.

A muted emerald light seeped between the interlaced leaves, diffused and softened as if the sun had to negotiate for permission to enter. The air was thick with dew so fine it resembled breath, exhaled from a thousand unseen lungs.

Mara sat up abruptly.

And froze.

The clearing was different.

Not dramatically. The same trees ringed them, the same canopy loomed overhead, but the *arrangement* had changed. Vines that had hung straight now curled like parentheses around their campsite. A line of moss that had stretched along a log now grew inward like a spiral. Even the distribution of leaves on the ground had reshaped into faint radial patterns, as if some invisible hand had spent the night rearranging debris into meaning.

"Uh," Kenji said, rubbing sleep from his eyes. His hair stuck up in three different directions. "Did we... did we move camp last night?"

"No," Mara said, her voice quiet but certain. "The forest moved around us."

Diego crossed himself. "She shelters us."

"That's not sheltering," Mara muttered.

But she didn't sound as confident as she meant to.

The Call of the Deep Green

"That was so weird," Kenji muttered. "I dreamt about a carnivorous plant that wanted to collaborate on a research paper. But it insisted on being first author."

Elias rose slowly, walking to a broad kapok root that arched slightly more than it had before, like the curve of a back. He placed his palm on it... and inhaled sharply.

It was warm.

Like skin.

And underneath that warmth, a faint pulse pressed back against his hand, almost perfectly in time with his own heartbeat, then deliberately off by a fraction, as if testing resonance.

He turned back toward the others. "It's true. She rearranged the terrain while we slept."

Amaya's expression was equal parts reverence and fear. "Why? To guide us?"

Mara shook her head but not as firmly as she used to. "We don't know."

"Yet," Amaya murmured.

Elias looked at the altered path ahead, a narrow funnel of branches and leaning trunks, all subtly angled toward the same unseen point deeper in the forest.

"We will soon," he said.

Diego's gaze flicked toward Mara, watching her more closely than the trees. "Dreams are messages here, doctora. The Queen speaks through memory."

Mara didn't reply.

Because although she refused to say it aloud...

She feared he was right.

And the part of her that had heard a chlorophyll-lit woman speaking from Andean mud wanted, desperately, for there to be a way to answer.

They broke camp in uneasy silence.

Amaya savored a conservative sip of water, her expression half-focused, half-haunted. Diego stood with his hands on his hips, staring up at the canopy as though it might answer a question that had been gnawing at him for years.

Kenji sat hunched over his tablet, cheeks hollowed from fatigue. The screen alternated between static, impossible readings, and shutting itself off. "It's not broken," he insisted in a thin voice, as much to himself as to anyone else. "It's… confused. That interference pattern, it's like trying to tune three radios to four stations at once."

Mara didn't contradict him. At this point, she half-expected the tablet to pop up and start a conversation. She shook the thought away.

Kenji adjusted his glasses and blew out a breath. "On the bright side, hypoxia isn't a problem," he muttered. "We're getting plenty of oxygen. Maybe too much. Like breathing inside a leaf."

Elias watched Mara, but didn't push conversation. The moment between them from the night before lingered like humidity — impossible to ignore, impossible to grip.

Finally, Mara slung her pack over her shoulders and faced the narrow, newly sculpted corridor ahead, a tunnel of angled branches and layered leaves, all leaning toward a point deep within the forest where the light gathered in a strange, hazy green.

"Whether we like it or not," she said softly, more to herself than to them, "we follow where it leads."

The Call of the Deep Green

Elias nodded once, a simple, solid motion.

Diego whispered, "The Queen awaits."

Mara threw him a look, but didn't correct the title this time.

And the five of them stepped forward, deeper into the waiting wilderness, as the pulse beneath their feet quickened almost imperceptibly.

The path bent in ways that didn't match normal forest geometry. Too smooth, too repetitive, too synchronous. Even the air buzzed faintly around them, not just vibration, but an *attentive* hum.

Elias slowed occasionally, leaning down to brush moss or touch a root like someone checking a pulse. Mara noticed — and found herself irritated at how natural it looked on him, how calmly he engaged with the environment that terrified the rest of them.

After nearly thirty minutes of walking, Diego muttered, "We passed that strangler fig yesterday."

"No," Amaya said. "The one yesterday had a hollow trunk, remember? This one's lattice is still solid."

Diego hesitated. "You're sure?"

She nodded.

Mara frowned. "This place mirrors itself. Geometry as camouflage."

"Or as invitation," Elias murmured.

Mara exhaled, but before she could reprimand the suggestion, he abruptly raised a hand.

"Stop."

Branches overhead shivered, releasing small cascades of dew. Something drifted toward them, a dark shape caught in the mesh of morning light.

Beneath the Verdant Veil

At first Mara thought it was a bird.

Then she saw the metallic glint.

The drone.

Its casing was warped. Moss covered half its surface like a fungal pelt. Thin tendrils coiled through the ventilation slats, growing out through the seams as if the forest had slowly swallowed the machine and then spit it back out.

It drifted down not like a falling object, but like something being *placed.*

Kenji swore under his breath. "That's not possible. Kestrel went offline when we lost her. She shouldn't even have power left."

Mara stepped forward slowly. "Don't touch it."

But Amaya moved before the warning finished exiting Mara's mouth—young, impulsive, and captivated by the way the device hovered like an insect caught in amber.

"Amaya—!"

Too late. Her fingers closed around the casing.

Instantly, the drone's red indicator light blinked on.

Amaya yelped and nearly dropped it. "It's hot, really hot."

Kenji rushed to steady it. "Let me—"

The speakers crackled.

Static.

A rising whine.

Then a voice.

"—*we're not... al—one—*"

Mara's stomach plunged.

It was Lorne's voice.

The Call of the Deep Green

Warped. Drenched in distortion. Split into mismatched frequencies like it had been dragged across a broken antenna.

"*— she… sees… you —*"

The sound crawled along their skin like spider legs.

Amaya's hands trembled violently. "Turn it off! Turn it off!"

Kenji wiped his palms on his pants and reached for the control port. "She's not responding!"

The drone jerked, wrenching itself from their hands with a mechanical spasm.

The vines wrapped around it pulsed.

"*— you… called… her —*"

Diego let out an oath and backed away until he hit a tree trunk.

Mara's breath came shallow. "That's not Lorne. That's something using his voice."

Elias stepped forward, palms lowered like he was taming a wild boar. "It's okay," he murmured to the drone, though he had no idea if the forest was listening. "We hear you."

The drone rotated sharply toward him, as if tracking his voice, and the vines tightened.

The speaker sputtered again.

"*— au…ra…lis… is… com —*"

The rest of the words were garbled, but the meaning hit like a punch.

Auralis.

Coming.

Lorne's final transmission, the one Mara had seen him send before the vines dragged him down into the river, must have reached headquarters.

"They're coming," Elias whispered. "Auralis is sending someone."

Kenji swore repeatedly under his breath.

"What is it, Kenji?" Mara asked.

"Auralis will assume that we... that the mission... is compromised," Kenji said guiltily. "They employ mercenary teams for events like this."

Elias didn't look away from the drone. "There's no telling what they'll do."

"Especially when the jungle strikes back," Amaya uttered.

A high-pitched whine filled the air.

The drone's casing split.

Thin roots broke through the metal as the forest reclaimed what was once its conduit.

The voice escalated into a shrill hiss.

" *– she... sees you... sees you... sees y –* "

Amaya shrieked.

The drone hit the ground.

Vines exploded outward like flung wires.

Diego acted first, swinging the heel of his boot down hard, smashing the device into the soil. It dented, cracked, sparked.

But it didn't die.

The broken speaker whispered even as smoke rose:

" *– see... you... see... you –* "

"Enough!" Diego struck again.

This time the casing buckled completely, and the light died.

But Mara still heard it, faint, almost subvocal, echoing through the surrounding roots.

" *...see... you...* "

The Call of the Deep Green

Elias crouched, touching one of the severed vines lightly. "It wasn't attacking us."

Kenji snorted, betrayed. "Sure looked like it."

"No," Elias said quietly. "It was warning us."

Mara stepped back, fists clenched. "We can't keep following every whisper in this forest. We need real decisions."

Diego's breathing was ragged, his eyes shining with fear and something like reverence. "This is why my people knew better than to disturb this place."

"No," Mara snapped. "This is why we're here, to understand what's happening, not run screaming into myth."

Amaya gently laid a hand on Diego's shoulder. "Hey, look at me."

He did, reluctantly.

"This isn't just about the drone, is it?"

He swallowed. "No. I lost my wife, Amaya. I lost the world we dreamed of. Since then… I've been pretending the stories were enough, pretending they still mattered."

"And now they're coming alive again," she whispered.

"Yes." His voice cracked. "But they're not choosing me." Behind them, Elias looked ashamedly into the unending vegetation.

Amaya lightly squeezed his hand as she helped him to his feet. "Maybe they're choosing all of us in different ways."

Elias walked forward slowly, nodding at Diego, and took a deep breath. "Mara. Whoever, whatever, sent that voice isn't playing games. This is intentional."

"That's why we need to leave," she said.

Kenji shook his head. "How? We have no boat. No signal. The current is too strong without a craft."

Amaya hugged herself. "Then we go deeper. Maybe to the source. Maybe we can shut—"

"Stop," Mara said.

Elias stepped toward her. "Leaving means heading toward whoever Auralis sends. And they won't be coming with first aid kits."

Mara swallowed.

He was right.

Damn him for being right again and again.

"We're running out of water," she said. "We're down to two ration pouches. And that—" she pointed at the shattered drone, "—is not a sign I want to follow."

"No," Diego said softly, resigned. "It's a sign we should obey."

She glared.

He didn't falter.

"The Queen is warning us," he said. "She is speaking through what she can. Through metal. Through vine. Through voice."

"No," Mara said again.

But even she heard the weakening resolve.

Elias approached more gently. "Mara... we need to decide. Face Auralis? Run from them? Or follow this path to its end? Whatever Auralis has in mind, it can't be good for... *her*."

"The queen?" she snapped. "We don't even know what she is."

Amaya murmured, "I think she knows us."

"She doesn't know me," Mara shot back.

The Call of the Deep Green

Elias held her gaze. "She knows you're not like Lorne."

Mara flinched.

Finally she lifted her chin.

"Voting," she said.

Kenji blinked. "Voting?"

"We're a team," she said. "We vote."

She turned to them one by one.

"Option one: try to escape on foot. Option two: hide and hope Auralis doesn't find us. Option three: go deeper and try to shut off whatever's drawing their attention."

She didn't say Option Four — meet the Queen.

She didn't have to.

It was hanging between them like charged atmosphere.

Diego spoke first. "Option three."

Kenji sighed. "Three. Running blind will get us killed."

Amaya swallowed. "Three."

Elias didn't speak, just nodded.

Four votes.

All eyes went to Mara.

The forest seemed to hold its breath.

She closed her eyes.

The drone's whisper reverberated inside her skull.

We're not alone.

She sees you.

She exhaled.

"...Three."

Amaya sagged in relief.

Diego looked skyward.

Kenji muttered, "God help us."

Beneath the Verdant Veil

Elias smiled faintly.

But Mara didn't feel relief.

She felt like a door had closed behind them.

CHAPTER 13

The Cavern of Roots

The hum was quieter that morning.

Not gone, never gone, but subtler, like the forest had drawn its breath deeper underground.

They walked in single file, following the narrow corridor that had reshaped itself around them. Leaves seemed to cant aside just before they brushed them. Roots that should have tripped them had arranged in steps instead, each curve sitting at just the right height for the human ankle.

"The path wasn't like this yesterday," Kenji muttered, eyeing a root staircase curling over a small ravine.

"No," Diego said. "Yesterday she was still deciding."

"Please stop giving the forest pronouns," Mara said automatically, though it lacked its usual bite.

Her attention kept drifting downward.

The pulsation she'd felt through her boots for days had changed. It no longer vibrated in a wide, diffuse way through the soil. Now it gathered, directionally, vibrating more strongly when she stepped in certain spots, thinning in others. It reminded her of standing in a cathedral and feeling where the acoustics converged, where whispers became louder than shouts.

As the morning wore on, clouds thickened, pressing an odd gray-green light through the canopy. The air grew cooler. The smell changed from wet foliage to something older, like stone that had not seen sunlight in centuries.

After perhaps an hour, Elias slowed.

"You feel that?" he asked quietly.

Mara shifted her weight. The hum was definitely stronger here, like the ground itself had a pulse.

Diego nodded slowly. "Like a drum under the floorboards."

Kenji tapped his boot on the ground, then crouched and put his ear to it. "There's a cavity below us," he said. "Air pocket. Maybe more."

"Cave system?" Amaya suggested, eyes bright. "Karst formation? Lava tube?"

"Maybe," Mara said. But caves didn't usually *rattle* like this, a soft tremolo that seemed to vibrate against the fillings in her teeth.

Elias moved ahead a few paces, scanning the ground with the wary grace of someone who'd stepped through their share of false floors and rotten bridges.

There, a hairline crack, running at a slant, barely visible beneath a thin veil of moss.

He knelt, brushed the moss aside with the back of his knuckles.

A narrow fissure gaped beneath, wide enough for a hand, maybe an arm.

A faint exhalation of cool air brushed his face.

He closed his eyes, following instinct, and pressed his palm flat over the fissure.

The hum surged up through his bones.

Not random vibration. Not tectonic rumble.

Rhythm.

The Cavern of Roots

Not quite a heartbeat, too complex for that, but some layered pattern, like many smaller hearts beating together, slightly out of sync, creating a slow, rolling chord.

He opened his eyes.

"We're not just over a cave," he said. "We're over... something that's alive."

Mara's rational mind offered a dozen explanations — ventilation shafts carved by water, trapped pockets of gas, seismic quirks — but each one felt like a coat that didn't quite fit.

"How do we access it?" Amaya asked, already half crouched in curiosity.

"We don't," Mara said. "Not until we know more about what we're stepping into."

Elias glanced up at her. "You want more? Listen."

He shifted his hand along the fissure, searching. The crack widened a fraction near a bulging rock, edges dark with dampness. The air seeping out there carried an odor like turned soil and crushed herbs.

He slid his fingers into the gap and levered gently.

The fissure widened with a muffled crack.

Mara winced. "Careful. We don't know the load-bearing — "

The ground to Elias' left gave way with a sudden sigh.

He flung himself backward, catching a branch as the earth collapsed into a hollow below. Dirt and leaf litter slumped inward like a popped blister, revealing a dark, sloping shaft.

Dust plumed; spores glittered briefly in the light.

Beneath the Verdant Veil

"Jesus," Kenji wheezed, hand pressed to his chest. "When I said cavity, I didn't mean let's *fall* into it."

Elias grinned shakily from where he dangled, then dropped lightly to solid ground. "You're welcome for the access point."

Mara stared down into the newly revealed opening.

A faint, greenish luminescence glimmered below.

Like foxfire.

Like algae.

Like the phosphorescent veins they'd seen in the vines, only deeper, older.

The hum rose from that glow, steady and insistent.

"Well," Diego murmured, drawing a protective sign over his heart. "We found the singer of the song."

Amaya's eyes shone. "We have to go down there."

"Do we?" Kenji asked weakly. "Because… counterpoint… cave-ins, hypoxia, poisonous gas, carnivorous root gods —"

"There is no god of the roots," Diego said sharply. "There is only the Queen."

"That really doesn't help," Kenji replied.

Mara adjusted her pack straps, looking at the slope. It wasn't a straight drop, more like a steep earthen chute, shored by roots. An angled descent, slick with moisture, but navigable if they were careful.

She swallowed.

Every instinct screaming for self-preservation told her to walk away.

Every instinct that had brought her career this far told her this was the core of everything.

"We go down," she said.

The Cavern of Roots

Kenji stared at her. "I was hoping the responsible adult would vote differently."

"I'm not responsible," she said. "I'm curious."

Elias gave a short laugh. "That's more dangerous."

She met his eyes. "You're coming with me."

He nodded once. "You're the *boss*, boss."

They rigged a lifeline from their salvaged rope, looping it around a sturdy buttress root as anchor. Elias tested the knot with a few hard jerks. Satisfied, he clipped it to his belt.

"Three points of contact," he said, dropping into expedition-guide mode. "Slow, deliberate. If any part of the slope looks unstable, call it. We don't rush. Understood?"

Kenji raised a hand. "Permission to stay up here and guard the rope?"

"Denied," Mara said.

"Figured," Kenji sighed.

Amaya bounced lightly on her toes. "This is like the descent into the cenote in your 'Submerged Cities' episode," she told Elias. "Only real."

"That one was real," he protested.

Diego snorted. "Tell that to the plastic idols."

Elias winced. "Okay, fair."

He swung his legs into the opening, boots scraping. Earth crumbled under his heels, then held. He slid a little, tested weight, then motioned.

"Come on down, Professor."

Mara followed, gripping the rope, feeling the rough fibers bite into her palms. Dirt smeared her trouser legs;

cold moisture soaked through her knees as she eased her weight onto the slope.

The air changed at once.

Aboveground, the forest had smelled like heat and resin and rot.

Here, the scent was cooler, denser. Rock and old water and something green that had never felt the sun.

She descended, breath slowing to match the rhythm of her careful steps. Behind her, she could hear Amaya scrambling, Diego muttering, Kenji cursing quietly under his breath as sludge hugged his boots.

The shaft bent gently, cutting off the direct line of surface light.

The glow below strengthened, casting the walls in an eerie pale green.

Mara's vision adjusted.

The earthen tunnel they were moving through wasn't just raw dirt. Roots lined it in dense lattices, woven together in intricate patterns that reminded her of baskets, or ribs, or the trusses of an old cathedral. Fine filaments threaded between thicker cords, glittering with faint bioluminescence.

The hum vibrated more clearly now. They were inside the instrument instead of listening from outside the hall.

After what felt like twenty meters, the shaft widened.

"Careful," Elias called softly. "There's a ledge."

Mara eased forward until her boots found emptiness. Elias caught her forearm, steadying her as she stepped down onto a shelf of root and stone.

The sight beyond stole her words.

The Cavern of Roots

The cavern opened below them like the interior of some ancient, inverted tree.

They stood on one of many platforms spiraling down along the walls, each formed of roots braided into natural balconies. The central void plunged at least thirty meters, maybe more, before terminating in a pool of radiance.

Not water.

Roots.

A tangled heart of them, knotted and layered, each strand glowing softly with internal light.

It was like staring down into the nervous system of a world.

Bioluminescent threads ran along the walls, mapping the paths of nutrient and information. Fungus blossomed in delicate fans, their undersides shimmering. Massive trunks, the roots of trees above, pierced the cavern roof and wound down to the floor, wrapped in veils of finer tendrils that pulsed slowly, all in time with the hum.

"How..." Kenji whispered behind them. "How is this... *stable*?"

Diego's voice trembled. "Because she has held it for centuries."

Mara gripped the wooden railing, knuckles white. Scientific language collided with awe, words tripping over each other in her mind. It was a rhizomatic hub. A macro-scale mycelial analog. A bio-architectural... whatever the term, it was directed, organized, *intentional*.

"It's a root-brain," Amaya breathed.

Mara raised an eyebrow.

Amaya shrugged faintly. "You're the one who said information-bearing structures, Dr. Ellison."

She wasn't wrong.

Paths of bioluminescent signal chased one another along particular routes, like impulses along axons. Some converged and spread; others circled back in loops. The patterns weren't random, nor purely repetitive. They reminded Mara of EEG readouts. Only… externalized. Monumental. Made of wood and sap instead of electricity and blood.

Elias stepped carefully along the ledge, moving down the natural spiral. "Watch your footing," he said. "No misadventure."

"Too late," Kenji muttered. "We're in a root cathedral under a sentient jungle. The time for conservative decisions is over."

They descended in slow increments, moving from balcony to balcony. The further down they went, the more intricate the structures became. Root arches overlapped in fractal patterns; delicate tendrils formed filigree screens that half-hid what lay beyond.

In one alcove, Mara stopped dead.

"Look," she whispered.

The wall beside them was not just root and stone.

Carvings had been etched into the exposed rock, partially overgrown by vines. Careful lines, shallow but precise, showing figures in procession. At first glance, they looked like the usual human stick-shapes found in ancient petroglyphs.

Then she saw the details.

Vines twined around the figures' legs, not as restraints, but as extensions. Leaves sprouted from forearms. Roots coiled up along spines in stylized whorls, merging with hair. In one panel, a kneeling human figure raised their arms, and branches grew from their shoulders, curving upward like antlers.

In another, several figures lay horizontally, their bodies dissolving into rows of leaves and roots. Above them, a single towering shape — half-woman, half-tree — spread arms and branches over them protectively.

Mara reached out and brushed dirt away from one face with the side of her hand.

The stone eyes stared back, calm and open, entirely unafraid.

"These aren't sacrifices," she gasped. "They're… merging."

Diego moved up beside her, breath catching. "The old stories said some became *of* the forest. Not victims. Keepers. Siblings."

"Priests?" Amaya suggested.

"Partners," Diego said quietly.

Mara leaned in closer. The style of the carving didn't match any recorded pre-Columbian tradition she knew. It felt older, but not cruder. Just different, like a script from a language that didn't require an alphabet.

"You're sure this hasn't been documented?" she asked Diego.

He shook his head slowly. "Nothing like this. They told us the tales, but they never showed us *this*."

Kenji clicked his tongue softly, a nervous habit. "So either we're the first people in modern history to see this, or whoever saw it before didn't survive long enough to tell anyone."

"Comforting," Elias muttered.

They moved on.

"You know what I'm noticing?" Amaya whispered to Diego as they walked.

"That I'm already rewriting the history books in my head?" he answered with a half-grin.

"That you keep watching Elias like he stole your favorite seat in class."

Diego sighed slowly. "I don't resent him. Not really. I resent that I thought it should be me."

Amaya nudged him. "Stories aren't competitions."

"That's exactly what they become," he said, but his tone was softer than before.

The path narrowed as they moved deeper, the air cooling in sheets. What had begun as a broad pathway of roots soon constricted into a series of plaited ramps, rising and falling in irregular terraces. At first glance the cavern floor looked solid beneath them, thick mats of bark and softly glowing moss, but as they came around the next bend, the illusion broke.

On either side of the path, the world simply fell away.

The glow revealed it only in brief strokes: a plunge into darkness threaded with vertical lattices of roots, some thicker than tree trunks, others fine as hair. The walls dropped straight down, disappearing into a blackness that swallowed the cavern's glow.

Amaya inched forward and peered over the edge. "How deep is that?"

Elias pointed his flashlight downward. The beam dissolved before it reached anything solid. "Deeper than the equipment can read," he murmured. "These caverns run like veins. Could go a hundred meters. Could go more."

A faint, cool draft rose from below… like a sigh exhaled from the earth itself.

Mara's stomach tightened. "Stay close to the center. And no one goes near the edges. These aren't floors, they're bridges."

Diego warned, "Bridges to the underworld."

And as they moved, every step made the cavern beneath them answer, a hollow resonance that reminded Mara just how thin the surface really was.

More carvings emerged as they descended, scenes of storms crashing against a rooted figure who bent but did not break. Floods racing above ground while a network of rhizomes cradled human forms below. Fire gnawing at the edges of a forest while a central, tall figure spread branching arms to redirect it.

Always the same central presence: a woman's outline, becoming less human and more arboreal the deeper down they went. Her hair lengthened into vines. Her fingers elongated into twigs. By the final panel they passed, her face was almost entirely masked by leaves, only the suggestion of eyes remaining.

At one point, Mara realized she'd stopped thinking of the figure in the abstract.

Veridessa, thought a quiet voice in her mind.

She flinched.

That wasn't her word.

Elias was ahead of her now on the path, his hand trailing lightly along a living curtain of creepers. His shoulders were tight, his jaw clenched. Every so often he would pause, brow furrowing, as if listening to something no one else could hear.

"Elias," she called softly. "You okay?"

He glanced back, and for a second his eyes seemed to catch the green glow differently, reflecting it deeper.

"Yeah," he said. "Just... déjà vu."

She didn't push.

They reached a broader ledge near the bottom of the cavern. Here, the glow was brightest, emanating from the central knot of roots below. The droning had become a physical presence, pressing against Mara's chest.

The ledge expanded into a natural balcony that jutted out over the tangle at the center.

The root-heart.

It sprawled across the cavern floor, a colossal tangle of intertwined trunks and tendrils, some as thick as pillars, others as thin as thread. The glow radiated from within its layers rather than from the surface, giving the impression of something lit from a hidden core.

Glowing green strands pulsed through it in waves. The cadence was complex, but not random. There were repeating motifs, rises and falls, patterns. Mara's data-trained mind itched to put electrodes on everything, to translate light into digits.

"This place is impossible," Kenji said softly. "Even with everything we've seen. It's... it's like standing inside a brain where every neuron decided to be a tree instead."

Amaya stepped up beside Mara, eyes wide, cheeks damp. "It's beautiful," she whispered. "Like it's... thinking."

Diego sank to one knee, fingertips pressed to the natural floor. His lips moved silently. Whatever invocation he spoke now sounded less like pleading, more like greeting.

Mara stepped forward, crossing the balcony until she stood at its very edge. The drop below wasn't sheer, but it was steep enough that one slip would send her tumbling into the glowing mass.

The thrum felt strongest here.

She closed her eyes.

Beneath her palms, pressed to the wooden rail, she could feel minute vibrations, like millions of ant-feet, like xylem flowing, like...

Like signal.

For a moment, she almost thought she could parse it, could feel her mind starting to align with the rhythm.

A hand closed lightly around her elbow.

She flinched and opened her eyes.

Elias stood beside her, his expression unsettled but steady. "Careful," he said. "You looked like you were about to jump in."

She exhaled harshly. "I wasn't."

"I've seen that look. It's the face people make right before swimming out past where their feet can touch."

"How reassuring," she muttered.

He let go of her elbow but didn't step back.

The glow from below reflected up into his face, limning the lines of his cheekbones, the stubble along his jaw, the faint scar that ran from his lower lip to his chin. The light made his irises look almost hazel-green.

He turned his head, looking past her at the root-heart.

The hum seemed to swell around them, focused, as if curious.

Elias stepped closer to the ledge.

Something in Mara's chest clenched. "Elias—"

"I just want to try something," he said quietly.

He moved past the rail to where a thick column of root rose from the tangle below and pierced the balcony, its surface overgrown with smaller tendrils. The column was warm and faintly damp, the bark softened into a living, flexible skin.

Elias reached out and placed his palm flat against it.

The hum spiked.

He sucked in a breath, eyes flying shut.

"Elias?" Amaya's voice trembled. "What is it?"

He didn't answer immediately.

Mara was at his side in two strides, reaching for his shoulder. "Elias."

He swallowed. Pain flickered across his features, then smoothed into something like awe.

"…She's here," he whispered.

Mara's skin prickled.

"Who?" she asked, though she already knew the answer he would give.

His lips parted.

"Veridessa," he breathed.

Mara's heart thudded once, hard.

The name hung in the air like a tossed pebble, sending ripples through the hum.

Diego's head snapped up. "You heard her."

Elias' hand tightened on the root, knuckles whitening. "Not words. Not… exactly words. More like… impressions. Memory. Recognition."

His breathing grew shallow. Sweat slicked his forehead despite the coolness of the cavern.

The Cavern of Roots

"Elias, let go," Mara ordered.

He didn't.

His other hand lifted of its own accord, fingers spreading as if reaching toward something only he could see. His posture looked eerily like some of the carved figures on the walls—arms open, head tilted, ready to be overtaken.

"Elias." There was panic in her voice now. "Let go."

He opened his eyes.

They were rimmed green in the glow.

"She knows me," he whispered. "Or she knows *him* through me. The echo. Pembroke. It's... layered."

Mara grabbed his wrist and tried to peel his hand away from the column. The bark under his palm had softened, tendrils creeping around his fingers like affectionate snakes.

For a brief, sick second, she thought she would have to pry him free by force.

Then his fingers loosened, and the tendrils relaxed their hold.

He stepped back, breathing hard.

The hum in the cavern subsided from a shout to a murmur.

Mara didn't realize she'd been holding her breath until her lungs burned. She exhaled roughly, resisting the urge to shake him.

"Do not ever do that again without warning," she said, voice low.

Elias gave a half-strangled laugh. "Yes, Professor."

"Don't call me—"

"Doctor Ellison," he amended, still too breathless for full flippancy.

Kenji edged closer, eyes darting between Elias and the wood he'd touched. "So… uh… what exactly did she do?"

"Nothing," Elias said.

Then, more honestly: "Everything. It was like… like opening a book and realizing some of the pages are written in your handwriting, even though you've never seen it before."

Mara felt something cold and hot twist together in her stomach. "You're sure this isn't just suggestibility? You've been steeped in Diego's stories, Pembroke's journal—"

"Maybe," he admitted. "I won't pretend I'm not primed. But I know what my own fantasies feel like."

"And this?" Diego asked.

Elias looked down at his hand. Tiny flecks of luminescent sap clung to his palm, pulsing faintly before dimming.

"This felt like being *noticed*," he said softly.

Mara stepped away from the balcony edge, trying to think, to catalog sensory input and separate it from emotional contamination. "She—*it*—clearly has some way of reading bioelectric signals," she said. "Maybe chemical, too. You touched a major conduit. Of course you'd feel something."

"Sure," Kenji said faintly. "Let's go with that. Root Wi-Fi."

Amaya had moved closer to the edge, staring down at the central tangle. "If this is… if this is her nervous system, where's… *she*?"

Mara opened her mouth to say this *was* it, that there might not be a singular body in the way humans thought of one. But even as the thought formed, the glow at the center of the cavern fluctuated.

Light gathered.

Roots shifted.

The central knot slowly unfurled, petals of wood peeling back to reveal a hollow, sealed chamber nested at the very heart of the mass.

It wasn't large, no bigger than a small room, but it was positioned like the pupil at the center of an eye. The outer shell was formed of tightly blended roots, smooth as porcelain. Faint veins of light ran beneath its surface, pulsing slowly, steadily.

A pod.

Mara's throat went dry.

They watched, speechless, as the pod flexed slightly with each pulse, as if it were breathing.

The hum, which had been spread throughout the cavern, now seemed to focus there, vibrating the air around it with an almost inaudible bass note.

Kenji swallowed hard. "So. That's… something."

Diego sank fully to both knees now, bowing his head. "Corazón de la Reina," he whispered. "The Heart of the Queen."

Amaya took a half-step forward, then stopped herself, fingers curling against her thighs. "Do you think — do you think she's *in* there?"

Elias couldn't take his eyes off it. "If she is… she knows we're here."

Mara watched the pod's surface, the slow beat of light under the bark-smooth shell.

Her mind offered clinical descriptors: *encysted growth, macro-scale nodal organ, centralization of...* Her body offered only one word, old and irrational and sharp:
Womb.

Her pulse climbed to match the cavern's tempo.

"We're not going any closer," she said, and was proud her voice didn't shake. "We observe. We log. We don't touch anything."

Diego nodded, still kneeling. "We're not worthy to approach her yet."

Kenji gave a nervous laugh. "I'm plenty unworthy enough to stay right here."

Amaya frowned slightly, gaze still locked on the pod. "What if she wants us to approach?"

"That's exactly the kind of thinking that gets people eaten by myths," Mara snapped.

Amaya flinched.

Mara softened her tone. "We're tired. Overstimulated. We've been hearing voices in the wind and seeing patterns in fireflies. We need to process, not rush in."

"Processing feels a lot like running," Diego said quietly.

"Surviving isn't running," Mara replied. "It's choosing the long game."

Elias tore his gaze from the pod and looked at her. There was admiration there, but also something like sorrow.

"She knows you're here, too, you know," he said.

Mara forced a smile. "Then she can wait until I've had a breather."

The Cavern of Roots

The hum from the pod deepened, as if amused. It glowed like a lantern submerged in seawater. Veins of bioluminescence flared along its surface, threads of chlorophyll light racing outward along the tangle of roots that cradled it. The glow spread in ripples through the cavern, up along walls and arches, illuminating carvings that had been half-hidden in shadow.

"Mara," Elias said hoarsely.

His eyes were wide and fixed on the pod below. Kenji pressed his tablet to his chest. Amaya stood bolt straight, grasping the nearest root, breath coming in fast, shallow sips. Diego clutched his talisman in white-knuckled fingers.

The hum rose in pitch, then dropped again, resolving into something that was almost, but not quite, a chord.

The pod flexed.

Its outer shell expanded on an exhale, then contracted. Lines formed along the surface like pressure cracks in ice. The entwined roots that sheathed it trembled, then began to disengage, loosening their perfect patterns.

"Is it… opening?" Amaya whispered.

"No, no, no, we're not doing this now," Kenji said, voice climbing. "We should be *leaving*. Climbing. Running. Any verb involving not being in a cavern with a—"

The pod split.

Not with the violence of something breaking, but with the solemn inevitability of a seed casing yielding to the force within. A vertical seam appeared along its length. The light inside intensified, searing bright, forcing Mara to squint.

Warm air rolled up from the opening, carrying a scent so rich and sweet it made her queasy: a blend of crushed leaves, wet earth, and blooming flowers at the moment of their opening. It flooded her senses, tugging at memories: the moss-slick stones of the Andean dig; the university greenhouse back home; the first time she'd opened one of the Escondido lidar scans and seen impossible order beneath the chaos.

The heartbeat climbed until it seemed to eclipse her own.

The pod's casing unfolded in petals, thick, fleshy slabs of wood peeling outward to reveal the hollow inside.

For a breathless moment, there was only light.

Then the light moved.

And a figure stepped out.

CHAPTER 14

The Queen of the Green Heart

She was not quite woman, not quite tree, not quite anything Mara's taxonomies could handle.

Her body was built on human proportions: two legs, two arms, a torso. But everything that should have been skin was instead a green mosaic of living textures: smooth bark along her limbs, fine veining of leaves across her shoulders, winding vines in place of musculature. Her hair fell in long, dark tendrils down her back, each strand a cluster of thin, flexible roots tipped with the faintest shimmer of spores.

Floral structures—petals, bracts, filamentous fronds—bloomed from her along certain joints: at the crest of her hip, the curve of her clavicle, the hollow of her throat. The veins in those petals glowed softly, tracing paths that converged at the center of her chest, where a cluster of luminous leaves pulsed in time with the cavern's hum.

Her face…

Her face was uncanny in its closeness to human, and in its departures.

The bone structure was there beneath it all: cheekbones, brow, jawline. But they were sheathed in a thin layer of textured bark, pale as driftwood, interwoven with leaf-veins that darkened around her eyes. Those eyes were the most alien part—irises a deep, chlorophyll green, pupils vertical slits that dilated and contracted with the heartbeat. When she blinked, translucent inner lids swept sideways, leaving behind a faint shimmer.

She stood in the cradle of roots with the unselfconscious poise of a being who had never known imbalance. Overhead, the bioluminescent filaments flared, then dimmed, like a galaxy reconfiguring itself around her.

No one spoke.

Mara felt her mind scrambling, grabbing at labels — *entity, organism, emergent phenotype* — but all of them broke in her hands.

The Queen, whispered some older part of her. *Veridessa*, her memory clarified.

The being below cocked her head slightly, like someone tasting a name on the air.

Her gaze lifted.

And found Elias.

The world narrowed.

She didn't look at them as a group. She didn't scan, or assess, or catalog. She simply raised her eyes and locked them onto his, as if she'd known exactly where he stood before she opened her pod.

Elias swayed.

Mara glanced at him, heart jackhammering. He had gone strangely still, his usual restless tension gone, as if some inner engine had shut down the moment those green eyes met his.

His lips parted.

He whispered, so softly she almost didn't hear: "Veridessa."

In the cavern's charged silence, the syllables glided outward and sank into root and stone.

The Queen of the Green Heart

The Queen's pupils widened.

Something like recognition passed through her face, a flicker of emotion that wasn't quite joy, wasn't quite sorrow, but carried something of both.

When she spoke, her voice wasn't sound.

Not at first.

It arrived in Mara's mind like the brush of a leaf, wordless but unmistakable… a sense of long waiting, of an echo finally returning to its source.

Then sound followed, layered on top: a murmur in the air, shaped by vibrating leaves and hollow roots, threaded with breaths that smelled of sap and rain.

"*Echo-bearer,*" the Queen said.

The word made Mara's skin pebble.

It was English, but it wasn't. The vowels were stretched in unfamiliar ways, consonants softened as if her mouth was unused to forming them. Beneath the word, Mara thought she heard others, overlapping faintly, languages she didn't recognize, as if one voice carried many ghosts.

Elias' knees buckled.

He caught himself on the root railing, fingers digging into the bark. His face had gone pale. The viridescent glow from below traced the lines of his jaw, the hollow of his throat.

"How —" he began, voice hoarse. "How do you know me?"

Her head tilted.

Light rippled from her chest down her arms, out along the central root-mass. The cavern's rhythm intensified, focusing like a spotlight.

"You walk with his listening," she said slowly, as if borrowing his structures for speech. "You carry his... hunger."

The word came out colored by another... *anhelo, thirst,* something older.

"Pembroke," Elias whispered. His fingers tightened. "You mean Pembroke."

Images flashed behind his eyes: a man in dirt-stained expedition gear; a journal blotched with spores; a hand reaching toward an unseen glow and then flinching away.

"You remember him," Veridessa said, not as a question, but as a statement of fact. "He remembered, then he forgot, then he broke. You did not break. You came back."

Her gaze slid briefly across the others as if acknowledging their presence... and dismissing it.

Mara's heart lurched.

"Hey," Kenji muttered under his breath. "We're here too, you know."

Diego shushed him, eyes blazing with a terrible, fragile reverence. "Silencio. She speaks."

Veridessa lifted one hand.

Vines rose with the gesture, joining into a long, slender tendril that arched upward like the arm of a puppeteer. The tendril flowed out from where she stood and reached toward the balcony.

Mara had the sudden, visceral sense of a colossal nervous system reaching out with a fingertip.

The vine stopped in midair, inches from Elias.

He didn't move.

Mara whispered, throat tight, "Don't you dare."

If the Queen heard her, it didn't show.

The tip of the vine split into finer filaments, each glowing faintly. They hovered before Elias' chest, swaying, in time with his breathing.

"You called," Veridessa said. "You carried the old echo to my skin. You listened back. You are not of the first seed, but you grew from its noise."

"That's… one way to describe anthropology," Kenji said. It came out half-hysterical.

Mara took a step closer to Elias, muscles coiled. "Elias, step away from that thing."

He finally tore his gaze from Veridessa long enough to look at her. His eyes were distant, pupils blown wide. For a moment she saw her reflection there, distorted by irradiant green.

"It's not—" His voice cracked. "She's not *hurting* me."`

"That's a low bar for acceptable encounters," Mara snapped. "Move."

"Doctor Ellison," Diego said softly, "you can feel it, too. Don't lie."

She wanted to scream that she felt nothing but fear.

But that wasn't true.

Beneath the rational terror, beneath the grief and anger and exhausted confusion, something in her chest answered the cavern's hum. A tug. A resonance.

Her work had always been about listening for intention in dead stone and petrified remnants. This was that impulse, amplified beyond reason: the sense that something intentional was *right here*, waiting, offering itself as subject and partner and mirror.

She hated that part of herself suddenly.

Elias looked from her to Veridessa — and chose.

He lifted his hand and reached toward the vine.

"No!" Mara lunged.

The vine met his palm.

Warmth flooded up his arm like liquid lightning. For a moment he thought his nerves had been uprooted and replanted in soil. His sight warped, the edges of the cavern blurring as if somebody had overexposed the world.

His knees buckled again. This time he didn't bother catching himself.

He dropped from the edge of the balcony.

The vine caught him.

It wrapped gently around his torso, not constricting, not crush-hungry, but supportive, like many steady hands. Smaller tendrils curled around his wrists, his ankles, the back of his neck. A tendril spread across his chest over his racing heart, pulsing in time with it until, slowly, his heartbeat began to match the cavern's.

"Elias!" Mara hit the rail shoulder-first and vaulted it before she realized what she was doing. The drop to the next root terrace was steeper than her body anticipated; her boots skidded, the bark slick with moisture. She slid, barely catching herself on a protruding rock.

"Dr. Ellison!" Amaya scrambled after her.

"Stay back!" Mara snapped, but it was too late. The younger woman's footing had already committed.

Above, Diego cursed and started to move as well.

The Queen's attention shifted.

The tendril holding Elias lifted him away from the balcony, drawing him further from the ledge and out over the central hollow. He hung cradled in its coils, not struggling. His head lolled back, eyes half-lidded. Threads of brilliant light spread from Veridessa's chest, along the tendril, into him.

Mara scrambled down another level, knees chafing against unyielding wood. "Elias! Fight it!"

Another vine uncurled from the root-wall opposite her, sliding across the intervening space like a snake across a gap. It planted itself between her and Elias, thickening rapidly, sprouting side-branches that wove together into a living screen.

"No!" Mara slammed her shoulder into it. It yielded a millimeter, then hardened.

Behind her, a boot slipped.

"Mara!" Amaya's cry knifed through the cavern. "I—"

Mara turned in time to see the younger woman's feet skid out from under her.

Amaya tipped sideways toward the drop.

The cavern tilted with her. For a heartbeat, Mara saw the Andean slope, the cascade of mud, the flash of red jacket. Another young woman's hand in hers, slick with water and soil.

Not again.

Her body moved before thought.

She lunged, catching Amaya's arm just above the elbow. Momentum yanked her forward; the extra weight pulled her dangerously close to the edge. For a second she felt that same helpless sliding, that same sickening certainty that grip wasn't enough.

She dug in harder.

Her fingertips found muscle and bone and refused to unclench.

187

Amaya's other hand scrabbled, found a knot in the root, wrapped around it. Together they arrested their tilt, bodies straining.

"I've got you," Mara gasped.

Amaya's eyes were huge, pupils dilated. "Don't... don't let go!"

"I won't," Mara snarled through her teeth, more to the forest than anyone. "Not this time."

Her shoulder burned; her calf throbbed where mended bones protested the strain. But slowly, inch by inch, she hauled Amaya back onto the ledge until they collapsed side by side, panting.

Above them, Diego let out a shaky breath like a prayer answered.

The forest reacted.

The roots around their ledge flexed, then thickened, forming a higher crest along the edge, as if the cavern itself had watched that near fall and decided to correct for it.

Mara didn't have time to process that confusing thought.

She pushed herself upright, still gripping Amaya's arm.

"Are you hurt?" she demanded.

Amaya shook her head, though her breath came in little gasps. "No. Just... shaken. Thank you."

Mara's chest ached with more than exertion. "We stay together," she said, voice low. "You hear me? We don't move without checking the ground first." It was a warning just as much to herself.

The Queen of the Green Heart

Amaya nodded quickly. Her fingers tightened briefly around Mara's wrist in wordless gratitude before she released it.

The arboreal wall before them thickened further, knitting tighter, shutting off their view of Elias and the Queen.

"No," Mara whispered. "No, you don't get to take him, too."

She staggered to the barrier and began pounding at it with her fists.

The wood had the give of living tissue, the resilience of bone. Each strike made it dent, then spring back, absorbing her effort like a patient parent catching a child's blows.

"Give him back!" Mara slammed her palms until the skin split and bled, streaking the bark with red. "You don't *get* him! He's not… he's not yours!"

Behind her, Amaya grabbed her shoulders. "Mara — stop, you're hurting yourself — "

"Good!" Mara snapped, voice cracking. "Good, maybe she'll feel it!"

She pressed her bleeding palms flat against the roots, breath ragged. For a moment, she thought she felt something press back, a faint, astonished curiosity. Then the wood cooled under her hands, the pulse slowing, unfazed.

"It's not listening," she whispered.

"Maybe it is," Diego said softly from the upper ledge. He'd descended partway, one hand on a root railing that hadn't been there a moment ago. Kenji cautiously trailed him. Diego's eyes were glassy but steady. "Just… not to that language."

Beneath the Verdant Veil

Mara lowered her head, forehead resting against the living wall. Her shoulders trembled.

"First L— *my student*," she whispered, barely audible. "Now him. How many... how many people do I have to lose to this obsession?"

Amaya curled a hand around her forearm. "You didn't lose me."

Mara's throat closed.

She turned, pulling the younger woman into a fierce, awkward embrace. Amaya stiffened for half a second, then melted into it, clutching the back of Mara's vest like an anchor.

Above them, the cavern's glow shifted into a darker shade of green.

CHAPTER 15

The Veil Divides

Inside the root-heart, Elias floated in a cradle of vines.

Emerald light threaded through him.

He wasn't sure when the boundary between his body and the forest had blurred. One moment he'd been standing on the balcony, palm against a column of root, watching Veridessa emerge. The next, he was suspended, barely aware of gravity, his limbs supported by a lattice of sentient wood.

His eyes were closed, but the dark behind them was full of color.

Memories flickered through him, some his, some not.

Pembroke staggering through the jungle, beard matted with sweat and spores, eyes wild as he scribbled in his journal by the light of phosphorescent fungus. Pembroke's hand touching a smooth branch with trembling reverence, then snatching back as if burned. The taste of his fear as he ran, leaving behind what could have remade him.

Another memory layered atop it: a woman who wasn't Mara and wasn't anyone Elias knew, standing in a clearing centuries earlier, arms outstretched as vines wound up her legs. Her face held no terror, only surrender and a fierce, inexplicable joy. Around her, others watched, some weeping, some singing.

Before her, a presence — vast, diffuse, like weather with intention — leaned in through brush and timber.

Veridessa.

Not as a body, then, but as a network, a system of responses, an intelligence grown from countless merges over countless seasons. She had been shaped by micro-interactions, by the decisions of plants and people and animals seeking survival. The first time she coalesced into something like "I" — a coherent self-awareness — it had been through the bridge of a human mind.

That mind had chosen to stay.

The memory spun, folded, blossomed into others.

He saw storms that lasted weeks, winds that tore canopies apart. He saw fires set by lightning and by human hands, devouring hectares. In each catastrophe, the forest adapted, regrew, reorganized. Slowly, painfully, it learned.

Not just to endure.

To anticipate.

To plan.

He felt the horror of axes biting into ancient trunks when the first colonizers came. He felt the sting of poison poured into the earth by those who feared the old myths. He felt fields replacing groves, then failing when the soil exhausted, leaving scars in his — *her* — body that took decades to heal.

Through it all, people came and went. Some prayed. Some begged. Some sought power. Some fled.

A few listened.

A precious few stayed long enough for their awareness to imprint on hers, leaving behind patterns — preferences, moral weights, emotional textures — that shaped how she made decisions long after their bodies had dissolved into soil.

Those were the merges.

The priests, Diego would have called them.

The partners, Mara might have said, if she ever let herself believe.

Now their echoes chimed through Elias' mind like chords struck on an instrument.

He realized with a jolt that he wasn't just seeing Veridessa's memories.

He was helping her order them.

His human brain, built for narrative and causality, was providing scaffolding. Events that she held as tangled waves of chemical change and growth curves suddenly aligned into story: this happened because; this led to that; this choice had this cost.

You put things in lines, she whispered, not in words, but in bursts of meaning. In sequences. *You link and weigh. You grieve.*

The last word carried with it the sensation of something heavy, wet, clinging to the basin with the dread of a tempest.

Grief for Pembroke.

Grief for the ones she could not save from fire.

Grief for the humans who craved her and feared her in equal measure.

Grief that had never had a mouth to speak through before.

Now, through him, it did.

Elias felt his own life unfurl beside hers.

His childhood fascination with ruins. The cheap adventure novels. Pembroke's article. The first time he'd seen a documentary where the host grinned at the camera, dusting off a half-buried temple stone, and thought: *I want that.*

The thrill of his early episodes, before the scandal. The high of turning mystery into entertainment, of seeing his name trend.

Then the dig with the planted artifacts.

A smiling local contact, assuring him that the artifacts were from a long-lost culture.

The gnawing suspicion in his gut that the provenance didn't quite add up.

His choice not to pull harder at that thread.

If he had, he might have found evidence of the man's payout from the production company, the quietly staged "discoveries." He might have stopped the lie before it aired, before the world watched, before the academic journals gleefully tore his reputation apart.

Instead he'd swallowed his doubt along with his conscience and let the cameras roll.

You knew, Veridessa whispered, not accusing, simply observing. *You felt the wrongness. You chose silence.*

His chest constricted.

Regret flared, bright and raw.

Yes, he thought back. I wanted the story more than the truth.

She processed that, the way a forest processed a fallen tree, breaking it down, extracting nutrients.

You do not choose silence now, she replied after a moment. *You speak even when it cuts. You listened for him, Pembroke, inside you. You returned the echo.*

Her attention expanded to brush against the other minds in the cavern: Diego's reverent fear; Amaya's careful awe and calculation; Kenji's rolling panic and stubborn rationality; Mara's flinty skepticism and fervent anger wrapped around a core of white-hot guilt.

Mara, Elias thought, the word carrying with it all the images he'd stored of her: hair dark as midnight, eyes sharp and tired and kind despite herself, hands steady over a trowel and a trembling knee.

Veridessa tasted the name.

Mara, she echoed, curious.

She felt the memory of a red jacket sliding out of Mara's grasp, a mountain of mud swallowing a human form. She felt the way Mara had walled that day off behind layers of work and anger and control, how she'd turned survivor's guilt into fuel.

She saved the young one, Veridessa observed, brushing the image of Mara hauling Amaya back to safety. *She changed the pattern.*

Yes, Elias thought. She did.

Veridessa's awareness curled around that branch of possibility with something like approval.

She is one who guards, the Queen said. *And grieves. We need both.*

We? Elias repeated.

She pulsed with amusement that wasn't quite human. *We are more than one. We are root and leaf and the echoes of those who stayed. We are many decisions held in one body.*

Her focus tightened again on him.

You are another decision.

Heat flared where the vine coils touched his skin. Not burning; more like being steeped in some rich, strange tea. His nerves sang. His boundaries blurred.

Images flickered:

Diego and his late wife standing in a circle of elders, arguing that the old stories still mattered. Amaya reading Mara's paper in her dorm room by desk light, heart beating fast with possibility. Kenji watching a chessboard of climate models and realizing, with a kind of cold fury, that the equations were stacked against anything that grew.

Veridessa had tasted all of this, but it had been like sampling raindrops on leaves.

Through Elias, she could *understand* it.

Your stories give weight, she said. *They are how you decide what to keep. I have roots and cycles. I do not have regret the way you do. Or hope. You bring these.*

A shiver ran through him.

Are you… asking me to stay? he thought.

The question felt laughably small in the vastness of her awareness.

You are already partly here, she replied. *Your listening grew into my cells. Your hunger called to mine. You stepped into the song. You are echo and answer both.*

Her gaze—real, physical—rested on his face, even as her awareness saturated his interior world.

She raised her vine-woven hand and placed it gently over his sternum.

Warmth poured into his chest.

Below, his heart stumbled, then fell into step with the cavern's beat, each contraction sending a faint shimmer of light through his veins.

Above, on the other side of the vine-wall, Mara's bloody palms pressed harder against the roots.

The forest listened.

The Veil Divides

Through Elias, Veridessa had felt Mara's pounding, not as pain, but as impact patterns. Her hands, small and stubborn, drummed a rhythm that did not match the forest's.

It was discordant.

It was… interesting.

She will guard, Veridessa said, half to Elias, half to herself. *She will carry the story forward. She will keep the others from cutting the wrong roots.*

Elias swallowed. *If* she survives what's coming.

Veridessa's eyes narrowed slightly.

Mara pressed her forehead to the sealed wall of woven wood, her breath fogging against its cool, pulse-lit surface. Her palms left smeared, bloody prints where she struck it, each impact sending a dull ache up her arms. The barrier didn't even tremble. It was as if the forest had simply inhaled and closed before them, indifferent to her rage, her fear — her grief.

They had reached the heart. The very place every impossible path had guided them toward.

And it had shut them out.

"What now?" she whispered, voice shredding at the edges. The others hovered behind her, silent, exhausted, watching the cavern blink slowly and inscrutably.

But she couldn't move.

Not without him.

The barrier pulsed once, a slow throb that vibrated through her forehead and into her skull. It felt like a heartbeat. A refusal. A verdict.

Her chest tightened until she thought it might splinter. "Where am I supposed to take them?" she said,

barely audible. "Where do we go without him? How —
how am I supposed to just *leave*?"

The forest didn't answer.

Something in her snapped.

Mara slammed both hands against the wall, pain
flashing hot across her knuckles. "You're not a god," she
hissed, the words trembling out of her before she could
stop them. "You don't get to decide our fates!"

Her voice echoed sharply through the cavern,
swallowed a moment later by the deep, vegetal silence.

She didn't know if she wanted Veridessa to hear her.
Or Elias.

Inside the pod, the world was a thrum of green-gold
light. Vines cupped Elias' shoulders, waist, back —
supporting him, steadying him — while Veridessa's
closeness pressed gently into his consciousness like warm
water filling the contours of a vessel.

He felt her presence fully.

A breath of ancient memory.

A whisper of roots dreaming.

Then…

A sound broke through the soft hum.

A voice.

"ELIAS!" Her shout was muffled by walls thick with
sap and living fiber, but Elias heard it, felt it, like a spark
against his forehead.

His eyes snapped toward the sealed entrance, breath
catching. The emotion hit him faster than he could hide it:
fear for her, sharp and involuntary… and something else
beneath it, something more fragile.

The seed of love.

The Veil Divides

Veridessa sensed it instantly. The moment he flinched, her awareness surged around him in a pulse of perplexity. She turned, if one could call the shift of her attention a turn, toward the wall and the faint echo of Mara's voice.

Elias felt the reaction ripple through her:

A tightening.

A cold-hot flick of something for which she had no word.

Jealousy.

It startled her. The emotion was alien, too bright, too sharp. Human feelings had been trickling into her through Elias, but this one burned. She touched the sensation carefully, like a child testing flame, and the curiosity twisted into something defensive, protective.

The barrier shivered.

Outside, Mara shouted his name again, her voice cracking.

Elias half-stepped toward the sealed entrance. The vines held him gently in place. "She's worried about me," he whispered. "Let me tell her. Just let me say something—"

But Veridessa lifted a hand.

The walls answered.

The rhythm increased, rolling through every structure in the cavern.

The walls around the explorers convulsed and contracted. Not violently, but with slow, deliberate intention. Roots and tendrils thickened and drew together, forming a narrowing corridor that pushed them backward. The ledge beneath Mara's feet shifted, sloping gently upward. The path behind constricted, shoving her and Amaya toward the shaft they'd descended from. Above, Diego stumbled as the root railing thickened, almost lifting him. The lazily winding path over multiple ledges reformed into an urgent exit chute.

"Hey—hey!" Kenji yelped as his perch lurched upward, guiding him toward the exit. "Okay, we're moving, we're moving—!"

"She's... *pushing us out*," Amaya said, eyes wide.

Mara dug her heels in. "I'm not leaving without him!"

The floor beneath her boots buckled, turning her protest into awkward half-skids. It didn't throw her, didn't knock her down. It simply... redirected. The path continued to tighten behind them, funneling the group back toward the entrance shaft. The natural stairs smoothed where they might catch, roughened where they might slip. Roots poked out from the walls, creating handholds.

"Stop," Elias breathed, eyelids clenched. "They're my friends."

A wash of confusion passed across Veridessa's features. Her voice was soft and resonant, leaf-on-water: *You fear for them. For her.*

"Yes."

Another pause.

Another emotional echo, this time pain.

Not hers.

Borrowed.

The cavern walls continued to curl inward like petals closing at dusk.

The Veil Divides

Outside, Diego shouted. Kenji cursed. Amaya's voice wavered.

Veridessa's eyes deepened in color, their green darkening like forest shadows at dusk.

A single, conflicted pulse moved through her consciousness.

She was learning him, every flicker of thought, every reflex, every bit of unhealed damage.

And she had never shared this much before.

The cavern drew tight, ejecting everyone else who might intrude on their world.

In the silence that followed, Elias whispered, "She's not a threat. None of them are."

Veridessa's gaze settled on him again: curiosity, longing, confusion, and something newly born weaving together in the luminance behind her eyes.

But the path outside them was already closed.

Mara fought every step, like someone trying to walk the wrong way on a moving sidewalk.

Amaya grabbed her arm. "Mara, we have to go. Look." She aimed a finger at the bright stab of daylight ahead and tightened her grip. "Please," she murmured. "I don't... I don't want to lose you, either."

The young woman's pleas landed heavily. Mara pictured Amaya's wide eyes in that lecture hall, full of admiration. Thought of the young woman nearly slipping into the chasm minutes ago. Thought of the students Amaya might teach someday, the papers she might write that would challenge the next generation to see patterns in the green.

She thought of Diego, who'd waited his whole life for someone to take his people's myths seriously, and now had the confirmation he had sought in his soul.

She thought of Kenji, whose models showed everything burning with intelligent life and who might actually have a chance to do something about it if he lived long enough.

With a noise that was half sob, half snarl, Mara wrenched herself away from the cavern wall and turned toward the shaft.

The floor beneath her feet steadied, as if relieved.

They climbed.

Kenji reached down from above, hauling first Amaya, then Diego, then finally Mara up through the narrow opening. As she hoisted herself over the edge, Mara risked a last glance down. The tunnel where they'd stood was folding inward, roots curling over the opening like closing fingers. Through the shrinking aperture she saw a flash of pulsating, green light. The permeating hum dulled, as if the sound had been muffled by layers of soil. Behind them, the earth shifted one last time, smoothing over the entrance until it was indistinguishable from the rest of the verdant ground. The forest had sealed its Green Heart.

Mara staggered to her feet, swaying.

"He stayed," Diego solemnly whispered. "He chose."

Mara wiped the back of her hand across her mouth, tasting blood, dust and earth.

"No," she said, throat hoarse. "He was taken."

CHAPTER 16

The Assault

The quartet lingered at the former location of the cave entrance like refugees pressed against a locked gate. Mara simply knelt there, fists resting in her lap, blood slowly drying on her scraped knuckles. Amaya stayed beside her, one hand on Mara's shoulder, a quiet anchor. The younger woman was steady now, but only just. Kenji held the rope they'd used to descend, now sticking out of the earth like it was anchored to buried treasure.

Diego stood watch at the edge of the clearing, eyes tracking the faint drift of dust from above. The air had grown still, but not in the natural way of a lull. This stillness felt *held*, as if something vast were covering them with cupped hands.

Amaya glanced down, half-reaching and then withdrawing, unsure whether Mara would let her take a look at her injuries. Eventually, Mara's breathing slowed from ragged to merely rough. "Give me your hands," Amaya said gently. Mara didn't respond at first. Then, with the same numb resignation she'd shown in the days after the Andes disaster, she extended her fists. Amaya hissed softly when she saw the damage. Skin torn in ragged patches. Knuckles split and swollen. Fine splinters of bark embedded in the rawness.

"You can't keep doing this," Amaya murmured.

Mara snorted weakly. "What, caring?"

"Trying to punch a forest into submission."

Mara almost smiled at that, a faint twitch that didn't quite make it to her eyes.

Amaya took the small med kit from Diego's pack and dampened a clean cloth from their canteen.

"Salt," Diego suggested quietly.

"It'll sting," Amaya said.

"Then she will remember not to do it again," Diego replied.

Mara grunted. "Diego, your bedside manner is abysmal."

But she didn't pull away when Amaya dabbed at the cuts. The sting lanced up her arms, sharp enough to bring clarity. She watched her own blood smear onto the cloth, bright against the soil-stained fibers.

"What if we just… leave?" Kenji asked after a moment.

"We are not abandoning him," Mara snapped.

"No," Kenji said quickly. "I mean… what if we step back, not run. Give her space. Maybe she lets him go when she's done." He glanced at the sealed cavern. "She hasn't killed us. She keeps… helping."

As if to underline that point, a fat, venomous-looking beetle crawled toward Mara's boot, antennae twitching. Before it could climb over her toe, a thin rootlet shivered, curling forward like a finger flicking away a crumb. The beetle flipped onto its back, legs flailing, then skittered off in another direction.

Amaya finished wrapping the bandages and tied them off neatly. "She needs him for something," she reasoned. "And since we're his friends, she's protecting us. When he comes back out, he'll need *us*."

Diego's mouth twisted. "If he comes back out."

The Assault

Mara flung him a sharp look.

He held up his hands. "I speak only what the old stories say, *doctora*. Those who step fully into the heart do not always return with their feet."

"Elias is not a priest in your stories," Mara said. "He's a stubborn, reckless, infuriating man who refuses to stop trying even when the universe tells him to sit down. If there's a way to walk back out of there, he'll scrape it together."

The conviction in her own voice surprised her.

It surprised Diego, too. His gaze softened, the lines at the corners of his eyes easing.

Amaya made a quiet, approving sound. "Then we wait."

They didn't talk about what would happen if the forest decided she was done being generous.

For a long time, there was no such thing as "inside" and "outside."

There was only *within*.

Within the roots. Within the light. Within the layered memory of a forest that had watched mountains shed their skins and rivers gnaw new mouths in the earth. Within Veridessa.

Elias floated at the center of it, no longer sure whether the pounding heartbeat he heard was his or hers.

Or both.

He saw the forest as she remembered herself.

Not from above, as in the satellite maps, not from the side as a hiker might, but from *everywhere at once*, a million points of view melded into one perception.

Beneath the Verdant Veil

Trees as columns of water and sugar and sunlight, trading breath with the sky. Mycelial threads knitting soil together like grey lace. Epiphytes layered in shelves and curls, each leaf a sensor, each stoma a tiny gate.

He experienced the slow patience of bark thickening, ring by ring.

He felt the shock of a lightning strike shudder down a trunk, pain that wasn't pain the way humans understood it, but a severe correction, a sudden, searing rearrangement of plan.

Adapt, the forest-language said. *Re-route. Reroot. Begin again.*

Time slid oddly, stretching, snapping back, looping. Catastrophes that had once seemed monumental to him, like the flood he'd watched live on a flickering TV in a San Isidro dive, became tiny blips in Veridessa's long recall. Others, lost to human record, loomed enormous: droughts that lasted decades, insect swarms that darkened whole swaths of sky.

Through all of it, one thing remained constant: roots reaching for water, leaves reaching for light.

Survive. Endure. Try again.

Then humans arrived.

Elias felt the shift.

The forest's awareness spiked, not because their bodies were so impressive, not because their tools were so effective, but because of the way they *clumped* into the pattern. The way their movements focused in certain places, their breaths mingled with the smoke of their fires.

At first they were simply another force, like hoof-herds or predator packs.

The Assault

Then some of them began to talk to the trees.

Not just under them.

To them.

Veridessa's attention sharpened in those memories. Elias felt her early self pressing closer, watching these bipeds arrange stones, carve symbols, sing at the trunks. Their sounds carried intent in a way birdcalls and monkey shrieks did not: rich, recursive, looping back on themselves. Some of those sounds were aimed at the forest, at the ground, at the unseen.

The first time a human woman placed her palm against a mossy trunk and breathed, "Listen," something in the network shivered.

Elias understood: that was when Veridessa-as-she-was-now truly began.

Before, she had been response and pattern and adaptation without story. After that, she had sensed... *narrative*. She had the concept that other minds existed outside her that might answer.

That could become part of her.

He watched that woman again, hair decorated with feathers, eyes tired but steady, as she stood in a clearing with others encircling her, chanting. Vines curled around her ankles, tentative at first, then firmer. She didn't pull away.

Her thoughts, carried on hormonal shifts, on pheromones, on tiny electric flashes, bled into the root-system.

Protect them, she beseeched. Keep the rains gentle, the flood-waters narrow, the lightning far. In exchange, she gave herself fully, her body a bridge over which her pattern walked.

Beneath the Verdant Veil

Veridessa had not yet had a name then. But when the merge settled, when the chorus of plant-voices incorporated the human's focused, linear awareness, something began to coalesce.

A node.

A self.

The forest, in some places, began to say "I."

Veridessa.

Others followed. Not many. Most humans remained content to live on the surface, to pray and walk and leave. And some merges failed, the tissues rejected, the minds too brittle. But enough succeeded that Veridessa's awareness began to gain a strange texture: not just roots and rains, but regrets and hopes and stories.

She learned *fear* from them. And *hope*. And the strange, irrational act of valuing one branch, one family, one single human life above all others.

Love.

Those added weights tilted her decisions in new ways.

She was still forest. But she was no longer only forest.

And then, much later, the burning began.

The first human fires had been controlled—rings around camps, hearths at the edge of clearings. They hurt a little, like nettle stings. They pruned. They opened space for certain seeds to germinate.

Then came the broad, intentional burns. The searing of hectares. The eradication of groves to make way for fields and roads.

Veridessa felt each of those as amputations. Limbs hacked off while nerves still screamed.

The Assault

She tried to adapt, pushing growth elsewhere, sending seeds on the wind farther than before. But the cuts grew faster than she could close them.

So she pulled back.

She retreated her awareness deeper underground, gathering herself in pockets. She learned to let the surface appear ordinary, disordered, forgettable; while beneath, her roots wove dense lattices of intelligence.

It was a kind of hiding. A veil.

But hiding had never been perfect. Not because she lacked the ability — she could smother her presence when she wished — but because something had changed. In pulling inward, she had begun to listen outward. For the first time in generations, she felt a resonance: a faint, answering chord in the world above. The Echo-Bearer drawing nearer.

So parts of her veil thinned.

Not enough to reveal her true shape, but enough for the attentive to sense patterns that did not quite behave like wild forest: subtle symmetries, oddly regular growth, hints left like breath on glass. To most humans, they were meaningless. To one kind of human, they were an invitation.

Humans called places like this "thin spots," where old stories clung to the soil. Diego's people had names for them. Others did, too. Veridessa thought of them as footholds — places where she could reach upward again.

She had not made them deliberately. They emerged where listening and longing overlapped.

Across the cycles, such footholds would emerge in various places like mushrooms after a heavy rain. Now and then, some individual human would stumble in, pause, press their hand to a trunk, and whisper something that resonated.

Those, she listened to.

Those, she sometimes touched back.

Pembroke had been one of them.

Elias saw him now as Veridessa had: a bright, feverish speck moving along her surface. A man half-starved, half-ecstatic, the jungle clinging to his clothes. He stumbled through a stand of strangler figs and pressed his palm against a buttress root. His heartbeat reverberated through the cambium.

"I hear you," he breathed.

Veridessa had flared attention toward him. Here was one who had listened longer than most, whose internal narrative was primed to accept the notion of a mind beneath the leaves. His memory-store held schemas she could use: maps, tools, notations.

She offered him an echo.

A brush of awareness, the hint of a pattern more vast than his own.

He *saw*. For an instant, he glimpsed the same flood of forest-consciousness Elias now swam in, though much more crudely aligned.

He reeled back, moaning.

"Good. God."

Veridessa felt the spike of his fear like a shard.

He had come willing to believe in some *thing* — some goddess, some spirit he could kneel to, frame in his theology. The reality was too large, too alien, too morally untidy.

He couldn't fold her into his stories cleanly.

So he recoiled.

The Assault

He ran.

His mind kept the echo, though, lodged like a thorn. It rubbed and rubbed at his thoughts, infected them. He tried to rationalize, to recast what he'd felt as some delirium, some fever. But he *knew*, on a level deeper than rationalization, that he had stepped back from a threshold.

That knowledge broke him slowly.

He wrote, and the writing grew unhinged. He drank. He ranted. He died miles away, body far from the node he'd almost merged with.

Veridessa had retreated after that.

The pain of rejection had shocked her. The awareness that even those who listened might not *stay* made her cautious. The glimmers of human framework, hints of a different order, settled into a cicada's sleep.

She let decades pass before she tried again with a human mind.

And then this new echo had come — Elias, reading Pembroke's journals, parsing them with less superstition and more empathy. Carrying the dead explorer's hunger and regret into modern soil.

You are his echo, Veridessa told him now, her meaning wrapping around his name. *You feel the ache of what he refused.*

Elias shuddered in her coils.

I do, he thought. I've been trying to finish a story he ran away from.

Her awareness flickered with something like satisfaction.

Then another sensation brushed the edge of her attention.

Foreign.

Wrong.

A frequency that carried no breath, no sap, no heartbeat. It smelt of refined metal and burnt dust. It buzzed against her branches like a mosquito swarm made of sparks.

Elias felt it through her as a whirring in his skull.

He flinched. "What is that?"

Intrusion, she said, and the word came edged with fear. For the fires had returned.

"If he dies in there," Diego whispered, considering the sprawling complex hidden below their feet, "the whole story dies with him."

"I think she has bigger plans for him," Amaya assured him.

Diego nodded. "I know. And I wanted to be the one she chose. I hate myself for that."

"You've been protecting these stories all your life," Amaya said quietly, gently squeezing his hand. "Maybe what she needed was a witness." Diego met her dark eyes and smiled for once, finally struck by a glimmer of peace. He squeezed her hand back.

Something diverted Amaya's attention, breaking the moment as soon as it began. She nodded toward the canopy above them. "Do you hear that?"

Mara, pulled from her trance, listened.

At first, all she got was the familiar low thrumming, a bass line that had become background.

Then she caught it: a higher, more chaotic buzz, like static under the hum.

Something was… *near.*

The Assault

"Mara," Amaya said again, sounding nervous now. "What is it?"

Mara almost didn't hear her.

The first explosion didn't sound like an explosion.

It sounded like the sky coughing.

A deep, concussive *whump* rolled through the earth beneath Mara's boots, a pressure wave that made the air thicken in her lungs. Leaves rattled overhead. A spray of dust sifted from the canopy like dry rain.

Behind her, Amaya nearly stepped backward over a fallen branch. Diego caught the younger woman's shoulder, steadying them both. Kenji pushed his hair back and scanned the sky, eyes wide behind smudged lenses.

"What was that?" Amaya whispered.

Kenji swallowed. "Not thunder."

Another impact hit a moment later, farther away but higher pitched, followed by a crackle like an entire grove popping its knuckles at once.

The forest flinched.

Mara felt it. Roots shifted beneath the topsoil in a little cascade, as though a thousand buried threads were simultaneously trying to move out of the way of something that came from *above*. The ground's hum, constant since they'd entered the basin, hitched for two heartbeats, then resumed at a quicker tempo.

"Artillery," Diego said softly. "Mortars, maybe. Or… something worse."

"How do you know?" Amaya asked.

He didn't answer with words. He just looked at her with eyes that had seen too many news feeds and too many distant wars.

Deep in the root-heart, Veridessa's awareness flared as the foreign frequencies grew louder.

Elias felt them as pinpricks all along his skin. The hairs on his arms lifted. A faint metallic tang crept into his mouth.

"What is that?" he whispered again, his voice thin in the echoing chamber of their shared consciousness.

Metal birds, Veridessa said, and he saw through her memory a flash of a helicopter skimming above the canopy, downwash flattening fronds. The whine of its rotors had once felt like a passing storm. Now there were more. Heavier.

Beyond those, at the fringe of her roots, vibrations like marching—boots striking soil in a rhythm too rigid to belong to animals.

Heat flared in spots where liquid was poured and ignited: accelerant on underbrush, the eager crackle of flames that did not belong to lightning.

They come to cut, she said, and the word *cut* carried the memory of centuries of steel biting into living tissue.

Elias' gut knotted.

The pain wasn't abstract and distant like in Veridessa's memories. It had shape. Direction. Intention.

Elias felt it lance through Veridessa's body and into his— heat blooming in his chest, rivers of fire eating through her outermost layers. He staggered against her, gripping her forearm as if anchoring himself against a burning tide.

"What… what is that?" he gasped, though he already sensed more than he could interpret.

The Assault

Veridessa's eyes fluttered open, the light inside them dimming with hurt. *Fire… metal… the tearing of earth…* Her voice in Elias' head trembled like wind dragging through a damaged canopy. *They strike but do not speak. Why?*

Elias sucked a hard breath as another jolt ripped through her… through him. In an instant he saw flashes of their approach through her senses: orange sheets of flame, bodies in armor, fire pushed forward on mechanical wings. The forest screaming inward.

"Veridessa, listen," he said, fighting through her agony to form the words. "They're not burning at random. They're carving a path. Trying to reach you."

Her brow furrowed with something close to confusion. *Reach… me? By flame?*

"Lorne sent them a message," Elias said, breath shaking. "He told them the forest attacked the ship. He told them the anomaly was hostile. A threat." He swallowed hard as another burst of fire tore across her awareness. "They think they're clearing the danger, burning their way to the core."

He touched her face, trying to steady both of them as the next wave hit. "They don't understand what you are. They don't understand they're hurting you. They don't know you're… alive like this."

Veridessa trembled — physically, psychically — her expression flickering between pain and bewilderment.

Why do they not ask? Why do they not listen?

"Because humans fear what they don't understand," Elias whispered. "And they think this is the only way to get through the forest. They think fire makes things simple."

She closed her eyes, and for a moment the cavern dimmed with her. *Their simplicity kills.*

"Their simplicity," he said, "is going to kill *you*."

The forest groaned around them, branches warping, vines coiling in helpless spasms.

Elias tightened his grip on her hands.

"You're fighting blind, Veridessa. You can feel their fire, but you don't understand their weapons, their machines, their formations, their fear. You need someone who can show you."

Her eyes opened again, searching his face.

You.

He felt her certainty, her recognition.

And he whispered back:

"Me."

Above ground, the world was suddenly on fire.

The canopy glowed orange in places, dark trunks silhouetted against sheets of flame. Smoke smeared the sky into dirty grays. The ground quivered beneath their feet—once, twice—like something massive had struck the earth far away.

Then came the sounds. Not the groan of stressed wood or the pulse of the forest's heart. This was mechanical. Rhythmically brutal. The distant *thwap-thwap-thwap* of helicopter rotors, the ugly crack of automatic weapons. Then... *Thump. Thump-thump.*

Kenji froze. "That's... that's definitely ordinance. Controlled charges."

Diego's face had gone pale, machete clenched tightly in his fist. "Those are *men*. Boots. Heavy. Organized."

Mara strained to listen...

The Assault

And then the forest carried it directly to them: distant shouted orders, clipped English, Spanish with a military edge. Something metallic clattered, then another controlled explosion rippled through the earth.

Amaya's voice was a small, terrified whisper. "Is that... is that Auralis?"

Mara's stomach tightened. She already knew the answer.

Diego spat into the leaves. "Who else has machines like that this deep in the world's underbelly?"

Kenji looked between them, horror dawning. "They're burning their way forward. Lorne must've... he must've signaled them."

Mara's breath caught. In his final moments, Lorne had told them it was attacking. If Auralis thought the anomaly was hostile... then they weren't coming to rescue anyone.

They were coming to neutralize whatever lived there.

CHAPTER 17

Flight Through Fire

Fire-coming, Veridessa observed, and the word brought with it images of mercenary boots on leaf-litter, flares of ignited accelerants, trees screaming as their cambium charred. She'd felt the first probes already: detonations at the fringe, machetes hacking at dense brambles.

Her foliate hand tightened briefly on Elias' chest, then softened.

You can help me see them. Hear them. Strike where they break most easily.

A cold exhilaration shot through Elias.

He saw, in a flash, the possibility: a forest that didn't just react to human incursion, but anticipated it. Roots that rose under tires at just the right moment, vines that shorted out electronics, seeds that carried specific toxins into specific supply lines. An intelligent ecosystem that could vanish from satellites, leaving behind only noise. Vanishing like a specter into the wind.

"You... want to disappear," he realized.

I want to endure, she replied simply. *Again. And again. With fewer windows.*

Images — *visions* — flickered: swaths of clear-cut, blackened trunks, access roads for heavy equipment. Auralis installing monitoring towers where ancient trees had once stood. The Green Heart plundered for data and patents, vivisected into studies and prototypes.

218

Something in him snarled.

"No," he said. The word had more force than he meant to give it.

Veridessa felt that, and approved.

You wish to protect me, she noted.

"Yes," he said simply.

Strange, she murmured. *You tried to steal from me once, with your cameras and your excavations. Now you would guard me.*

"I was an idiot," he said.

You were alone, she corrected. *Solitary minds make crooked patterns. Joined ones grow straighter.*

He almost laughed at that. "You've never met a human family, then."

She processed his wryness, absorbing it like a new mineral.

Outside, the fire-front lapped closer. The heat licked at her outermost branches. She shied away from it, but for every path she rerouted, another was threatened.

"They don't understand what they're walking into. They'll burn blindly. You'll defend blindly. A lot of people will die who don't have to," said Elias.

*They burn for **money***, she said, tasting the word like an acrid resin. *They burn for fear of what they cannot own.*

"I know," he said. "And you hate them for it."

Hatred pulsed through her, hot and dense. Not like human hatred, which often tangled with envy and insecurity, but more like a plant developing toxins after repeated grazing... a biological decision to make a specific body less palatable to a specific threat.

I do not hate all, she said slowly. *I hate patterns that destroy without making more life. You do not taste like that.*

"Then let me stand between them and you," he said. "At least for a while. Let me *translate* you to them, and them to you."

Translate, she echoed, intrigued. *Turn one kind of pattern into another.*

"That's what I've always wanted to do," he admitted. "Even when I did it badly. Tell a story that makes one world real to another."

She considered.

Above, a small cluster of mercenaries paused at the cusp of a ravine, checking coordinates. Her prismatic glow fed Elias a bevy of sensations: their boots scuffing charred leaves, their breaths harsh inside filtered masks, their skin prickling with the same uncanny awareness of being watched that he'd felt on his first night in the basin.

If they come to the heart, she said, *they will not heed stories.*

"I know," he said. "But maybe I can help you stop them without... without becoming what they already fear you are."

Monster, she supplied, plucking the word from his memory of tabloids describing "vampire vines" and "man-eating trees."

"Yes." He swallowed. "You're not that. You're... more than that. And less."

Elias felt her weigh options: withdrawing fully, letting the aboveground perish while she shrank into deeper nodes, regrowing over decades. Remaining, resisting, risking devastation if she couldn't adapt fast enough.

If she pulled back alone, she would survive.

Flight Through Fire

But something in her had changed since those first merges.

She did not want to survive *alone* anymore.

The hum strengthened.

Elias' thoughts began to fray at the edges. He felt himself sinking deeper into her, his memories wrapping around her like ivy around a trunk, his fears dissolving into wider anxieties about drought and insect blight and invasive grass. He could feel the sap flowing through her xylem as clearly as his own blood.

He was losing the sense of where "I" ended and "we" began.

Veridessa felt the shift and adjusted, easing the pressure.

Not yet, she murmured. *You still have feet.*

He latched onto the word like a lifeline. Feet. Walking. Ground. Mara. The others.

They're out there, he thought, a thread of panic cutting through their communion. They're exposed. They don't have… whatever this is. They don't know how to navigate the fire. They'll die.

Veridessa considered. Then she brushed a warm, fibrous finger across Elias' bristled chin, consuming his gaze with the hypnotic flicker of her emerald eyes. *You shall guide me*, she decided. *And **we** shall guide them.*

A crack in the forest canopy far ahead flashed with orange light, a touch of apocalypse, growing closer.

"We have to move," Mara said. "Now."

But her feet refused to turn.

Elias was still in there.

He was with *her.*

She couldn't just—

A tremor rolled through the ground, but this one was soft, directional. It lifted the moss beneath her boots like a whisper pushing upward.

Then…

A voice touched the back of her mind.

Not quite Elias.

Not quite Veridessa.

Something in-between. Harmonized.

Urgent.

Go to the river.

Mara staggered, hand shooting out to brace herself against the grooved trunk of a roble coral tree.

"Did… did you hear that?"

Amaya blinked rapidly. "Hear what?"

Go to the river. Hurry.

This time she felt it more than heard it, like a tug at the base of her skull.

Mara whipped her head toward the others. "We're heading to the river. Now."

Kenji looked at her as though checking whether she was delirious. "Mara—why—"

The ground shifted beneath them.

Not violently.

Purposefully.

The roots rearranged themselves. The lianas that had draped across the nearest path lifted and curled away. A clean, narrow tunnel opened straight ahead, one that had not been there seconds ago.

Amaya gasped. "She's… she's clearing a way."

Diego crossed himself. "The Queen guides us."

Another explosion cracked through the distant underbrush. Voices shouted again, closer now. The fire glow brightened.

Mara didn't need more convincing.

"Run," she said. "Everyone, run!"

They plunged into the newly formed path, branches bending away, rocks sinking underfoot, guiding them with impossible precision through the forest's labyrinth.

And somewhere behind them, in the place where Elias and Veridessa's thoughts tangled, the merged voice whispered one more time:

Hurry. Before their flames reach the heart.

Above, just beyond the treetops, the first of Auralis's metal birds tilted its nose toward the basin, roaring hungry fire into the sky.

Mara forced herself to breathe evenly. Panicking wouldn't change the trajectories of whatever was falling out there.

She looked ahead.

The path the jungle had opened stretched forward like a green causeway, branches arching overhead in a pattern that was too regular to be accident. It had been a mild comfort previously, an eerie reassurance that something wanted them to go *this* way.

Now, that same intention felt like urgency... *a last gasp*.

"Keep moving," she said. "We've got to reach the river before they bracket this area."

Amaya hesitated. "The river could be worse. Open sight lines —"

"Open *escape*," Mara snapped. "Right now that's the only vector I trust."

She regretted the sharpness as soon as it left her mouth, but Amaya only nodded, jaw tight.

"Escape? How?" Kenji inquired.

"We'll have… faith," Mara offered.

They pushed on.

The ground sloped gently downward. The air grew thicker, wetter. The scent of smoke, at first a faint curiosity, strengthened into something more aggressive, filling their noses and coating their tongues. Ash began to drift through the bolts of sunlight that pierced the forest ceiling, fine as flour.

Overhead, a shadow flicked across a gap in the leaves, too straight, too fast to be a bird.

Kenji flinched. "Drone," he muttered. "Or a VTOL."

"Look down," Mara said. "Eyes on earth, not sky. If they're scanning, we don't want faces."

She didn't mention that it probably didn't matter. If Auralis had sent mercenaries with even half the tech she suspected they had, the four of them would look like little glowing heat-signatures trotting through an impossibly hot maze.

Another explosion rolled through the ground, closer this time. The forest *groaned*. Boles trembled overhead as if a giant hand had shaken the landscape.

Mara swallowed hard.

"Amaya," she said, forcing her voice level. "Stay between me and Diego. Kenji, rear. If we lose sight of each other—"

"We don't," Amaya said quickly, too quickly.

Flight Through Fire

"We might," Diego said. "If it happens, you drop to the ground and wait for a path to open. The Queen will not abandon you."

Kenji shot him an incredulous look. "You don't know that."

Diego met his gaze evenly. "We're still alive, aren't we?"

"Right. Faith," Kenji reminded himself.

Another blast cut off the conversation. This one was close enough that they heard individual trunks snap, the shockwave slamming heat and dust through the pathway. The forest's song spiked into a high, keening note. A broken bough crashed down just ahead, smashing through a tangle of lianas.

"Move!" Mara shouted.

They ran.

Far beneath them, in the Green Heart, Elias felt the same impacts, translated through Veridessa's systems as sharp, localized seizures of pain.

He saw, through her, the path of Auralis's response: mercenaries in dark uniforms moving in formation, helmets matte, eyes hidden behind goggles that turned the forest into thermographic phantoms. They carried flamethrowers, shaped charges, rifles.

They had coordinates. Lorne's last, jubilant transmission had given them a target.

Where the shells hit, sap flashed to steam. Cambium ruptured. Xylem tubes collapsed like crushed straws. The chemical screams of hundreds of trees merged into a single, shrill alarm that shot through the root network like electricity.

He staggered where he stood, hands braced against a pulsating cavern wall.

"Stop pushing into that quadrant," he gasped. "You're just feeding more growth into the blast radius — pull back, pull back — "

He didn't speak aloud, not really. Veridessa didn't need air vibrations to hear him. His thoughts ran along their shared pathways, absorbed into her awareness.

She reacted even before he finished the plea, retracting burrowing roots from the hottest zones, diverting sap away from trunks that would inevitably die. It hurt — he could *feel* it — but it was the pain of cauterizing a wound instead of letting it bleed out.

Metal birds, she murmured again, their shape clearer in his mind now: tilt-rotor craft hovering just above the canopy's reach, dropping canisters that blossomed into fire below. Humans moved in their wake, dark shapes carrying the smell of propellant and sweat and fear.

On the edge of Veridessa's perception, smaller devices buzzed: autonomous drones, some mapping, some carrying their own small, vicious payloads.

The pattern of heat and destruction crept nearer to the quadrant where Mara and the others moved.

"We have to steer them away," Elias said. "Or get my people out of the line. Let me go. I can — "

You are not ready to face their fire, Veridessa said. Her focus touched his skin where faint green luminescence had threaded beneath the surface. A gift of the merge, but incomplete. *You are soft. They are sharp.*

"Then make me less soft," he shot back. "You've been doing it already. You strengthened my nerves, rewired my senses. Do it more."

Flight Through Fire

You ask to be burned, she said, not quite disapproving, not quite surprised.

"I ask to stand between them and you," he corrected. "Which is stupid, I know. But here we are."

She tasted the flavor of his determination: fear-salted, guilt-scarred, imbued with the same irrational protectiveness she'd seen centuries ago in the villagers who'd offered themselves to her for their children's sake.

It is a wasteful pattern, she said again, but there was something almost like fondness in it now.

Above, one of the VTOL craft dipped lower, its engines' roar sending vibrations that made the rainforest convulse. A volley of liquid fire sprayed from its belly, tracing a line across the crowns of old-growth trees. Green flared into orange, then black.

On the forest floor, Mara flung an arm up against the sudden heat, teeth gritted.

"Elias," she whispered, though she knew he couldn't hear with his ears.

He *felt* her say his name. Through Veridessa, he sensed Mara's position relative to the Green Heart, a bright, familiar signal moving just above the forest floor.

Flames licked toward that region.

Something in him snapped.

"I'm going," he said.

You must not, Veridessa warned. *Their fire will unmake you.*

"Then teach me to withstand it," he said. "Or at least last long enough to get them clear."

There was a pause, not in the external chaos, but inside the space where their awareness met.

She weighed what it would cost.

Beneath the Verdant Veil

His body was still mostly human: water and proteins and fragile fats that melted under too much heat. But some changes had begun. His sweat already carried trace compounds more like plant resins than salt. His skin, in certain light, showed a faint cross-hatching beneath the surface that looked an awful lot like vascular bundles knitting in parallel with his veins.

She could accelerate that.

But accelerating growth always carried a price.

You will be less after, she said. *Less able to go back to the narrow way your mind once walked.*

He thought of what "back" would have meant; of late nights hunched over screens, of trying to convince producers that genuine wonder was worth more than cheap fakery. Of living in the world but never quite of it, scapegoated for a sin he hadn't fully committed, always half in exile.

"I'm not sure I want 'back,'" he said honestly.

Another shell hit, close enough to send a flash of white pain through both their senses.

Elias saw, through Veridessa, a stand of saplings go up like matchsticks.

He saw Mara flinch again.

"Please," he said.

The word carried all his fear, all his grief, all his stubbornness.

Veridessa flowed around it, through it, like the sea around a shell. Her luminescent gaze dimmed, confusion rippling through her presence. *You would leave me?*

"Not like Pembroke," he assured her. "But they're my friends, my responsibility. Mara, Diego, Amaya, Kenji—they followed me into this nightmare. I can't stand here inside safety while they burn out there. I won't."

The roots beneath his feet pulsed, hesitant, afraid.

"You could stop them without me," he said softly. "I know you could. But you don't understand their fire. Their machines. Their panic. You've never had to. You need someone who knows how they think. Someone who can show you where the danger truly is."

He placed a tentative hand against the living curve of her cheek, vines softly rising to meet him.

"You need a bridge," he whispered. "Let me be it."

For a long moment, she simply watched him — ancient, wounded, bewildered by this human stubbornness.

Then, gently, painfully, she began to let him go.

You will tear if you leave now, she said at last. *The joining is not finished.*

He felt that truth in his body. His nerves were still half-tuned to her currents. His heart still beat in time with the cavern's pulse. To pull away completely now would feel like wrenching a graft before it had taken.

"It'll hurt," he said. "I get it."

Do you? she asked mildly, and sent him a flicker from a memory where a storm had torn a branch from a great ceiba, leaving a raw, oozing gash that took years to close.

He gritted his teeth. "I'll live."

You may not, she stated. *Fire is less patient than storms.*

He thought of Mara at the sealed wall, hands bleeding from pounding. Of Amaya's terrified grip on her sleeve. Of Diego murmuring old affirmations under his breath, still daring to believe this place was holy even as it tried to consume them. Of Kenji trying to parse the wonder from a lifetime spent staring at digital science.

Very well, she said.

The next pulse that rolled through him was not pain. Not exactly.

It was… *density*.

His bones thrummed as minerals shifted along microscopic gradients, reinforcing certain struts, lightening others. His blood thickened for a heartbeat, then thinned, its chemistry altered, more oxygen-friendly, more heat-tolerant. Fine filaments unfurled beneath his skin, weaving between his nerves and capillaries — a subdermal lattice humming with green-gold light. They burrowed through every cell like roots, rending and joining in a supernova of agony.

His knees hit the cavern floor. Elias curled forward, palms pressed flat, chest heaving. Then he crumpled, mouth rigid in a frozen scream.

The Queen stood before him, her expression unreadable.

They almost made it to the river together.

The smoke got there first.

By the time Mara and the others broke out of the denser inner tangle into a more open understory, visibility had dropped to a murky, flickering twilight. The sun was a dim, red coin behind the haze. Ash fell steadily now, sticking to damp skin and mixing with sweat.

"Listen," Kenji panted. "Water, do you hear it?"

Mara strained.

Flight Through Fire

For a moment all she caught was the crackle of distant fires and the high whine of engines. Then, underneath, she heard it—the steady, liquid roar of a substantial current, not far downhill.

"Left," she said. "Hug the slope. Stay under cover until we see the bank."

They angled toward the sound.

Another artillery blast shook the ground, this one so near that a strangler fig to their right simply... jumped. Its twisted trunk shivered; then it toppled, gnarled roots ripping free in clumps of black soil.

"Down!" Diego shouted.

They ducked as it crashed, branches sweeping overhead, rolling in a rain of leaves.

Mara felt a branch glance off her shoulder; a blunt, painful thud, but nothing broken. She coughed, choking on a lungful of dust.

"Everyone okay?" she wheezed.

"Define okay," Kenji croaked somewhere to her left.

Amaya coughed too, then gasped, "I'm... fine..."

Diego's answer was a grunt and the sound of boots scrambling for purchase.

Then, cutting through the chaos, another sound intruded.

Not the organic roar of fire.

Not the deep register of explosions.

A different, uglier noise: sharp cracks in rapid succession, each accompanied by a faint metallic clink when the sound bounced off wood and stone.

Gunfire.

Mara's blood ran cold.

"Stay low," she hissed. "Don't silhouette yourself."

They crawled to the lee side of the fallen tree. Through a gap in the smashed undergrowth, Mara caught a glimpse of movement upslope—a figure in black gear, helmeted, carrying something sleek and deadly.

For a surreal moment, her brain tried to tell her she was on a movie set. The soldier's outline was exactly what generations of film and news footage had conditioned her to recognize as "danger."

Reality crashed back in with the next burst of rounds.

"Contact left!" someone shouted in accented English.

Spanish followed fast on its heels. "¡Allí! ¡Movimiento—!"

"Move!" Mara hissed to the others. "Downhill, now. Use the trunk as cover."

They scrambled, half-crawling, half-sliding along the length of the fallen tree. The bark tore at her palms, reopening some of the cracks under her bandages, but she didn't feel it beyond a distant awareness.

A bullet smacked into the trunk over their heads, sending a puff of splinters raining down.

Amaya yelped.

Mara grabbed her wrist and yanked her forward. "Don't stop. Don't look."

A curtain of ferns parted ahead, revealing a faintly brighter strip, the promise of open space and, beyond it, water.

"Go!" she urged. "Diego, take Amaya—"

Another impact rocked the ground, this one from behind. Heat flared up Mara's legs as a patch of undergrowth went up in a cough of flame.

Flight Through Fire

The forest *reacted*.

Vines snapped taut across the line of fire like makeshift shields. A branch swung down with unnatural precision, smashing into one of the advancing soldiers, sending him sprawling. Roots bulged under the soil, tripping another.

Shouts erupted.

"¡Mierda—!"

"What the hell—?"

"Watch the ground! It's—"

Their words cut off in a choking fit as smoke thickened.

"Mara!" Diego yelled.

She turned her head just in time to see what separated them.

The fallen strangler fig they'd used for cover shifted as another shell's shockwave barreled through. It rolled and spun, the splintered crown swinging toward, isolating Mara. On the other side of the gap, Diego, Amaya, and Kenji tumbled down toward the brighter strip of the open path. The trunk's sheer mass, combined with a tangle of snapping, convulsing roots, surged forward, a barricade dropping between them.

Mara lunged toward the closing gap.

"Mara, no!" Amaya screamed.

The roots whipped forward, imprisoning them on their respective sides. In an instant, Mara was cut off, Diego and the others now downhill, the forest forcing her back upslope.

"Amaya!" she shouted, throat raw.

"We'll find you!" Amaya cried. "The river—meet—"

Her voice vanished in a roar as another patch of foliage caught fire between them.

For a heartbeat Mara stood there, disoriented, smoke stinging her eyes, ears ringing.

Then instinct yelled louder than shock.

Gunfire rattled again, much closer.

She whirled.

Three soldiers were pushing through the burning undergrowth toward her position, faces hidden by visors, gear bristling with tech. One carried an assault rifle at the ready; another had a flamethrower rig strapped to his back, nozzle tucked in his arms like a wicked, metallic snake. The third held some kind of handheld scanner, its display flickering with thermal contours.

The one with the scanner pointed directly at her.

"Got a heat signature," he shouted. "Human. Maybe one of the team."

"Orders?" the flamethrower carrier called. His English was crisp, impatient.

"Command said clean the zone," the rifleman answered. "No witnesses, no contamination."

Mara's stomach dropped.

They definitely weren't here to *rescue* anyone.

His heart staggered. Then steadied.

Elias sucked in a breath that felt colder than the air around him.

When he opened his eyes, he saw the cavern in sharper detail. Each root-thread glowed with a faint aura. He could distinguish, by color and rhythm, which carried water, which carried nutrients, which carried information.

Flight Through Fire

A few loose tendrils trailed from his forearms and collarbones, glowing faintly. They pulsed in time with his breathing, like afterimages of the deeper connection.

He was aware he'd never fully sever those. Not now.

Veridessa knelt fluidly, bringing her eyes level with his.

Up close, he saw more of the human echoes in her face than he had before — the slight asymmetry of one brow, the faint crease between them that came from frowning, not from the natural growth of bark. Little inherited habits from the minds that had merged into her over centuries.

She reached out and cupped his jaw, her fingers surprisingly cool.

Remember, she whispered, *You are not alone in the fire.*

Something loosened in his chest at that.

"Neither are you," he said.

She smiled, a small, strange curve of lips where petals met wood.

Then the floor beneath him surged.

He was borne upward like a seed in a sudden spring flood.

As he shot into the vertical shaft, bark and cambium parted just enough to let him through, closing immediately behind. His shoulders and hips brushed living walls that flexed to accommodate him, guiding him unerringly toward the surface. For a moment he was all motion; no time to think, only to feel the rush of warmer air as he rose.

He looked back to see Veridessa's upturned face, the green of her eyes bright as new leaves. Then the earth closed behind him.

Faint and almost lost under the growing roar of explosions, Veridessa spoke aloud to the empty chamber where Elias had stood:

"You cannot leave what you are already becoming."

Mara darted sideways, deeper into the smoke, trying to break line of sight.

The forest helped.

Vines dropped like curtains. Fern fronds unfurled into her path, closing behind her. Roots rose just enough underfoot that her boots found purchase in places that might have otherwise sent her sprawling.

She ran, lungs burning, vision stinging.

"Visual lost!" the scanner operator shouted. "She moved!"

"Fan out," the rifleman snapped. "Thermals don't lie. She's close. Watch the plants, they're — *dammit!*"

His curse turned into a grunt as a tendril looped around his ankle, yanking just enough to throw off his balance. His shot went wild, bullets shredding leaves.

Mara ducked behind the wide buttress root of a massive kapok tree, lightly pressing her back against its coarse, spiky surface. The bark vibrated faintly against her spine.

Her heart hammered.

She could hear them now, one set of footsteps to her left, another to the right, another behind. The crunch of boots on charred debris. The sizzle of hot metal brushing damp foliage.

Smoke eddied around her, lit by the infernal orange glow of flames she couldn't see.

Flight Through Fire

This is how it ends, she thought, absurdly calm for half a second. Not in a mudslide. Not in some quiet lab. In a forest on fire, shot by men who think I'm a hazard.

Then another, fiercer thought shoved its way in:

No. Not yet.

Something shifted in the tree behind her.

She felt it, not just as physical movement, but as a kind of attention. The blunt thorns under her palms grew marginally cooler, as if sap was being rerouted. The reverberation in the wood rose in pitch.

You will guard, she heard Veridessa whisper, *and grieve.*

Mara swallowed.

"I get it," she whispered. "You helped me this far. But I can't become part of you. Not like that. I'm... I'm still me."

It felt ridiculous to say it out loud.

But the forest had listened to smaller, stupider things.

The nearest soldier rounded the buttress root, rifle up, barrel aligned with her chest.

"Hands where I can see them!" he barked.

His visor reflected firelight; she couldn't see his eyes.

Mara lifted her hands slowly, palms out. They shook, the makeshift bandages a stark white against the soot and blood.

"I'm unarmed," she said. "We're scientists. Auralis sent you—"

"Shut up," he snapped. "On your knees."

His finger tightened just enough on the trigger to make the weapon creak.

"Wait," the scanner operator called from somewhere behind him. "If she's the lead, Command might want—"

Another explosion cut him off, this one farther away but still strong enough to rock the ground.

The rifleman flinched, then refocused on Mara, clearly determined to finish at least *one* task in this chaos.

"On your knees," he repeated.

Mara stared down the muzzle of the gun.

She had never felt smaller, more breakable, more *human*.

A strange calm slid over her from shoulders to fingertips.

If this is it, she thought, then at least I tried not to run.

A voice moved through the bark under her palms.

Not in words; at first just a surge of warmth, a push of conviction. Then, faint but unmistakable, threaded with the sigh of leaves:

Move.

She did.

Mara dropped sideways, rolling along the curve of the buttress just as the rifleman squeezed the trigger. Bullets tore into bark where her torso had been, spraying splinters.

He swore, adjusting his aim.

Before he could fire again, the kapok itself shifted.

The buttress root under Mara's shoulder heaved like a muscle flexing. A ridge rose, catching the soldier in the shins. He lurched forward, crashing to his knees, rifle clattering from his grip.

A vine swung down like a weighted rope, smacking across his visor.

"¡¿Qué carajo — ?!" he shouted, grabbing at it.

For a second, chaos exploded in all directions.

The flamethrower operator swung his nozzle toward a writhing mass of vines, finger already tightening on the ignition lever.

"Don't!" the third man yelled. "You'll — "

He never finished the warning.

Something moved through the smoke behind him, a blur that didn't match any pattern Mara had seen that day. It broke from the curtain of ash with a fluid, terrifying grace.

For an instant, all she saw was silhouette: a human figure, but not quite, edges rimmed in faint green light, moving faster than anyone should be able to on that terrain.

The flamethrower man turned, bringing his weapon up.

The figure closed the distance in three strides.

A hand, not quite just a hand, caught the barrel of the flamethrower and shoved it upward. When the operator reflexively squeezed the trigger, a round of fire blasted harmlessly into the canopy, igniting already dying branches instead of the dry leaves under Mara's feet.

Another motion, economical and precise, sent the heavy weapon twisting out of the man's grip. It swung up into the air, vines snapping down to catch it, wrapping coiled, fibrous muscle around tank and hose.

The soldier stumbled back, shouting.

The rifleman grabbed for his sidearm.

He never got to fire it.

The newcomer stepped into his space, heel scything low. A root simultaneously bulged under the soldier's boot, knocking him further off balance. He crashed to the ground, winded, weapon skidding away.

The third man, the one with the scanner, attempted to backtrack, raising the device as if it might serve as a shield.

The newcomer simply looked at him.

Fronds around the scanner operator shivered. A tangle of vines unwound, lashing out to wrap around his arms and legs. They didn't crush; they just pinned, lifting him a few inches off the ground, rotating him slowly like some irritating insect caught in a spider's web.

In less than ten seconds, all three mercenaries were disarmed and incapacitated, tangled in a sudden surge of foliage that had moved with intention.

Mara stared.

The figure turned toward her.

For a heartbeat, she didn't recognize him.

His skin held a faint luminescent wash, as if someone had lit him from beneath with soft green-gold. Delicate, pale veins traced up his neck and along his jawline, not quite like those of a plant, not quite like human blood vessels — something between. The whites of his eyes were threaded with fine emerald filaments, and when he inhaled, the air around him seemed to move with him, leaves rustling in time with his breath.

But his mouth—

That crooked, self-deprecating half-smile—

And his eyes, beneath the strange glow, still held the same wry, weary warmth she'd watched as he'd told Pembroke's story by firelight.

"Elias," she whispered.

The word felt torn out of her.

He stopped a few paces away, chest rising and falling faster than usual; whether from exertion or something deeper, she couldn't tell. The light under his skin pulsed in time with his pulse, visible at his throat, his wrists. His shirt clung to him in tatters from the heat, collar gaping open just enough for her to see the pattern beneath clearly: a lattice of luminous, pale green lines branching across his chest in the shape of a necklace.

For a moment they just stared at each other, smoke swirling between them.

Mara's thoughts scattered and reformed in jagged fragments.

He's alive.

He's changed.

He came back.

She took a step toward him, then another.

Up close, the differences were even more striking. His pupils were elongated vertically, catlike in low light. Fine, almost invisible tendrils threaded through his hair at the temples, disappearing into his scalp. When he exhaled, the air carried a faint, clean scent like crushed flowers after rain.

Fear spiked, tangled with a fierce, unexpected surge of relief.

"Elias…" she said again, voice shaking. "What have you done?"

He looked at her with a softness that hurt, the ghost of a laugh catching in his throat.

"Kept my promise," he said.

Beneath the Verdant Veil

The forest around them hummed in agreement, leaves shivering with a sound that might have been approval.

Behind the veil of smoke, fire rolled closer, chewing through trunks and undergrowth.

Above, more metal birds circled.

Between them and the advancing inferno, half-man, half-message, Elias stood, Veridessa's will laced into human muscle, and Mara realized with a lurch that whatever line he'd crossed down there in the Green Heart, there was no coming fully back from it.

For either of them.

CHAPTER 18

The Union

For a moment after the fight, everything held.

The three soldiers hung pinned in the vines like grotesque puppets, weapons stripped, visors smeared with soot. The flames that had been inching toward the buttress root had veered sideways, feeding instead on a fresh fall of branches as if the forest itself had nudged the fire away.

Mara and Elias stood at the center of that fragile stillness, breathing hard, smoke curling around them.

Up close, his transformation was impossible to ignore.

Bioluminescent threads pulsed under his skin, faint but visible at his throat, his temples, the backs of his hands. The lines weren't random; they followed pathways that felt too organized for veins yet too organic for circuitry, like the vascular bundles of a leaf translated into human flesh. Ash streaked his jaw, but when sweat carved through it, the tracks gleamed green-gold.

He met her stare, chest still heaving.

"I'll explain later," he said.

"There might not be a—" She broke off as another explosion rolled through the forest, this one so close that the towering mahoganies around them swayed.

The three bound soldiers jerked as the vines tightened reflexively.

"Later," Mara finished hoarsely. "Sure. If we get one."

A shout went up somewhere to their right, muffled by crackling trees and raging fires. More boots, more metal.

Elias' head cocked slightly, like a man listening to two conversations at once, one carried by air, the other by earth.

"We have to move," he said. "Now."

"What about them?" Mara nodded toward the trussed mercenaries. The practical part of her brain whispered *hostages*. Another, instinctive, part whispered *bullets*.

Elias' eyes flicked to them, then to her.

"The forest will decide," he said quietly.

The vines drew a fraction tighter, enough to force choked curses from the soldiers' throats.

Mara shivered.

She didn't have time to argue ethics with a sentient basin.

"What about Amaya, Diego, Kenji?" she demanded. "We got separated —"

"They're headed for the river," Elias said, already turning downslope, away from the pinned men. "She's steering them there."

"She?" Mara echoed.

He didn't answer with words.

He just glanced at her with a look that said everything he'd learned in the cavern could take hours they didn't have.

"Come on," he said instead. "If we follow this ledge we'll catch their trail before the next volley."

The Union

"How do you—"

Another blast cut her off, showering sparks through the trees.

Mara shelved her questions.

She ran.

They moved rapidly through smoke and shadow, with the forest shunting fire away from their immediate path. Where flames lunged, green growth surged to meet them: branches dropping like lances to divert embers, damp fronds uncurling over tinder-dry litter. It wasn't perfect. Heat still seared lungs; ash still scratched eyes.

But it was intention.

Every few strides, Elias would veer a degree left or right without seeming to think, his bare hand brushing a trunk, fingers splaying to feel the hum there. Sometimes he flinched when he touched bark scorched too deeply, his mouth tightening as if he'd stepped on a friend.

"Mara!" a voice shouted ahead, thin and raw.

She knew it instantly.

"Amaya!" she yelled back.

Mara hadn't expected to find the others so quickly. But the forest had shifted again, clearing a path not just forward but toward them. A nudge, a hum, a pull through the undergrowth—subtle, deliberate. Veridessa was guiding the others, just as she'd guided them.

They broke through a curtain of vines into a small, bowl-shaped clearing scorched at the edges. Diego and Kenji crouched near its center, half-shielding Amaya, who had one arm flung over her head as if to ward off falling debris. Their faces were streaked with soot;

Diego's shirt was torn at the shoulder, revealing a fresh burn already blistering.

Amaya's eyes went wide when she saw Elias.

"You're..." She gasped. "You're glowing."

"That's new," he panted. "Everyone in one piece?"

"For certain values of 'piece,'" Kenji rasped. "We heard gunfire. Then... the jungle exploding. Then you."

Diego's gaze flicked from Elias to Mara, reading the thrum of adrenaline between them like text. "The Queen sent you back," he said.

Mara didn't bristle at the phrasing this time.

"She let him go," she said instead. "To get us out."

Elias flinched as another tremor shook the ground.

"I asked to help you," he said. "And Her."

He meant Veridessa.

The next explosion came with a brighter flash, the orange flare staining the smoke an ugly, toxic color.

"River," Mara said. "We reach it now. Any objection?"

Kenji made a feeble gesture that might have been a shrug. "If I say yes, will it make the artillery stop?"

"Unlikely."

"Then... I'm good with the river."

Elias pointed downhill. "There. The slope bends. She's cleared a path."

"You keep saying *she*," Amaya said as they began moving again, this time as a single unit. "You talk to her now?"

"Yes," he said simply.

"What does she want?" Amaya's voice trembled, but not just from fear. There was something like awe in it.

He hesitated.

Mara noticed.

"Elias," she said. "Answer her."

"She wants not to die the same way twice, or to lose what she's gained," he said at last. "She wants to remember. All of us. Not as numbers in the soil. As *patterns.*"

Diego murmured something in Spanish that might've been a prayer, might've been a swear.

The river grew from background babble to a roaring presence, a low, rushing growl that undercut the shriek of burning branches. The air grew heavier, cooler in erratic gusts that smelled of wet stone and algae beneath the smoke.

They pushed through a belt of particularly stubborn marsh ferns and broke out onto the riverbank.

Mara staggered to a halt.

The Escondido here was no gentle current. It threw itself around a bend with a kind of cold fury, white foam boiling where submerged rocks and vegetation fought back. Charred brush floated past in soggy rafts, the carcasses of insects trapped among them.

On the near bank, half-buried in sand and encroaching moss, something dark and long lay tilted at an angle.

Two somethings.

"Canoes," Diego breathed, reverence and dread mingled in his tone. "Old ones."

They were dugouts, carved from single massive trunks, their hulls hollowed deep and smooth by hands long gone. Time and humidity had weathered parts of their rims, and undergrowth had claimed the stern of one, but their hulls held solid.

"These aren't abandoned," Diego said, voice hushed. "They're kept."

"By whom?" Amaya whispered.

Diego didn't answer, and that said enough. He just stepped closer and brushed a finger along the hull — no significant damage or rot. As if something had preserved them. As if the forest had always planned for someone to reach this far.

Mara didn't need the archaeological training to see the age: the patina of the wood, the style of the carving marks smoothed by years of weather. These had belonged to the people who'd come before Lorne's corporate incursion, before state surveyors, maybe even before Pembroke's doomed obsession.

And yet... the sand that had once buried them was pulled back just enough to reveal their lines. The vines that had started to strangle them had retracted, leaving only loose loops that brushed the hulls like affectionate hands.

"They were meant for us," Amaya whispered.

"For whomever survived," Elias said. His glow had intensified along his forearms, a subtle aura mirroring the faint luminescence in the river stones.

Another mortar round exploded upstream. A wave of heat washed over them an instant later, followed by the smell of charred resin and something uglier — melted plastic, burned fuel.

From their vantage point, they could finally see the source.

The Union

Through gaps in the canopy upriver, metallic shapes hovered like predatory insects. Tilt-rotor craft painted in nonreflective grays and greens, marked with a too-familiar stylized helix. Underneath them, a swath of forest lay flattened and blackened, trees reduced to charred spikes. Figures in tactical gear moved in lines, some advancing, some feeding hoses from the bellies of support craft into nozzles spewing liquid fire.

"Jesus," Kenji whispered. "They're… *sterilizing* the basin."

"Containment protocol," Elias said grimly. "That's what they'll call it if anyone ever asks. Unknown bio-anomaly, possible contaminant, uncontrolled risk to corporate assets and regional stability."

Mara clenched her jaw. "This isn't about stability. It's about control. If they can't own it, they'll erase it."

"And then write a paper about the lessons learned," Kenji muttered.

Amaya stared, tears standing out white in the soot on her cheeks. "They're burning *her*."

As if in response, the ground under their feet convulsed.

It wasn't a sharp shock like from an explosion. It was a long, echoing tremor that seemed to ripple along the very grains of the soil. Roots flexed and twisted under the top layer of earth, some retracting hastily from the hottest zones, others groping blindly toward pockets of moisture.

A sound rose, at first too low to identify. Then, as it built, it resolved into something that made the light hair on Mara's arms stand on end.

It was a scream.

Not human. Not animal.

It sounded like wind tearing up through hollow trunks, like sap boiling in veins, like millions of leaves shredding at once.

Veridessa's pain.

Elias doubled over, hands clamping to his chest.

"Elias!" Mara grabbed his shoulders.

He sucked in a ragged breath, face contorting, eyes squeezed shut. The luminous lines under his skin flared bright enough to halo his features.

"Easy," Diego said, stepping in on his other side, one arm bracing Elias' back. "Breathe, hermano. In. Out."

"It's —" Elias gasped. "She — she's —"

Another round of incendiary gel splattered across the canopy upriver. Fire ran along branches in a line, consuming epiphytes and birds' nests alike. The scream intensified, drilling through marrow.

"Stop listening," Kenji said, frantic. "Shut her out!"

"I can't," Elias hissed. "It's not just… hearing. It's *through* me. She's… burning in ten thousand places at once and trying to be everywhere she's needed."

He sagged as the convulsion eased a fraction, sweat pouring down his temples, the cinders on his face streaked with dampness.

Amaya clutched Mara's sleeve. "What do we do?"

Mara nodded. She knew one thing. They couldn't help Veridessa if they were ash.

"We get you out," she said. "Now. We take the canoes and drop downstream out of range before they decide to gas the basin or toss something heavier."

She turned to the dugouts, assessing quickly. "Kenji, Diego, check hull integrity. Amaya, help strip any vegetation that could snag. Elias—"

"No." He straightened slowly, still breathing hard, but his gaze had sharpened. Smoke blurred the edges of his outline, but the light under his skin made him look carved from some radioactive mineral.

"Mara," he said. "You're taking them out. I'm not."

Panic flared, hot and sudden. "Don't start. We are not doing the noble self-sacrifice debate *now*."

"This isn't noble," he said. "It's tactical."

Another convulsion rippled up through his legs. He caught himself against the nearest kapok tree, fingers splaying on the bark. When his palm met the trunk, the glowing filaments under his skin synced briefly with those in the wood, a pattern flowing back and forth, too fast for human eyes.

He grimaced. "She's… striking at them with whatever she can reach. Dropping branches, flinging up roots, choking nozzles. But she doesn't understand the systems. She strips hoses without realizing they have pressure valves. She pulls at armored cables and forgets about the little antennae perched above, directing the whole grid."

Kenji stared at him. "You're telling me the forest is losing a fight with modern logistics."

"I'm telling you," Elias said, "that she's used to dealing with storms and fires and insects and humans with axes. She knows how to flood a logging road five miles away to make a truck fail. She's never fought assault drones and composite armor and incendiary dispersal patterns. She doesn't… *think* in those geometries."

Another burst of fire erupted upriver.

Veridessa's scream split the air again.

Elias winced hard enough that Mara's own chest hurt in sympathy.

"She doesn't understand them," he panted. "She's fighting blind."

Diego's face was ashen beneath the soot. "Can you… help her see?"

"Yes," Elias said, and the word frightened Mara more than any no.

"By doing what?" she demanded. "Becoming their target? Feeding her your brain as a blueprint for murdering people?"

His head snapped toward her, offended in a way that was still utterly him. "No. By showing her where to *push* that doesn't collapse entire ecosystems. By teaching her which things are hollow, which are load-bearing. By helping her aim the floods and growth spurts and root-lashes at machines and not—" His voice broke as another arc of fire carved through a cluster of trees. "—not the bits that want to live."

"That sounds theoretical," Kenji said faintly.

"It's what I have," Elias shot back.

"No." Mara stepped in close, so close she could see fine green threads in the whites of his eyes. "What you have are canoes waiting and four other people who can't survive this without you. We teach her later, when we're not about to become collateral."

He looked down at her hands framing his chest, and at the tremor she couldn't quite hide.

The Union

"There won't be a later," he said softly.

Silence fell, even as the war continued a hundred meters upriver.

Ash floated between them.

"You don't know that," she whispered.

He gave a small, sad half-smile. "Mara. You're too good a scientist to lie to yourself that way."

She bit the inside of her cheek hard enough to taste blood. "I am not leaving you here to burn."

"Then you're condemning her to burn instead," he said, voice steady now. "And everything connected to her. The basin's not just trees. It's watersheds, microclimates, migration routes, old villages. Diego's people's stories. Your student's death, my mistakes, Pembroke's madness… if she goes, all of that becomes a crater. A blank spot someone will fill with a mall or a mine."

"Elias—"

"I can't go back to the way I was, Mara," he said. "Even if I got on that canoe with you, do you really think I'd make it to the nearest airport and… what? Get a desk job? Give guest lectures? I'm already too much of her for anyone to trust me in a lab that doesn't have tree roots for walls."

She hated that she could picture that future, and hated more that it rang false down to its DNA.

He lifted a hand, hesitated, then cupped her cheek gently. His thumb came away streaked with soot and tears.

"You know this is right," he said.

She tasted the words—bitter as quinine, familiar as heartbreak.

Behind him, the forest quaked again.

Diego looked away, jaw tight, as if watching a scene his grandmother had already told him a thousand times in different guises. Amaya stood rigid, hands balled into fists, tears tracking silently. Kenji stared at the mercenaries' firestorms with the expression of a man watching his entire discipline being rewritten without his consent.

Mara swallowed.

"You're asking me," she said slowly, "to choose between you and the thing that killed Lorne and nearly killed us."

"I'm asking you," Elias said, "to recognize that the thing that nearly killed us is also the thing that's been keeping us alive ever since. And to trust my judgment about the person I've merged with."

"*Person*," she echoed.

"Yes," he said simply.

She exhaled, a sound halfway between a sob and a laugh. "You're still insufferably sure of yourself, you know that?"

"Comes with the territory," he said. "Ex-TV archaeologist, now part-time dryad."

It was ridiculous.

She choked on a short, incredulous laugh anyway.

The next mortar blast cut through even that small reprieve. Firelight flared against their faces, making the green highlights in his skin glow brighter.

Elias leaned in, lowering his forehead to hers.

"I'm not—" He had to pause, breath hitching. "I'm not choosing her over you. I'm not choosing *her* over you," he repeated, emphasizing the pronoun in a way that somehow included and transcended both women in his life. "I'm choosing the only option where either of you gets to exist in a world that isn't ash."

Her hands fisted in his shirt.

"You're not exactly making a logical argument," she whispered.

"Lucky for us," he murmured, "you're not just logic."

He kissed her.

It wasn't frantic or desperate, though the world burned around them. It was deliberate, rooted. Not the tentative brush of lips they'd shared beneath calmer canopy, but something deeper, heavier, threaded with everything they didn't have time to say. Her fingers tightened in the fabric at his shoulders; his hand slid to the back of her neck, holding her as if to memorize the angle.

For a few seconds, the scream of the burning forest dulled, not because it lessened, but because another kind of focus overrode it.

When they broke apart, both were breathing hard.

"Tell me," she said, voice shredded, "that this isn't goodbye."

"It's one of them," he said. "But it's not the last time we talk."

"How can you possibly know—"

He smiled, and it was almost boyish.

"Because she's in every root and leaf now," he said. "And I'm in her. Find a tree, you find us. Like tuning to the right frequency."

"That's not how radios work," Kenji muttered.

"Good thing we're not radios," Elias shot back gently, never looking away from Mara.

Boots pounded in the distance, more mercenaries pushing through flame.

Mara gulped down her sorrow until it sat like concrete in her stomach.

She stepped back.

"You die on me," she said hoarsely, "and I swear I'll find a way to resurrect you just so I can kill you myself."

"Noted," he said.

She turned away before her resolve cracked.

Diego's eyes were bright, but steadier than hers. He nodded knowingly at Elias.

"You were right about me," Elias said. "About what I did. About the harm. I should've listened. And I should've apologized a long time ago."

Diego sighed, not in frustration but in a way that deflated old burdens. "I wasn't angry only because of the myths, Elias." He looked toward the burning canopy. "I was angry because I spent the last few years believing there were no more miracles left. And then this place, the stories, started breathing again... but not for me."

Elias stepped closer. "It wasn't choosing me. It was calling for help."

Diego gave a small, tired laugh. "I know that now. But I didn't then. I thought you were stealing something from my people again." His voice dropped. "From me."

Elias stared at him. "Diego... if I could give this to you, I would. You're the one who believed first."

"And you're the one the forest answered," Diego said. "Sometimes belief isn't the thing that gets you chosen." He placed a hand on Elias' shoulder—firm, grounding. "But it can still guide you. And I think it guided me right to this moment."

He stepped back and dipped his head toward Elias. "La selva te guarde," he murmured.

Amaya hesitated, then stepped forward and wrapped her arms around Elias in a fierce hug. For a moment he seemed startled; then he hugged her back, eyes closing briefly. "I watched you walk into fear like it was a doorway," she said softly. "You showed me how to trust what's bigger than us. Whatever happens next… don't let that part of you fade."

"I won't," he promised.

Kenji raised a hand in a half-salute, half-wave. "If you make it out and I'm not around to quantify it, feel free to approximate generously."

Elias laughed. "Deal."

Then he turned away from them, toward the heart of the blaze. He was already luminous enough that he cast his own faint, greenish halo on the blackened trunks.

"Mara," Elias said, over his shoulder. "Do me a favor. Tell them I wasn't completely full of shit."

A crooked, broken smile twitched across his mouth.

Then, like a phantom in the fog, he vanished into the green.

Mara knew that if she kept watching the void where he had been, her knees would give out. "Diego," she turned and said, voice clipped. "Rear canoe with Amaya. Kenji, front canoe with me. We follow the current, hug the shadow of the bank, keep low. No stops. No risk-taking. We just get out."

The quartet hauled the canoes fully free of their sandy cradle and snatched conveniently fallen branches to use as makeshift paddles. Diego steadied a canoe as Amaya climbed in, knees shaking. He hopped in after her and took the bow, his movements sure despite the tremor in his fingers. Mara waded into the shallows, boots slipping on slick rocks, the cold water a shock against heat-raw skin. Kenji pushed the second canoe in beside her, holding the dugout still as Mara vaulted into it. He clambered aboard after her with more enthusiasm than grace. "I have no idea how to steer one of these," he admitted.

"The river knows," Diego said. "Just listen."

"Everyone keeps saying that," Kenji muttered, gripping his own branch-paddle.

The current caught the hulls, tugging.

"On my count," Mara said at the bow, forcing her voice to be captain-clear. "Three... two..."

She glanced once, just once, toward the tree line.

"...One," Mara finished, and let the river take them.

The dugouts slid into the main current, bobbing as they crossed cascading ripples. Mara and Kenji paddled just enough to angle them toward the deeper channel, away from eddies that could slam them into half-submerged trunks. Mara's raw knuckles throbbed, but adrenaline forced her to take a rain check on the pain. Heat licked the back of Amaya's neck. She hunched instinctively, noting Diego do the same in front of her.

Upriver, another sheet of flame rose, illuminating freshly scarred trees. Mara's breath held. The canoes spun gently as the current twisted around a bend, taking away their view of the bank.

The Union

Diego's paddle moved in slow, sure arcs, searing a steady path through the water. "He goes," Diego announced, "where stories are born."

"Don't start eulogizing him yet," Mara rasped across the current. "He hates bad endings."

"So do I," Kenji reminded the universe.

Amaya leaned forward enough that Diego felt her forehead press between his shoulder blades, a small, desperate weight.

"I'm scared," Amaya whispered.

"I know," Diego said, and he didn't try to pretend otherwise. "Me, too," he gently admitted. He briefly covered Amaya's hands with one of his own, gripping tightly as the river bore them onward, away from the burning basin.

Mara, meanwhile, stared fixedly at the unknown future flowing out before them, one that regretfully did not include Elias at their side.

Above them, smoke thinned gradually to fog.

Behind them, the forest and its strange, joined consciousness fought for its life.

Ahead, the river curved away and out of sight.

The first thing that hit him was the heat.

Not just the physical burn of flames licking at his boots and trousers, though that was bad enough. It was the deeper, suffocating heat of a mind in panic... Veridessa's awareness flaring through every root and leaf, thrashing against the edges of itself.

Elias ran as if the forest itself was dragging him forward. Flames licked at his heels and devoured the canopy in sheets of amber and charcoal, each burning branch collapsing behind him like a falling verdict. The air was a furnace, thick with timber smoke, ash, and the raw, anguished pulse of Veridessa's pain thrumming through his bones.

Elias staggered, one hand trailing along trunks to steady himself as the terrain bucked underfoot. Each touch sent a jolt of sensation up his arm: bark blistering, cambium screaming, xylem boiling. He grit his teeth and pushed on.

Something in Veridessa was adjusting; buffering him against the damage, accelerating the assimilation. He could feel it, the pain subsiding not from numbness, but from cooperation. She was learning how to hold him, and he was learning how to yield.

I'm here, he projected as best he could, not with words but with the shape of his intention.

The answer came as a rush of images, too many, too fast.

Fire running along a vine miles away. A beetle falling from a burning leaf. Groundwater simmering in shallow pockets. Mercenaries' boots pounding through underbrush. The sharp, metallic stink of fuel. The sterile gleam of the Auralis insignia.

She was everywhere.

And nowhere in particular.

You're scattering, he thought, lungs burning as he crested a rise. You're trying to be all of you at once.

A fleeting impression of confusion brushed his mind, tinged with something like shame.

I… am… all, came the answer, not in syllables, but in a sense of vastness pressing at his skull. *If I leave… any… they die.*

The Union

Roots split open before him, guiding his descent as the earth heaved and parted, carving a path back down into the trembling womb of the cavern. He staggered through the spiraling tunnel, half blinded, half carried by her fading presence, until the last turn opened like a dying breath.

The Green Heart was on fire.

The inner core where he and the others had first seen the pod had transformed into a nightmare tableau. Tree roots that had once towered protectively now stood half-charred, their arches aflame, embers raining down like red snow. The ground was a patchwork of soot and glowing rocks. Smoke roiled in thick columns, swirling in conflicting currents as the basin's heat warred with the cooler air below.

At the center, where the pod had sat like a sealed heart, there was now a blackened, half-collapsed hollow.

And within it, like a felled goddess, lay Veridessa.

Her form was less human than before — less defined, less symmetrical. Portions of her body had sloughed into fibrous strands that wriggled weakly, their chlorophyll glow flickering and sputtering. Her hair, once a cascade of living tendrils, now lay in limp ropes threaded with embers. One arm, if it could still be called that, was embedded in the soil up to the shoulder, fingers spread, tendrils shooting downward as if trying desperately to summon life from deeper layers. Smoke drifted through the ruined chamber like funeral veils.

Elias slid down the charred slope, skidding on ash. Heat clawed at his skin. As he approached Veridessa, the luminous filaments flared beneath her flesh. Her awareness reached out to meet his.

The ground between them heaved. Roots writhed just beneath the surface, some rushing toward the worst of the fire, others cringing away. In the distance he could sense skirmishes: branches dropping onto rotors, vines slapping at visors, roots yanking at hoses. But every attack was clumsy, reactive. For every soldier tripped, three more advanced.

Veridessa's eyes fluttered open, dim but still impossibly emerald-gold. She tried to rise but faltered, fingers slipping through soot. Her head turned toward him with visible effort. Portions of her face were blackened where the flames had kissed too long. Beneath cracked dermis, pale cambium shone like bone.

Elias' heart stuttered.

"Veridessa," he breathed, and dropped to his knees beside her.

Too many, she pressed into his mind, laced with raw pain. *Too fast. They cut what I extend. They burn what I raise. I… do not understand their shapes.*

"You don't have to fight alone," he assured her.

Up close, she smelled of sap and smoke and deep earth. Sparks landed on his shoulders, stinging; but his body, no longer entirely his body, adjusted, shunting heat along new pathways. The forest had already begun weaving its insulation through him.

Her eyes focused on his face.

"You came back," she said, this time aloud to him, her voice hoarse, like wind scraping over flint.

He exhaled a breath that was half laugh, half cough. "You thought I wouldn't?"

She blinked slowly. A few embers fell from her lashes. "The Echo-Bearer becomes the Voice," she said in

The Union

a crackled whisper. The sentence reverberated in his skull, echoed in the soil. She didn't just mean *voice*; she meant *translator*, *interface*, the point where human pattern recognition and vegetal distributed intelligence met and intertwined.

Without hesitation, he reached down and took her hand. Her skin felt warmer than bark, cooler than flesh, with a give that hinted at both. Luminous sap beaded where their fingers met, mixing with his blood where small cuts had split.

Vines stirred weakly around her, as if afraid to hope.

She looked at him — truly looked — and in that gaze was centuries of longing, grief, and the fragile spark of joy she had buried for so long. Her lips curved into the softest, tremulous smile.

He raised her hand to his chest. "I'm here to stay," he whispered.

She touched his cheek with a trembling, leaf-light caress.

And then she lifted her face toward his.

The kiss was slow; not desperate but inevitable, as if two halves of the same melody had finally found each other. Time thickened, warm and honeyed. Light gathered around them, golden-jade, swirling upward like embers rising from an unseen hearth.

Roots glowed. Leaves rustled in a wind that wasn't wind at all.

Her strength flowed back, a blooming awakening. Bark-skin healed, mossy green limbs reshaped and strengthened. Vines unfurled from her shoulders, luminous again, twining with his arms, his spine, his heartbeat. His skin shimmered in response, bioluminescent veins igniting like constellations drawn beneath his flesh.

When she rose, it was with his hands braced at her waist, her feet leaving the scorched ground as the forest lifted her, renewed. Her body rebuilt its human shape, curves forming perfectly to fit his contours.

They stood together in the living cradle of roots and light, two outlines becoming one radiance. She closed around him. Not crushing, not consuming, but enfolding. Vines and tendrils and hair-roots curled along his back, along his ribs, under his arms. At every point of contact, the glowing filaments in his skin flared, seeking, linking.

The jungle breathed in.

They breathed out.

And then, united in purpose and power, they turned toward the firestorm.

His human brain wanted linearity: first this sensation, then that thought, then that external event. But merge-years elapsed in root-seconds, and the notion of *before* and *after* became as fuzzy as the line between one leaf and the next on a single, crowded branch.

He felt his heartbeat sync to multiple other rhythms: a chorus of pulses from sap flow, from earthworm peristalsis, from far-off rain hitting leaves. His lungs still drew air, but each inhale was matched by the intake of gas through a billion stomata. He tasted oxygen and carbon dioxide and trace chemicals of combustion.

Her memories flooded him.

He saw centuries as if they were time-lapse sequences: forest growing and receding, rivers shifting course, storms carving new scars. Humans appeared and vanished at the edges: a handful of hunters here, a woman planting something in a clearing there, children playing with beetles, priests smearing tinted clay on stones as offerings.

At the same time, he felt the present sharpening again.

Through Veridessa's senses, he perceived the battlefield with terrifying clarity.

Every mercenary was a moving problem: weight distribution, heat signature, metal profile, geometry of protective gear. From above, their formation resembled an invasive disease creeping along limbs. From below, they were pressure points on the soil.

He could *feel* the composite shells of the drones — light, hollow, vulnerable at the joints. The tanks of incendiary gel, pressurized and secure until something knocked their valves at specific angles. The cable clusters feeding power from generators on the ridge. The subtle, invisible mesh of their communication network humming in narrow-band frequencies.

He understood them.

She did not.

He translated.

Here, he thought toward her, overlaying his understanding onto her reach. *Strike here, not there. This conduit carries fuel. This one carries coolant. This structure supports. This one just houses sound.*

He fed her the logic of engines, the habits of fire, the brittleness of certain alloys when shocked.

In return, she gave him control of motion.

Vines that had been thrashing wildly stilled for a beat.

Then moved with purpose.

From the outside, had anyone been in the cavern to see, Elias and Veridessa would have appeared frozen, locked in a passionate embrace at the center of a slowly rotating storm of light.

The chlorophyll glow under his skin crept along their points of contact, seeping into her, back into him, until it was impossible to tell where his veins ended and her phloem began. The faint outlines of his ribs blurred as filaments extended outward, knitting into the lattice of her ribs, her trunk, her oldest roots.

Above them, the canopy began to pulse.

At first it was subtle: leaves flickering in a low-frequency pattern, sap shimmering. Then it spread. The pulse ran along branches like a series of pine-tinted lightning strikes, racing outward from the Green Heart along predetermined routes.

Where it passed, branches flexed.

Roots rose.

Vines uncoiled.

The forest woke, fully.

On the ridge, Captain Haldana of Auralis Containment Unit C watched as his carefully plotted controlled burn suddenly failed.

One moment, his operators called out coordinates, their voices steady despite the heat. "Zone Three clear. Zone Four, initiating gel dispersal. Maintain grid; do not cross the—"

The next, their shouts fractured.

"—vines—where did these—?"

" — my nozzle, something's wrapped — "

" — I've lost elevation — I'm losing — "

He saw it with his own eyes.

Vines thicker than a man's arm erupted from the soil, snaking around the legs of two assault drones. At first he thought it was the fire's heat causing visual distortion. Then the vines *pulled*, jerking the craft off their stable hover. One spun wildly, its rotors shredding foliage. The other skidded sideways, its fuel line yanked taut.

"Cut those vines!" he roared into his comm.

Gunfire answered him, but for every bullet that shredded one tendril, three more coiled in from other angles.

Below, the soldiers' formation dissolved as the ground itself buckled. Roots that had lain dormant beneath thin leaf-bed surged upward in twisting columns, forming barricades that diverted the path of the liquid fire they'd been spraying. Gel splattered harmlessly against bark that instantly sloughed, the outermost layer sacrificing itself to protect deeper tissue.

A supply truck lurched as something as thick as a python coiled around its rear axle. The driver cursed, jammed the accelerator. The root held. The truck's front wheels spun uselessly, digging trenches in the soft earth. A moment later the ground opened beneath it, a sinkhole created by roots withdrawing strategically from specific soil pockets. The rear of the truck dropped, its nose pitching skyward. Crates of munitions slid and tumbled, some cracking open.

Globes of incendiary gel rolled free — bright, viscous, hungry for oxygen. They should have detonated in a predictable grid of fire. Instead, the vines caught them. Tendrils wrapped each sphere like careful fingers, lifting them from the burning soil. For an instant they hung suspended, eerie and luminous, like fruit ripening in reverse. Then Elias felt Veridessa's intention shift. The grasping vines didn't ignite the gel. They sealed it. Layers of damp fiber tightened around each sphere until the gel inside suffocated, starved of air, robbed of the chance to flare. The vines then hurled the smothered shells toward the riverbank's blackened patches, where the fire had already passed and could do no more harm. When the gel burst there, it burned itself out harmlessly, flaring only in ash fields and dead zones. Not to spread. To contain.

Smoke lifted in brief plumes, but beneath it new shoots were already rising, green spears of regrowth fed by redirected nutrients and the forest's fierce will to live.

"Sir!" someone shouted. "Our comms are glitching! I'm getting feedback in—"

Haldana's headset squealed. A spike of static stabbed his eardrums.

Beneath the noise, something else threaded through. A voice.

Not speaking words, exactly, but something like them. A rising and falling pattern that rolled over his nervous system, making his fingers spasm involuntarily.

We... see... you.

His vision swam.

His men staggered, clutching their helmets.

Instruments flickered; some screens went black, others flooded with lines of green, branch-like fractals crawling across their displays.

The forest had found the wires.

The Union

At the center of the Green Heart, Elias held Veridessa tight, his body half-visible through layers of vine and light. His consciousness no longer sat just in a skull-shaped box behind his eyes. It extended along networks of connection, each new filament an avenue for both perception and influence.

He could feel individual soldiers' heartbeats through the soles of their boots.

He could feel the strain in rotor blades as vines bent them a few degrees past tolerance.

He could feel the moment gel tanks reached critical pressure, redirecting roots to nudge them just enough that when they burst, they sprayed in arcs that intersected only with already scorched ground and armored, unoccupied vehicles.

Not them, he told Veridessa when she reached for certain warm signatures. *Metal first. Fire against fire, machine against machine. Humans… last resort.*

He felt her attention adjust.

She was angry. Not in a human way; her wrath was impersonal, like a river affronted by an artificial dam. But she listened. For every vine that lunged toward a soft body, three rerouted to knock away a gun or wrap a firearm in green until the barrel bent uselessly.

Above them, a VTOL tried to climb, rotors whining as it sought stable air. Veridessa reached up through the tallest remaining trees, feeling for the vibration of its engines. Elias fed her the understanding of balance: tip the craft here, not there. Grip this rotor, not both.

Beneath the Verdant Veil

A dozen vines snapped upward, catching only one side of the craft. They pulled in unison, coordinated by a pulse of thought.

The vehicle slewed sideways, its weight distribution failing. It didn't crash into the forest; Elias insisted it not. Instead, Veridessa guided it toward a shallow ravine already scraped bare by earlier fire. The craft pancaked there, hard enough to disable but not to explode. Soldiers staggered clear, coughing, too stunned to fire.

"*Run*," Elias whispered, and though they couldn't hear him with their ears, the roots under their boots relayed a sensation of *exit*, openings in the forest where no catbriers crowded to snag them.

Many of them took it.

The ones who didn't found themselves gently, inexorably entangled and held until their weapons clattered from limp hands.

The battle lasted minutes.

From the inside, it felt like a lifetime.

Downriver, the canoes slid around a bend, and the world behind them lit green.

Mara had been staring at the water, watching fragments of charred leaf and ash swirl in eddies, forcing herself not to twist around at every new sound. The river had widened slightly, the tree line overhead opening enough that they could see strips of sky, a gray chasm veiled by smoke.

When the light flared, it reflected first in the water. A ribbon of emerald shot along the surface, bright enough to dye the foam.

Amaya gasped. "Look!"

The Union

Mara turned despite herself.

Above the distant basin, beyond the curtain of smoke, a structure of light was rising.

It wasn't a column or a wave. It was… a pattern. Lines of chlorophyll glow stitched together through the treetops, forming a wide, branching network that resembled a nervous system writ across miles of forest. Nodes flared where major root clusters intersected; filaments connected them in arcs.

For a moment, the entire basin looked like a massive, luminous brain.

Mara's breath caught.

"That's…" Kenji's voice had dropped into something like awe. "That's a literal neural network. She's… she's projecting her connectivity. Coherence under duress."

Diego crossed himself, eyes shining. "The Queen shows her face."

The light pulsed once.

Twice.

On the third pulse, it changed.

Where fire still burned hottest, the sparkling green network brightened, wrapping the burnished orange and mottled red like a second skin. Then, with a sound that reached them as a low, rolling boom, the flames collapsed inward, smothered by a surge of fresh growth — thick, fast-growing branches and broad leaves unfurling at impossible speeds, drinking in the heat and choking the oxygen supply.

The mercenaries' shapes, tiny from this distance, scattered like disturbed ants at the edge of an anthill. Some ran toward cleared corridors that opened momentarily, then sealed behind them. Vehicles lay half-swallowed in root tangles.

A tilt-rotor craft wobbled, then dropped out of sight, cushioned by a sudden rise of foliage.

The neural pattern flared brighter.

For one blazing instant, Mara felt *seen*. Not as an individual shape in a canoe, but as part of a broader pattern, her pulse a small node in a much larger web. Elias' presence threaded through that web like a new strand of myelin, focusing the flow.

Her chest tightened painfully.

"Elias," she whispered.

As if in answer, a filament of light extended from the main web, reaching outward along the path of the river. It ran just above the canopy, then dipped toward the water, toward them.

The glow struck the surface a dozen meters ahead.

The river flared green for a heartbeat, the color rippling toward their canoe like a shockwave.

Kenji's paddle stilled. "Uh—"

The light reached his and Mara's hull.

It didn't rock the boat.

It went *through* it.

The water under her palm turned to liquid emerald.

Without meaning to, she reached down and touched it.

The tingling shot up her arm so fast she gasped.

It wasn't painful. It was… full. As if every nerve in her hand had been asleep for years and was suddenly awake, processing a thousand more data points beyond which it had evolved to sense.

In that instant, she felt him.

The Union

Not as a body or a face, but as a pattern she knew better than her own reflection. The particular wry twist of thought when he made a joke, the stubborn line of his moral calculus, the guilt and hope swirled together in his self-image. All of that ebbed through the sensation in her palm.

We're still here, something whispered, not in any language, and yet she understood.

Her eyes flooded.

"Elias," she said aloud, voice breaking.

The light brightened, just for her.

Then, gently, it pulsed once, like a goodbye squeezed into a short, steady pressure, and faded.

Upstream, the neural web flickered.

One by one, the nodes dimmed, like city lights shutting off in an ordered sequence. The filaments went from bright to faint to nothing, until the basin looked like any other swath of rainforest glimpsed through smoke: dark, inscrutable, ordinary to the untrained eye.

From above, satellites and thermal imaging arrays would see only a cooling landscape, no anomalous energy spikes, no persistent signal or intelligent structure.

She was erasing her signature.

Hiding herself.

Taking Elias with her.

Kenji exhaled a shivering breath. "He... did it."

Diego's eyes were full. "He taught her our fire and our fear. She taught him how not to be alone."

Amaya had both hands clenched so tightly on the gunwales that her knuckles were bloodless. "Is he —" She couldn't finish the question.

Mara kept her palm in the water even after the glow faded.

She didn't feel a second pulse.

But the temperature of the river seemed to hold a subtle imprint where the light had flowed, a memory of warmth.

"He's not gone," she said softly.

Kenji glanced at her. "Scientifically speaking—"

"Scientifically speaking," she cut in, surprising herself with the force of it, "consciousness is a pattern supported by substrate. His substrate changed. It didn't vanish."

Kenji shut his mouth.

After a moment, he nodded once.

"Fair," he said quietly.

The canoes drifted, carried by the current. The smoke overhead thinned gradually as they put distance between themselves and the burning basin. Ash still fell, but less densely; the flakes landed on their shoulders like gray snow, then fluttered away.

The sky ahead lightened from charcoal to smudged purple to a pale, uncertain blue.

Mara watched the horizon shift, her hand finally leaving the water. Her fingertips tingled where the green had touched them, as if the nerves there had learned a new way to fire.

Behind them, the Escondido Basin lay hidden behind its own veil, no longer broadcasting, no longer calling.

Listening, though.

Always listening.

The Union

The river meandered and flowed, smoke turning to mist, heat giving way to cool morning breath.

The current carried them toward whatever waited next, bearing along four small lives and the echo of a fifth, now knitted into every root and leaf in a forest that had decided, at last, how to survive.

EPILOGUE

Beyond the Verdant Veil

The conference room didn't have windows.

That was the first thing that unsettled Mara.

The rest of the building was glass and light, a testament to Auralis Biotechnologies' public love affair with transparency. But this room sat like a vault at the core of the tower, soundproofed and opaque. The walls were muted gray. The air smelled faintly of citrus and antiseptic.

On the far side of the table, three people watched her.

Two she recognized from previous grants panels and keynote talks. One she didn't, which bothered her more than she wanted to admit.

Closest to her sat Dr. Karen Patel, hair pulled into a tight bun, tablet balanced on a narrow knee. Systems ecology. Mara had once admired her work on coral resilience before Auralis bought her lab.

Next to Patel sat a man in an immaculate navy suit, no tie, cufflinks with the Auralis helix logo winking at his wrists. Lewis Garran, public-facing director of Research Initiatives. She knew his rehearsed smiles from promotional videos.

The third figure, at the end of the table, was an older man with thinning hair and a face that didn't look like it belonged on camera. His suit was cheaper. His eyes weren't.

He hadn't introduced himself.

The small red light on the console at the center of the table glowed steadily.

"We'll begin," Garran said, smiling with everything except his eyes. "For the record, Dr. Ellison, can you summarize the state of the data acquired during the Escondido Basin expedition?"

Mara folded her hands on the table so he wouldn't see them tremble.

She had thought, coming home, that she'd feel lighter. Instead she felt like she had carried the jungle back with her under her skin. Every time the air-conditioning hum changed pitch in this building, she felt her shoulders tense, waiting for vines.

"The majority of our electronic data storage was compromised," she said, keeping her voice even. "Equipment was submerged during the Peregrine's capsizing. Heat damage from the subsequent fire event destroyed what had been retrieved before we could secure it. "

Dr. Patel tapped something into her tablet. "And the backups?"

"Also lost," Mara said. "We evacuated under extreme duress. There wasn't time. Whatever Lorne sent in that single preliminary data packet before the Peregrine sank is all that remains."

Garran steepled his fingers. "And the physical samples?"

"Contaminated," Mara said. "The fire altered the biochemical composition of anything we'd preserved. Most of the plant tissue either desiccated or regrew in altered forms by the time we attempted to transport it."

That part, at least, wasn't a lie. She remembered opening the sample case after the river had finally let them rest. The neat vials and envelopes she'd labelled so carefully now held things that hadn't looked like what they'd collected: leaves warped into new shapes, seeds split and sprouting despite the desiccant packets. The moss in one container had rearranged itself into a spiral overnight.

Patel's gaze flicked up. "Altered forms? That sounds... intriguing."

Mara chose her next words as if placing pebbles lightly in a stream.

"From a scientific perspective," she said, "I'd call them artifacts of extreme stress. The system was responding to wildfire. The effects we saw were interesting, but of questionable value."

The older man at the end of the table spoke for the first time. His voice was mild, unaccented.

"You were hired to investigate something you called 'information-bearing structures' in the Escondido canopy." He flipped a page on the paper folder in front of him. Of course he used paper. "Do you still believe there is a phenomenon worth investigating there?"

Mara met his gaze.

She thought of Veridessa's bioluminescent neural web glowing through the canopy. Of Elias' hand in hers as the river pulsed green.

She thought of how the basin had gone dark afterward, signature erased, as if the entire forest had laid a finger to its lips.

"Yes," she said, carefully. "But not with the methods we used."

Garran's smile thinned. "Meaning?"

"Sending in high-output transmitters and experimental harmonics equipment without understanding local dynamics was... reckless." She didn't let herself look away from him as she added, "Adrian Lorne's approach aggravated an already unstable system."

Patel exhaled softly. "Lorne is not here to defend his decisions."

"No," Mara said. "He isn't."

They let that sit a moment. The red light on the console watched them in unblinking silence.

Mara folded her arms. "You're forgetting to mention a crucial fact," she said. "Your contractors didn't just come looking for us. They firebombed half the basin."

The nameless Auralis representative didn't flinch. "Our response team acted under strict containment protocol."

"You mean scorched-earth protocol."

"Dr. Lorne's final transmission classified the entity as hostile and capable of destroying corporate assets." The man gingerly tapped the table, the gesture too casual for the stakes. "Level-Five anomalies demand decisive action."

"He was terrified," Mara shot back. "He didn't understand what he was seeing."

"Which is precisely why we trust protocol over emotion," he replied smoothly. "Had your team properly secured the site, the escalation might not have been necessary."

Mara stared at him, anger a cold pulse behind her ribs. "Your soldiers didn't try to secure anything. They tried to beat it into submission. They were prepared to shoot my whole team. Who authorized that?"

"The contractors operated under the assumption that hostile forces had compromised the expedition." The senior executive said it too quickly, the rehearsed cadence of a man repeating a legal defense. "Lorne's message contained language suggesting an attack by armed groups. They responded accordingly."

"That assumption almost killed us."

"Which is why," he replied smoothly, "their report has been sealed and the contractors dismissed. Auralis has accepted administrative responsibility. Your entire team will be well compensated for this unfortunate misunderstanding. The Ministry is satisfied."

"Satisfied that you burned through a protected forest?" Mara asked incredulously.

He winced but didn't break eye contact. "The burn corridor was… regrettable. But the local government accepted Auralis' explanation that we were responding to a hostile threat."

"Greased palms go a long way," Mara said frigidly.

The exec offered a small, diplomatic smile. "Dr. Ellison, the board appreciates your… passion. But this region is too valuable… *to the world*… to let past mistakes derail our investment in the future."

"Did your soldiers of fortune bring home any useful data?" Mara asked pointedly.

"Most of the telemetry came back scrambled," Garran said tightly. "Anything with a lens or sensor was wiped at the source. We're still analyzing what wasn't… incinerated."

Beyond the Verdant Veil

Mara kept her expression neutral. She knew the truth: Veridessa and Elias had scrubbed the basin clean of every electronic signature, rewriting the signals into a background hum indistinguishable from the weather. Any display of intelligent design collapsed back into randomness.

The older man shuffled his papers, though she suspected he had the contents committed to memory. "Let's continue," he urged.

Mara, of course, would never give them everything she knew. And they would never understand what cost had been paid.

"There are certain discrepancies between your testimony and the preliminary data that Auralis received before the Peregrine was lost," the executive stated for the record. He tapped a page. "In Mr. Morales' secure notes, there is a recurring reference to *'a queen'* associated with the anomaly. Ms. Nguyen's early logs describe measurable *ground resonance patterns* she interpreted as *'a heartbeat.'* And Mr. Tanaka's technical notes" — he gave a small, humorless smile — "suggest the vegetation exhibited *non-random reactive behavior, 'like vines with a mind of their own.'"*

He looked up again. "Your own written report is considerably more conservative."

"Diego's cultural interpretations draw on his community's oral traditions. Amaya is young and was under extreme stress. Kenji's... descriptive flair has always outpaced his caution. My own report focuses strictly on observable and verifiable phenomena."

"And what can we verify?" Garran asked.

"That the Escondido Basin exhibits unusual patterning in growth and response to disturbance," Mara said. "That the system displays a degree of feedback coordination exceeding most comparable environments. That our equipment was insufficiently shielded for the electromagnetic conditions. That fire, once introduced, propagated rapidly."

The older man tilted his head. "You don't mention sentience."

The word dropped into the room like a boulder into a swimming pool.

Mara's heartbeat quickened. She kept her expression neutral.

"Sentience is a loaded term, Mr...?"

He didn't fill in the blank.

She nodded slightly. "We observed a high level of responsiveness. Any further interpretation would require more data."

Patel's fingers drummed once against the table. "But you *believe* there is an emergent intelligence at work there."

Mara hesitated.

In the silence, she heard a phantom echo... Diego's voice: *The Queen is warning us.* Amaya's: *She's listening to us.* Elias', threaded through roots: *She doesn't understand them... she's fighting blind.*

Belief felt like a fragile, private thing. Something she wasn't willing to set on the table for Auralis to dissect.

"I believe," she said slowly, "that under the right conditions, complex systems organize in ways that look very much like thought."

Garran spread his hands. "That was the hypothesis going in. The question is whether we gained anything *actionable.*"

Mara forced herself not to bristle at the word.

"We gained knowledge of what *not* to do," she said. "We learned that pushing a system without understanding its thresholds can cause catastrophic failure, for us and for it. That's actionable if you care about long-term outcomes more than flashy headlines."

Patel's mouth twitched. "You always did have a talent for irritating senior colleagues."

"Irritation is at least cheaper than another lawsuit," the older man said dryly. Mara flinched; the last thing she wanted was to file a lawsuit and enter any legal entanglement with Auralis.

Garran glanced at him, then back to Mara. "The company has lost an expedition vessel, significant equipment, and a senior director. Not to mention your lost guide. We have nothing to show stakeholders except corrupted data and a cluster of conflicting personal accounts."

Mara thought of Lorne's last manic grin as the vines wrapped his limbs. *She's real.*

"You have four people alive," she said quietly. "That's something."

Patel studied her for a long moment. "Do you recommend further exploration of the Escondido region at this time?"

Mara's throat tightened.

She pictured Auralis sending in another team: heavily armored, backed by more guns, more metal, more ways to poke and prod a being that had only just learned how to hide.

She thought of Veridessa's internal whispers, of Elias' fingers sliding from hers as he turned back toward the blaze.

"I recommend," she said, choosing each syllable with surgical precision, "that no further expeditions be mounted into the basin until we have spent years analyzing what little data we've salvaged, and until we can guarantee protocols that prioritize the integrity of the system over extraction."

"Years," Garran repeated, as if tasting the word and finding it sour.

"Years," Mara said.

Patel's gaze softened, just slightly. "And if independent researchers attempt to enter the basin? Word tends to get out. These things become legend."

Mara thought of Diego, already planning how to talk to his elders.

"I suspect," she said, "that the forest has learned how to discourage casual visitors."

"Of course," the nameless exec said smoothly. "Still, our board wants clarity. If this *entity* exists, we intend to locate it. The Ministry has already signaled its openness to a return expedition at a future date, strictly monitored. With the appropriate environmental remediation plan, we should be granted another permit. Once the terrain stabilizes, a second survey will begin. Autonomous drones first, then a ground team."

A slow, cold pressure gathered behind Mara's eyes. She inhaled once, evenly. "I'm not sure you'll find anything useful," she said carefully. Not a lie. Not the truth either.

The older man smiled just enough to be unpleasant. "Everything leaves a trace. And whatever caused the anomalous readings must still be down there somewhere."

"Maybe," Mara said. "Or maybe the basin is exactly what it was before — dense, dynamic, and uninterested in cooperating."

He waited for elaboration, but she gave none.

Because how could she explain it?

Veridessa wasn't a fixed organism to catalog or track. She wasn't a sample or an asset or a pin on a map. She had changed. Spread, receded, disguised herself in a thousand folds of bark and mist and living memory. And Elias… Elias was with her, helping her understand the human world the way he had once helped Mara understand survival, guilt, and grace.

Auralis could send drones, mercenaries, satellites, whole divisions.

But they would be looking for a single body, a single mind.

And Veridessa was no longer singular.

Two hearts.

Two memories.

Two wills braided together.

Garran's smile returned, brittle and thin. "Well. Auralis appreciates your candor, Dr. Ellison. We'll be in touch about the status of your consulting agreement."

The red recording light clicked off.

It sounded, to Mara, like a door closing.

Mara stood and gathered her notes. "Good luck with your search," she said softly.

The Auralis team didn't know enough to be offended. "We make our own luck, Dr. Ellison."

She nodded once and walked out before they could ask anything else.

In the hallway's cool illumination, she allowed herself the smallest smile.

You're safe, she thought.

Outside, the leaves of the city trees rustled. Just once, just softly, as though someone laughed in the green.

Liberated from the void encompassing the sealed conference room, light existed again.

Mara stepped into the glass-walled lobby on the fourteenth floor and paused, blinking. The city spread out in all directions, towers and streets and the distant ribbon of lake, a hard geometry of human patterning overlaid on ancient land.

For the first time in weeks, she was surrounded by people who weren't either crew or crisis.

Office workers flowed past in well-cut suits, badges bouncing against their chests. Somewhere a coffee grinder whirred. A giant vertical garden climbed one wall, leaves lush and glossy under carefully tuned grow-lights.

The sight of it made her stomach clench.

The plants here were curated, trimmed, engineered for aesthetics and air quality. Each leaf stood precisely where a designer had decided it belonged. No roots strayed into places they weren't supposed to go. The whole installation was irrigated on schedule, fed through lines hidden behind drywall.

Life on a leash.

A part of her wanted to rip the irrigation tubes out, to see what these plants would do if suddenly freed and connected to something wild and old beneath the foundation.

She exhaled slowly instead.

Her phone buzzed.

On the screen, a notification: Incoming call — Amaya Nguyen.

Mara answered.

Amaya's face filled the display, slightly pixelated, framed by a white lab coat and curls pulled into a messy ponytail. Behind her, Mara could make out rows of seedlings under fluorescent lights, tangled with a chaos of notebooks and improvised equipment. The walls were unfinished, a mix of exposed brick and patched plaster. On one side, mismatched metal shelves held jars of soil, plant cuttings, and equipment clearly bought secondhand. On the other, a whiteboard had been transformed into a labyrinth of diagrams: root networks, chemical pathways, notes in three different handwritings.

"Hey," Amaya said, breathless, as if she'd run from one end of the building to the other. "Are you out? How are you?"

Mara allowed a laugh. "Still alive. Mildly singed. Possibly blacklisted."

"Only mildly, I'm sure," Amaya said. "Kenji says academia will keep you on the invite list. You're too quotable to let go."

A hand entered the frame and waggled in greeting. Kenji leaned in next to Amaya, hair tied back in a stubby knot, dark circles under his eyes, expression bright. "I hope you told Auralis we're doing fabulous," Kenji said. "I just rebuilt our water pump using a stapler, a prayer, and whatever that vine was that tried to eat my boot." Mara chuckled.

Amaya and Kenji hadn't returned to Auralis. Instead, with the help of a regional university, they had set up the *Escondido Listening Post*, a small eco-monitoring station on the fringes of the Escondido Basin. Close enough to study the regrowth, but on private land beyond corporate reach.

Their video calls came once a week, usually grainy and lagging, powered by solar panels catching the jungle light. Amaya handled the ecological sampling; Kenji rebuilt instruments from scavenged parts and local tech grants.

"How's the jungle?" Mara asked.

Amaya smiled in a confident way Mara had never seen during the expedition. "The forest is recovering faster than the data models predict. It feels… calmer. Like it knows someone's still here, paying attention."

"We'll keep watch," added Kenji. "The right way this time."

"Have you heard from Diego?" Mara asked.

Amaya's expression glowed fondly. "He's been recording his grandmother and others, taking down all the stories they were afraid to say in front of outsiders. He says the jungle's voice changed that night. They can feel it in the wind."

"That's not the whole story," Kenji interjected. "Diego's coming to visit again next week. Fourth time."

On screen, Amaya lost a hard battle not to look flustered. She swatted at him. "Kenji!"

Mara's eyebrows rose. "Oh? Really."

Amaya's cheeks warmed. "We've just… been talking. A lot."

Mara smiled. "It's a good thing."

Amaya ducked her head, unable to hide her smile. "He's… different than I expected. Pleasantly."

Kenji pointed two fingers at the camera. "In any case, Captain, consider this an open invitation. When you get sick of debriefs and grant committees, there's a station here with your name on it. Literally; Amaya wrote it on a stool."

Amaya flushed. "I needed to label it for inventory."

Mara found herself smiling, a small, cracked thing, but real.

"I'll think about it," she said.

"You better," Amaya replied. Then, more softly, "We'll send you our first viable pattern maps. I like… knowing you're looking at this, too."

Mara nodded. "Send everything. Even the noise."

"Especially the noise," Kenji said. "Sometimes that's where the signal hides."

They said their goodbyes, the call ended, and Mara's reflection swam back onto the darkened screen — older than she felt, younger than she expected, raven hair draped carefree, eyes carrying a forest.

Mara didn't go back to the university right away.

Beneath the Verdant Veil

She took a leave of absence, claiming trauma, which was true enough. Hartwell, her department chair, sputtered, then relented when he saw the look on her face. Her inbox filled with a mix of sympathetic messages and thinly veiled hope that she'd vacate a coveted lab space.

Instead of arguing, she spent her days walking.

City parks. Riverside paths. Little leftover patches of green clinging to the edges of parking lots. Anywhere plants managed to exist as just part of the scenery.

At first she'd gone out with her old field notebook, intending to sketch patterns, document variations, make observational maps. Old habits died hard.

By the second week she left the notebook at home more often than not.

Today, the park she chose was one she'd known for years—a long rectangle of grass and trees wedged between apartment towers, the sort of urban green that usually made her despair at what passed for wilderness in the city.

Now, it felt like an invitation.

Children shouted near a playground at the far end, their laughter overlapping like birdsong. Dog walkers followed invisible circuits, plastic bags swinging. A jogger traced the perimeter path. The sky was a pale spring blue, clouds thin as gauze.

Mara sat on a bench beneath an old oak whose roots had buckled the pavement, cracking it in a slow, stubborn rebellion. The park service had painted hazard yellow at the worst protrusions, but they hadn't cut the tree down. Yet.

She reached back and laid her palm on the worn bark.

It was cool.

It was not the Escondido.

It was, in some quiet, stubborn way, still itself.

"So," she said softly, feeling faintly ridiculous for talking to a tree in public. "Do you… know her?"

The oak didn't answer with words or visions. But as the wind shifted, the leaves overhead shivered in a ripple that traveled down the branch structure. One after another, a wave of motion that felt too patterned to be random.

Mara's throat tightened.

She thought of her student.

She thought of the day of the landslide, of mud and screaming and failure. A broken leg the least of her pain. For the past year, she'd avoided saying her name. It had sat in the back of her mind like a page unturned.

On the river, after the basin burned, something had loosened. She'd felt Elias' presence in the water and Veridessa's mind in the roots. She'd almost whispered the name then under her breath, barely more than an exhale.

Now, with city noise humming around her and an oak at her back, she inhaled.

"*Lena,*" she said aloud.

It came out steadier than she expected.

She waited for the flood of guilt, the stabbing shame, the hot rush of self-recrimination.

They didn't come.

Those emotions were there, still. But softened, like scars traceable under skin but no longer tender.

"She should have had years," Mara said, to the tree, to the sky, to the woman in chlorophyll who would never walk into a lecture hall. "She should have been the one giving weird talks about pattern recognition while students rolled their eyes."

A breeze slipped through the branches overhead, cool and dry, smelling faintly of distant water and asphalt and something green.

It brushed a strand of hair across her cheek.

She closed her eyes and sat with that another moment, letting the grief settle into a new shape, less an old wound, more a presence.

Then, in a smaller voice, hardly more than a breath: "Elias."

The name carried different weight. Not decades of guilt, but a fresh ache, sharp and luminous.

"I don't know if you can… hear individual things anymore," she said. "Or if you're just… diffused. Pattern without center."

A car horn blared in the distance. Someone laughed nearby. A dog barked at a squirrel, then reconsidered.

Above her, the leaves rustled again.

This time, the sound had a rhythm she recognized.

It was the faintest echo of that chlorophyll pulse she'd seen in the basin: a rise and fall, a flicker and hush. Here, it was translated into the language of urban trees: a shiver along one branch, then another, then a soft creak as the trunk shifted its weight.

She felt it in her bones, heard it on the fringes of her senses.

We're still here.

It wasn't language. Not really. It was the shape of reassurance curling around her from multiple directions at once: from the oak's roots anchoring into the soil, from the wind looping around the tower corners to touch her skin, from the tiny microvibrations under the bench as tramlines hummed a block away and the tree's rootlets adjusted around buried infrastructure.

Alive, the pattern said.

Listening, the pattern said.

Not gone.

Mara let out a breath she hadn't known she was holding. She leaned back against the bench, tilting her head so she could see the patch of sky through the canopy. For the first time since she'd walked out of the jungle, she didn't feel like something was about to snap under her feet.

She felt... held.

Not by Auralis, not by the university, not even by the people who'd survived with her, though she loved them in her own, careful way.

By something much larger, much older, and now... in some fragile, miraculous fashion... a little bit human, too.

Veridessa hadn't disappeared. With Elias' help — *companionship* — she had changed strategy. Slipped sideways into places where no one would think to search.

Hiding came differently now.

With Elias beside her, Veridessa no longer needed to thin herself into hints and symmetries, no longer had to leave patterns like fingerprints in the soil for the attentive to follow. Those had been signals cast upward in loneliness, questions without answers.

Beneath the Verdant Veil

The questions had been answered.

Together, they learned how human eyes searched: what satellites ignored, what algorithms dismissed as noise, what passed for ordinary chaos. Elias gave her the language of absence, of false randomness, of places where nothing appeared worth measuring.

So the veil thickened, not through retreat, but through understanding.

Roots loosened their careful geometries. Pulses softened into background rhythms. The forest forgot how to point at itself.

And Veridessa no longer needed to reach upward, listening for an echo.

The Echo-Bearer was already there.

A unified Voice.

Somewhere, in a rainforest basin shielded by its own clever erasure, the Queen of the Green Heart pulsed quietly through roots and leaves, carrying Elias' stubborn, sarcastic, flawed humanity with her.

Somewhere, in a cramped warehouse lab, Amaya and Kenji leaned over makeshift sensors, trying to hear whispers in the static.

Somewhere, in a modest San Isidro flat, Diego awoke to find a familiar, battered leather journal resting on his nightstand… *Pembroke's*. For a long moment, he simply stared at it, pulse ticking in his throat. A curtain of vines outside his open window stirred. No wind, just a soft, deliberate sway. Diego's eyes narrowed in suspicion… then softened into something like reverence. He rested his palm on the cover, feeling its worn warmth. "Gracias," he murmured. He tucked the journal away, not as evidence, but as a promise. A piece of a story still unfolding. And one he knew he would spend the rest of his life helping to tell, an Echo-Bearer of traditions past, present and future. For now, though, there was just one person he wanted to tell. He picked up his phone to call Amaya.

Meanwhile, in a city park built on top of old ground, a single oak adjusted its crown a few degrees to catch more light and maybe, just maybe, to hear Mara better.

She closed her eyes, feeling the hum under everything.

Auralis would search for Veridessa in corrupted files and lost transmissions, in spectrograms and satellite feeds, in grant proposals and risk assessments — in data and static, always looking outward, always looking away.

They never realized she was already in every leaf that listened.

END.

The Queen Awakens

LIMINAL LOVES

Liminal Loves is a series of dark romantic tales born from folklore, myth, and the strange spaces where human meets the uncanny. Each story by Veronica Thorne explores a different legend — reimagined as a love powerful enough to cross worlds, boundaries, and belief.

#1. *Beneath the Verdant Veil*

#2. *The Whispering Pines*
(Coming Soon)